DEMONIA

Kendal Grahame

This book is a work of fiction.
In real life, make sure you practise safe sex.

First published in 1995 by
Nexus
332 Ladbroke Grove
London W10 5AH

Copyright © Kendal Grahame 1995

Typeset by TW Typesetting, Plymouth, Devon
Printed and bound by
BPC Paperbacks Ltd, Aylesbury, Bucks

ISBN 0 352 33038 4

One

It was time.

Demonia sensed a glorious, sublime sensation as the damp air began to touch her awakening skin and the musty smell of her surroundings invaded her nostrils, a silent putrescence oozing from the death-cold stone walls. She opened her eyes slowly and absorbed the welcoming half-light, her vision gradually becoming sharper as she focused on the damp, grey stone of the ceiling above her.

It had been so long; so many, many years. Now the cycle was complete; now she would exist again; breathe once more the cool air of the night.

And she would thirst.

She ran her hands gently over the rough sides of the casket that had been her comfort and protection for more than two centuries, the sense of touch and the suppleness of life quickly returning to her fingers. The thick upholstery had long since turned to dust and tattered, straggly remains were left clinging to the wooden shell of the coffin. Her silken shroud, now grey and threadbare, hung about her perfect body, hiding nothing, merely accentuating the perfection of her alabaster-white skin.

She sat up slowly, the sensations of life causing slight stiffness in her movements. She looked purposely around the dingy, dismal cellar, taking in the images of the shadows, and gradually recalling why she had lain for so long in its fearful, damp embrace.

Professor Tankard! Demonia breathed his name through pursed lips and clenched teeth, her hiss of hatred breaching the ethereal silence. Tankard. It was he who had uncovered their secrets, and because of him the life force had been

1

snuffed out of so many of her sisters, like delicate candles in a great gale. Tankard the vampire killer – manic in his murderous ambitions to rid the world of an entity that he barely understood – had cut a swathe through their gentle community.

And he was so wrong, so very, very wrong. The sisters were not the threat to humanity that he perceived. They brought only pleasure and ecstasy to their always-willing victims. They were not of the same ilk as the evil ones, the vile and malevolent disciples of Baron Mansola, the Bavarian leech. It was he and his odious cohorts whom Tankard should have purged, not the harmless maidens of the night.

The professor would be dead now, of course, avenged by his own mortality, and no longer a threat to her kind. Now it was her time to begin again, to savour life and its myriad of sensuous pleasures, and to draw others into her fold.

The extermination of the sisterhood had been near total but, miraculously, Demonia had escaped along with just one other gentle sister who now lay in the smaller coffin on the far side of their gloomy tomb. She remembered with warm fondness their first meeting. Sweet Sinitia. Her waif-like innocence was coupled with a near insatiable lust for knowledge and a yearning to learn of the ancient and erotic secrets of true sustenance. Demonia remembered her delightful taste, and the joy she had felt when Sinitia suckled at her own wet flesh, drawing the juices of her arousal from her.

It had been on the occasion of one of the baron's soirées regular events through which he had been able to charm the unwitting townspeople of Gallows Hill, a suitably remote village set in the heathlands to the north of the ancient settlement of Hampstead, inhabited by less than two hundred souls who were soon to learn the truth of Mansola's evil. Demonia herself had only recently been initiated into the fold and although aware of the murderous intent of her erstwhile benefactor, had been powerless to refuse to serve his needs and those of his cohorts, blissfully enjoying their seemingly insatiable and lustful attentions.

She had been kneeling naked on the great couch, the

2

long, thick rod of a handsome young stud plundering the depths of her ever-welcoming pussy; the fourth or possibly the fifth such encounter that evening. Through the haze of erotic arousal that clouded her vision she had seen her; beautiful, barely yet a woman but possessing an aura of sensuous innocence that Demonia had found irresistible. The young girl had stood nervously in a corner of the room, her wide eyes taking in the sights of the bacchanalia with undisguised eagerness. She wore a white dress of diaphanous silk, the shining texture of the material serving to enhance the flawlessness of her ebony-coloured skin and the perfection of her slim but shapely body clearly visible through the gossamer-like layers of the rich fabric.

Despite the joyous pleasure Demonia had felt as her unnamed lover pumped his huge, throbbing stalk steadily into her from behind, she had sensed that she must be the one to welcome this embodiment of purity into the sisterhood.

She had let herself fall forward on to her stomach, allowing, with not a little reluctance, the long cock to slip from within her wet sheath before wriggling quickly from the couch. The man had seemed unconcerned, momentarily making a grab for her as she slid from his grasp, then clutching the arm of another naked nymphet and pulling her across his strong, muscular body. Demonia had struggled to her feet and walked, determinedly if unsteadily towards her quarry.

She had reached out and gently stroked the exquisite face, savouring the smoothness of her soft, black skin. The girl's large brown eyes had opened even wider, their expression an incongruous mixture of anxiety and lust. Demonia remembered that the girl was trembling.

Demonia had smiled, kindly. 'Do not fear, child,' she had said in a voice barely above a whisper. 'No harm shall come to you.' The young girl had relaxed in the warmth of her tone. 'What do they call you, sweet virgin?' Demonia had asked, stroking her face once more before allowing her fingers to trail sensuously down across the silk of her dress to her firm breast. Her nipple had felt hard, betraying her arousal.

3

The girl had shivered. 'I am called Sinitia; I have no other name.' She had spoken as though ashamed. Demonia remembered staring into her eyes and circling the long, thick bud of her nipple with her fingertips.

'What brings you to this place?' Demonia had breathed, her hand moving to the other breast, exciting it in the same, tender way. 'You must know what happens here?'

The black girl had nodded. 'It is my master's wish,' she had said, quietly. 'He wants me to, to . . .' She had looked at the floor, as though racked with guilt, then somehow drawn the courage to continue. 'To become his sex slave.'

Demonia's expression had become one of sympathy and understanding. The baron had won over the local gentry with promises of sexual excess, undoubtedly the key to his ultimate power, and had promised to fulfil their wildest dreams and fantasies. This poor wretch was merely part of such a pledge. Demonia had felt annoyed that such an innocent waif should be used in this way, clearly against her will, and resolved to do everything within her power to protect her.

She had known that she had such power – the simple, intimate touch of her tongue would suffice to break the hypnotic spell that held Sinitia. She had also been aware that the baron would be furious, having witnessed him unleash his wrath on other, unfortunate souls in the past. There was something beguilingly entrancing about this delicate flower of purity though, and she knew that she must care for her.

'Come,' she had said, with sudden forcefulness of will, as she took the slim arm of the trembling girl within her grasp. 'Come with me; you will be safe.'

They had walked slowly across the great hall, stepping carefully amidst the myriad of copulating bodies. Demonia remembered glancing furtively at the baron as he sat, eyes closed, the immense length of his penis being orally worshipped by three young wenches. She felt a slight twinge within her loins as she remembered the time, the one and only time, when he had impaled her with his huge staff, taking her virginity and with it her soul. Many times she had yearned for him to enter her again and stretch her to the very limits but no, he was to sate her lust but once before casting her aside to satisfy the pleasurable whims of the coven, like so many before her.

That night, she had led Sinitia into the darkness of the library, carefully closing the heavy, oak door behind them and turning the key in the lock. She had tested the door, then turned to face the nervous enchantress before her. She had walked over to her and slipped her arms around the narrow, sylph-like waist, kissing her lightly on the forehead. 'You are about to become part of the sisterhood,' she breathed, kissing her again. 'To join us in eternal ecstasy and perpetual delight.' Leaning forward, she had kissed the black girl fully on the mouth, coaxing the thick, pouting lips apart and slipping her tongue between them. For a moment, Sinitia had stood motionless, then quickly pulled away.

'No, please, I don't understand,' she had said, her voice shaking and her eyes filled with questions and concern. 'What do you mean, the sisterhood?'

'You will live forever, my child,' Demonia had soothed. 'You will savour the joys of sexual release with many men, delight to the sensations of their thick stalks entering your sweet body . . .'

'No, no,' Sinitia had interrupted. 'I . . . I'm afraid.'

Demonia had smiled gently then and taken the trembling figure within her arms again. 'There is no need to fear,' she had whispered, her hands stroking the firm, pert buttocks through the layers of sheer silk. 'In becoming one of us you will be saved from a far worse destiny.'

Her words must have inspired a terrifying reality within the young girl's consciousness and she had relaxed. Demonia had then kissed her wonderfully sumptuous lips once more and rejoiced as her mouth opened and their tongues met, dancing and darting around each other erotically as she felt a small hand slip cautiously around her naked waist. Demonia then gripped Sinitia's superb bottom firmly with one hand, allowing the other to trail slowly around to the front of her body. She had slipped it slowly,

5

oh so slowly, under the layers of material until her fingers touched the bare flesh of firm thigh. Their embrace had become ever more passionate, Sinitia gripping her lover's waist tightly as Demonia moved her hand upward and parted her legs slightly to ease the passage.

Demonia's fingertips had brushed the coarse hair between Sinitia's legs and she held still for a moment, the young girl gasping slightly within the wetness of their kiss. Then, Sinitia had begun to move her hips slightly, as though attempting to reawaken the movements of her lover's caressing touch. Demonia remembered slipping her fingers between the delicate folds of sex-flesh, thrilling to the moistness of the sweet nymph's arousal until she touched the thin membrane that was her virginity. She had then withdrawn her hand from the delightful warmth, pulling her face away from the long kiss and gazing once more into Sinitia's deep brown eyes.

'Please, don't stop,' the young girl had implored. 'It ... it feels nice.'

'That is for another to take,' Demonia had breathed. 'I will give you other joys.' Demonia remembered Sinitia looking a trifle disappointed but standing acquiescently, eagerly awaiting her lover's next move.

Demonia had deftly unclasped Sinitia's gold shoulder-brooch that held the layers of silk in place, stepping back to allow the material to drift, leaf-like, to the thickly-carpeted floor. Sinitia had stood submissively before her, her charms displayed in all their fragile perfection. Demonia's mouth had gone dry, so impatient had she been to taste the juices of her naïvely chaste conquest. 'You are beautiful,' she had breathed, taking the frail form once more into her arms and kissing her mouth obsessively. She had then stroked and fondled the lovely, bare bottom and her fingers had trailed between the soft globes of her buttocks, wetting the tip of one with the juices of Sinitia's lust before pushing it carefully into the tightness of her anus. Her other hand had snaked once more around her slim body to cup the warmth of her soaked pussy.

With just a little force she had pushed the young girl to

6

the floor, lying beside her on the carpet and running her hands over the flawlessness of her body.

'You will be so welcome,' she had said, her voice shaking with emotion. 'The sisters will be filled with joy when they learn that you have joined us.' Leaning forward, she had kissed Sinitia's mouth again, then with a purposeful elegance she had moved her lips down to the soft pillow of her breasts and suckled first one nipple and then the other, drawing each one between her teeth and rasping them against the tender flesh. Sinitia had groaned, closing her eyes to savour the moment.

Demonia had suckled heavily on one nipple and squeezed the other between her forefinger and thumb, coaxing them to full erection. They were long, thick and as black as the night, save for a hint of the deepest purple at the very tip. Demonia remembered sensing that she could lie her head within the warmth of these pert mounds for ever, but knew that there was more to do if she were to cause this virgin to yield completely so that she could take her within her loving guardianship. Slowly and deliberately she had run her tongue downwards over the flat, taut stomach to the silky-fine hair of her lower abdomen and then to the coarseness of her wet curls. She had breathed deeply, taking in the precious scent of Sinitia's arousal before slipping the tip of her tongue between the luscious folds of her hitherto unassailed pussy, licking them hungrily as the young girl's hips moved in compliant response.

'Oh ... oh it's wonderful,' Sinitia had groaned as she raised her legs higher to afford her lover greater access to her innermost treasures. Drinking the fluids of lust thirstily, Demonia had carefully raised her own leg until her hips were above Sinitia's face. Then she had gradually lowered herself, awaiting the ultimate joy.

At first there had been just a kiss; a simple, cautious touch of inexperienced lips to her aching pussy. Then the tongue; no more than a very brief lick, as though Sinitia was tasting a new; exotic fruit. Another wet caress, becoming ever more bold until, at last, the licking had become intense as she felt herself being suckled and the lips of her cunt being drawn into the soft mouth beneath her.

7

She had known then that she had won; that Sinitia was hers.

Drawing her head back slightly, she had allowed her tongue to flick steadily over the hard bud of Sinitia's clitoris. The young girl learned quickly and copied her actions. Their hands had fondled and stroked, their fingers gripping and clawing at the soft flesh of thighs and buttocks. Sinitia's hips then began to buck and the groaning, muffled cries that were almost lost within the bushy confines of Demonia's wet sex-flesh became ever more urgent. Demonia had licked harder and harder as Sinitia's thrusting movements became shudders and she moaned loudly, raising her bottom high from the floor and forcing her pussy against Demonia's loving mouth.

Demonia had felt that her own release was imminent, and knew that their unison would be complete. Sitting herself back on her haunches she had raised her arms above her head and cried out, grinding her crotch against the thick-lipped, suckling mouth of her sweet conquest. The pain of ecstasy had been almost unbearable.

Gradually, the throbbing had subsided and the climax had passed, and the two lovers had fallen into each other's arms, sobbing quietly as they recovered from their mutual bliss. Demonia remembered Sinitia's lovely face and the sweat running in little rivulets over her body; the wet sheen enhancing the blue-black perfection of her skin.

'Welcome, sister,' she had breathed. 'Now you are safe. Already you will be experiencing new yearnings, feelings that you don't yet understand. I will teach you and guide you into our world of succour and endless pleasure.'

'It is true; already I feel a strange warmth within my body, deep inside me.' Sinitia had held the palm of her hand against her pussy. 'The feeling is so strong, and yet so wonderful.' Demonia had smiled and pressed her own hand over the young girl's caressing fingers.

'Soon you will know the ultimate pleasure. We will seek out a fine young man with a rod of steel to impale you and to take the flower of your innocence. He will sate you with his succulence.'

8

'Yes, oh yes!' Sinitia's eyes had blazed with new-found lust. 'I watched you, on the couch. The man . . . he was so handsome . . . so big.'

'There will be many like him, I promise. Come, let us return to the great hall.'

They had been about to get to their feet when a sudden shaft of flamed torchlight had flared across the room as the door to the library was forced open, the wood of the heavy frame splintering like glass. Demonia remembered how they'd sat up in terror, their arms still entwined about their naked bodies. The unmistakable figure of the baron had stood silhouetted in the doorway.

'Well, my queen, you have chosen to defy me!' His voice was harsh.

'My lord . . .' Demonia had said, trembling visibly.

'Silence!' The barked order had caused the two women to gasp in abject dread. Mansola had moved forward, towering over the shivering figures of the two girls. 'You have made your choice. Now you may reap the rewards!' Gazing down at their cowering forms, his malevolent eyes had shone red in the flickering light. Demonia had tried in vain to avoid his leering stare, but it was useless. Slowly, her eyes had become heavy as the folds of darkness pressed heavily on her mind.

Just once did Demonia wake from the trance-like state as she lay within her coffin. Just once, as she heard the piercing screams of her sisters as Professor Tankard wreaked his terrifying revenge on the plague of vampires that had decimated the region and she knew that Baron Mansola and the other men would have gone to ground, safely hidden in the uncharted caves that riddled the hills surrounding the village, ready to rise again. And she knew that the sisters were lost, victims to a terrible mistake.

She closed her eyes and waited, expecting the sudden pain as the stake was driven through her heart, sending her into oblivion. Her one regret was that sweet Sinitia had never tasted the pleasures of man-flesh; that she would die a virgin.

The pain never came. Their tomb was perhaps too well hidden, even for the meticulous professor to unearth. Once more she drifted off into the sleep of the dead, and her dreams.

Demonia carefully eased herself out of the close confines of her wooden resting place and swung her long legs out into the air, her bare feet reacting slightly to the bitter coldness of the damp floor. She stood erect, breathing heavily as her lungs once again accepted life. The foul air quickly rejuvenated her, filling her body with an incongruous warmth.

She tore off the remnants of her shroud and closed her eyes, her hands running smoothly over her warming flesh. She felt her superb, flawless body – the very body that she knew would soon once more seduce many men and women into her power. She felt again the almost-forgotten yearnings as the succour of new life warmed her very nerve-endings, and remembered the power she could control with her sexuality and her devastating sensuality.

She cupped her magnificently large, firm breasts with both hands, enjoying the knowledge that their size had been the source of wonder and desire to so many in the past. She pinched and squeezed the long, hard nipples into immediate reaction, the sudden, erotic sensation causing her to shudder. Raising the heavy globes she bent her head slightly, pushing out her long tongue to lick each erect bud in turn, reliving the delight of a lover's suckling lips drawing them between the roughness of his teeth. Soon she felt the beginnings of a familiar, warm dampness between her softly curved thighs. She knew that life had returned.

She let her breasts fall back heavily and ran both hands down over her firm, flat stomach to her sex, nestling wetly in a thick bush of black hair that matched the long shining tresses that cascaded from her proud head. Her fingers quickly prodded and probed the puffy lips, the memories of ecstasy returning with each urgent touch. Her sex juices flowed as copiously as ever and her clitoris was excitely erect, responding to her delicate ministrations.

10

Her fondling became more aggressive, her need obvious and imperative. She opened her legs and crouched slightly, easing four fingers of one hand between her soaked pussy lips, the fingertips of the other hand rubbing rapidly against her demanding bud. She began to pump her fingers steadily in and out of herself; the hungry, wet sheath gripping her tightly as she recalled the exquisite sensation of having a long, thick penis invading her, filling her and exciting every nerve within her stunning body.

Soon, very soon, she would once again taste the juices of a lover and drink the erotic fluids which would give her both the satisfaction and the sustenance that she craved. Soon she would sit astride his compliant, muscular form, absorbing his long, thick rod within her tightly undulating sheath and riding her stallion to a frenzy of mutual bliss.

Or maybe her next lover would be a lithe, young girl and their bodies would writhe in mutual exhilaration as they suckled each other to the very pinnacles of total joy.

For the moment she needed blissful release. She needed to relieve herself after two hundred years of death-sleep and wild, frustrating sex-dreams when her mortal shell was frozen in time and her fingers were unable to touch the parts of her body which begged for erotic caresses.

She pulled and prodded herself with a ferociousness that would pain a lesser woman. Her fingertips rubbed furiously at her clitoris and her eyes were ablaze with life as she felt the first orgasm for so many years building at last within her beautiful body.

She felt the electrical sensations begin to tear at her. Every nerve ending was alive with sexual feeling and her juices flowed liberally over her caressing, self-loving fingers. Her cry of relief and satisfaction came from the back of her throat; a long, low sound that seemed to emanate from hell itself, increasing in volume and intensity as it built up into an ear-splitting scream.

Outside, the wind appeared to take up the force of her pleasure as an instant, roaring rush of air forced itself through a small, partly-glazed aperture that was her only link to the world outside. The branches of an ancient tree

11

slammed suddenly against the window, sending small fragments of what remained of the thick glass to the stone floor, the shards catching the cold glint of a harsh moon. The sound startled her, the shock causing her body to finally surrender to the inevitable, erotic joy of orgasm.

Her whole body shook with the force, her knees trembling as she pressed the palm of her slim, white hand against the throbbing mound of her cunt and yielded her entire consciousness to this single moment of sheer, abject pleasure. She gasped for breath, her legs buckling at the knee and her fingers forced hard within the soaked lips of her pussy. She knelt down on to the unyielding stone floor, her entire body trembling as she relaxed. The coldness of the surface against her sweating skin helped to return her senses to normality and her breathing became steadily more controlled.

Slowly, almost reluctantly, she eased her fingers from the soft kiss of her sex and put them to her mouth, tasting her passion. Her eyes closed and her newly-awakened heart thumped, sending the blood coursing through her veins.

Demonia stood up slowly, supporting her shaking body by holding on to the side of her coffin and gradually coming back down to earth. Her body was now completely alive, full of sensitivity and arousal, hungry for more pleasure and excitement. She tossed her head back, feeling the ends of her hair brush gently against her firm, pert bottom. The sensation reminded her of the joys she could experience from the perverse pleasures of pain – the kiss of the lash across her white flesh, the gentle touch of a lover's caress across the firm globes of her buttocks, the sensuous feel of a warm, wet tongue between them and the ultimate joy of intimate intrusion into that sweet, forbidden orifice.

She took another deep breath, her eyes closed. She was alive!

After a short pause, Demonia walked to the side of the other casket and looked lovingly inside at the calm, sleeping face of Sinitia. Her smooth, ebony features were as lovely as ever. She bent over the reclining form and kissed the full, thick lips gently, forcing her tongue between them

12

as she felt the mouth relax as though in submission. She kissed Sinitia passionately, their tongues sliding wetly against each other, and her hand cupped a firm, perfectly-rounded breast, the nipple hardening under her palm. Then she drew back and gazed in adoration at her lover's innocent face, the dark eyes open and shining with arousal. She leant forward and kissed her mouth, her tiny, pert nose and those beautiful eyes, then ran her tongue wetly over the cool nakedness of her perfect body towards the place she had dreamt of so many times during her long years of entombment; the sweet, black lips of her sex, untouched for so long, and soon to be awakened into a frenzy of lust.

Sinitia began to move her body slightly, raising her hips as Demonia's mouth found its target and pressed firmly against the softness of her pussy. Demonia's tongue probed between the lips as they opened to her wet touch, like the petals of a delicately-scented summer rose welcoming the freshness of the morning dew. The black girl's apple-firm breasts began to rise and fall as Demonia breathed life into her body, the warmth of new existence emanating from between the strong, sensuous legs. Gently she was brought into full consciousness; her skin becoming goose-fleshed and the long nipples hardening even more.

Demonia raised her head from her delicious task and looked into the face of her lover. Sinitia's eyes slowly opened fully, and she smiled as she focused on the gentle face before her.

'It is time?' she breathed, sitting up slowly in her deadly cot.

'It is time,' said Demonia, kissing her lightly on the mouth. 'Life has returned to us, as fresh and as sweet as before. It has been so very long; much will have changed and we have a great deal to learn. But first, my sweet child, I must give you relief to waken you fully.'

She returned her tongue to the warm and receptive wetness between Sinitia's legs and began to lick hungrily at the puffy folds of sex-flesh. She drank greedily at the fluids, savouring the taste that had for so long been denied to her, and swallowed its goodness with relish. Her young companion lay back again in her coffin, enjoying the pleasures of her newly-awakened life-blood. She pushed her mound firmly against the fluttering tongue and her juices flowed copiously, wetting her thighs and her lover's face.

Ah, sweet Sinitia, thought Demonia as she suckled her warm prize. She comes so easily, as before.

The black girl's entire body was shaking, her hips thrusting wildly against the suckling mouth as she orgasmed. Her cries of relief were no less terrifying than those of Demonia herself.

'Oh, my lovely Demonia,' she sobbed as she relaxed, 'how I have dreamed of the warm caress of your sweet tongue upon my cunt; and how I have longed to taste you, to drink the succulence of your pleasure from within your wonderful body!'

Demonia moved upwards and kissed her affectionately on her small nose. 'I, too, have dreamed,' she said quietly, smoothing the sweat from Sinitia's lovely face. 'Visions so real and erotic that I felt that I must tear my soul from the shackles of my mortal confinement.'

'My imaginings were strange, like those of the unknown,' said Sinitia. 'My greatest need was to feel the heaviness of a man as he pushes his huge erection into the very depths of my aching sex, as you promised I would.'

'You will, soon, my dearest,' said Demonia, once more moving down to lick the final droplets of sex-juice from the tightly-curled hair around her lover's pussy. 'The death-trance inflicted upon us by the evil baron is broken. Now we must quickly find a man to satisfy us, to feed us and give us strength.'

'The very thought of it is causing my loins to ache,' said Sinitia breathlessly. 'Pleasure me some more with your wonderful tongue!'

'Ah, my sweet, insatiable child, we shall have such a time!' cried Demonia with renewed lust as she buried her face back between Sinitia's strong thighs, suckling and swallowing as the lithe youngster almost immediately arched her back and threw herself into another orgasm. Her legs stretched over the sides of the coffin and her bot-

14

tom was raised high in the air as though trying to force her wet sex deep into the mouth of her lover.

Gasping in the dank air Sinitia at last relaxed and sat up, lovingly stroking the long black tresses on her lover's head. 'That was beautiful,' she said, stiffly easing herself from the crumbling casket. 'Just as I remembered it. How long have we been asleep?'

'Many years,' said Demonia, as she pulled her head away from its gentle trap. 'Too many to count.' She held her hand out and helped Sinitia to climb out of the coffin. 'Now, we must find clothing of this age and go out into the world, to see what wonders it holds for us.'

Sinitia gasped as she felt the coldness of the stone floor against her bare feet. 'We are truly alive,' she said. 'Truly alive!'

They walked slowly over to the large oak door and pulled back the heavy iron bar that had protected them for so long, the rust flaking against the sharpness of the metal clasps.

They tugged at the old door until finally it gave way to their efforts and creaked open wearily, allowing a sudden breeze of cool, night air to rush into the ancient crypt. They breathed in its freshness, their lungs filling with its life-giving goodness.

'I am hungry,' said Sinitia. 'We must find someone quickly.'

Demonia smiled reassuringly and guided her friend up the long flight of steep stone steps to the crypt gates. With one mighty tug she broke the padlock, throwing the old chain to the floor with a clatter.

'At least we still have our strength,' she said, smiling at her friend. They walked, naked, into the thick undergrowth that had once been a fine, closely-cropped lawn, the decaying manor behind them casting sombre shadows in the moonlight. They looked furtively around, anxious to find some sort of clothing.

Suddenly they heard noises; the groaning of a man and a woman nearby. Demonia put her finger to her lips and they crept, cat-like, in the direction of the sounds. They

15

neared the twisted, gnarled monuments that marked the ancient graves of the long dead – the sinister resting places of the baron's victims.

A sudden breeze blew warmly through the upper branches of the trees, causing the leaves to rustle. Sinitia trod heavily on a sharp stone and cried out; Demonia swung round and glared at her friend as they held themselves stock-still, hardly daring to breath. The groans continued; they had not been heard.

They found the source of the noises behind a large tombstone, amidst some long undergrowth. A young couple, neither above the age of seventeen, were lying naked in the grass. Their bodies were entwined in passion and their hips thrust together in perfect, abandoned unison, totally oblivious to the fact that they were being watched.

The intruders gazed down upon the rutting couple, watching enviously as the young man forced his happily submissive conquest on to her back, his backside moving swiftly up and down, the buttocks clenched as he swiftly thrust in and out of the lithe, wriggling body. The girl's rhythmic groans of pleasure tore into Demonia's mind, sending violent messages of lust and thirst to her brain. Her hand snaked between her legs and she began to finger her clitoris soothingly, her tongue running over her dry lips.

'Can we have them, Demonia?' implored Sinitia quietly. 'They look so fresh.'

'Yes, we shall take them.'

The two girls walked out from the shelter of the gravestone and stood before their intended victims, their legs apart and their hands on their hips. It was the girl who saw them first, their forms partly silhouetted against the night sky, and squealed with fright as she struggled from beneath the body of her lover. The boy swung round and fell back with shock on to his rear, his small cock waving ridiculously in the air. It glistened in the moonlight with his lover's sensuous juices.

'Who are you? What do you want?' he said, his eyes darting from one to the other, clearly savouring the sight

16

of their superb, shapely bodies emphasised in the harsh moonlight. Demonia put her finger to her pouting lips to hush him, licking the tip erotically. She noticed his erection swell as he gazed at them and watched his tongue run over his lips, clearly more in lust than fear.

Sinitia knelt before the shivering young girl, smiling gently as she stared into her eyes. Within seconds the girl's will was gone; she was in her power. Demonia watched as her friend pushed the teenager on to her back, opening her legs wide and burying her face in the wetness between her legs. Soon the sounds of gentle, oral love filled Demonia's ears as Sinitia drank from the sweet chalice, sucking the life-giving sex fluids deep into her mouth, and she knew that the simple touch of her own finger on the hard bud of her sex was no longer enough.

Demonia turned to the young man, staring at his eyes in the same hypnotic way that Sinitia had used to enchant the girl. He lay back obediently on the grass as she took his erection in her hand and watched her rub it slowly up and down, teasing the end with her thumb. She leant forward and took the stiff little wand in her mouth, running her tongue hungrily around the weeping end and savouring his flavour, glad in the knowledge that she had lost none of her expertise.

She started to rub his stem rapidly, wanting to make him finish quickly so that he filled her mouth with the life-giving fluids that she so desperately craved. She pressed her mouth down, taking his full length inside her warm wetness and her tongue played round and round his stiff erection, feeling it throb as he headed inexorably towards orgasm.

She bobbed her head up and down quickly, holding his stalk tightly between her pouting lips, drawing in her cheeks to afford him the most pleasant of sensations as she sucked on him. She heard the sounds of the young girl coming, and knew that Sinitia was drinking in the wonderful fluids, building up her strength. She suckled harder and harder at the stiff erection in her mouth, and at last felt the tell-tale throbbing as jets of sperm spurted to the back of her throat. She swallowed all he could give and sucked greedily on his wilting manhood until there was no more, feeling the warmth of his juices inside her eager body.

Their willing victims lay unconscious as the two sated vampires dressed themselves in their clothing. Fortunately, both of their conquests had been wearing simple jeans and T-shirts which although somewhat tight-fitting, would serve their purpose until better items were secured. The teenage couple would wake in about two hours, totally drained by their experience but otherwise unharmed and unaffected other than having to explain their nakedness.

Demonia and Sinitia sat quietly for a moment on the grassy bank. 'I feel so warm, so strangely satisfied,' said Sinitia, her eyes gazing blankly into the darkness. 'I don't understand.'

'This is our destiny,' said Demonia, solemnly. 'You will take sustenance in the erotic juices of men and women, and you will crave for it.'

Sinitia looked totally confused. 'But, the undead ... vampires, I thought ...'

'That they lived off the blood of the living? The men, yes, once they have tasted blood, that becomes their craving and their curse forever, but the female of the species receives her life-force from the fluids of Eros. Much better than sucking blood, don't you agree? It makes one glad to be female.'

'I agree, fair Demonia,' said Sinitia, standing, 'and I crave! Perhaps ...' She made to move towards the prostrate body of the young man. Demonia caught her arm.

'No, my child, they are drained. We must find others. Come, let us see what kind of world awaits us!'

Together, they drew back the creaking, rusted gate to the old manor house and stepped into the street. They looked around with bemused excitement. Where there had once been fields and thick woods of ancient oaks there were tightly-packed edifices to new prosperity soaring skywards, dwarfing what was now a single avenue of old houses

18

which somehow had remained untouched by progress. The manor itself, once lauded for its magnificence, looked sadly decrepit, its darkened portals all but hidden by the trees.

As they approached the bright, brash city centre, Demonia and Sinitia realised that much had happened in the world since they had slept and become entombed within the relative safety of the crypt, over two centuries previously. Like any traveller in time, however, they soon began to adjust to the situation – once they'd recovered from the shock of nearly being mowed down by speeding cars, their ears had become used to the deafening pop music blaring from almost every doorway and their eyes had grown accustomed to the searing, bright night-lights of London in the late twentieth century.

'What has happened?' asked Sinitia fearfully. 'What is this devilish place?'

'The years have torn the heart from the village and turned it into a city.'

'But what kind of place is this?' said Sinitia as the girls walked slowly along the damp, broken paving stones, absorbing the racy atmosphere and ignoring the calls and propositions from the many nefarious individuals who scurried about the streets like rats. 'What has happened?'

Demonia regarded the scene around her. 'We have slept, that is all. Things change.'

'I'm not sure that I like it. These people, they seem so bizarre.'

'No,' said Demonia, her eyes glinting evilly, 'this is a wonderful place. So many chances for wickedness to thrive. We shall do well, Sinitia.'

'But we are not wicked. You said we give only pleasure. I would not wish to harm anyone.'

'Nor shall you. It is not our way. But there is an aura about this place, something I cannot explain. I am certain that we will learn much.'

'I am sure you are right,' said her friend, nevertheless looking around her with great trepidation. 'But pray, Demonia, I need more sustenance, and I need the feeling of a man's fine stalk deep inside me.'

'What you say is true. You have waited too long to have your maidenhead torn by the rampant thrusts of a handsome lover. We must find one who is worthy of you.'

'I do not think I will have much trouble in achieving that,' said Sinitia as she watched the whores plying their trade to men who drew up in large, dark-windowed cars. 'We will watch what those women do.'

'The street women?' Demonia looked exasperated. 'I am afraid such an experience will never fully satisfy the likes of us. We need the pleasure of conquest, titillation and seduction!'

'Then we must hunt! We must find this man – my need is so great!'

'Indeed,' said Demonia, with barely concealed impatience. 'And there will be many opportunities to play our games. But we are still weak and we need further nourishment.'

'Very well, but let it be on our terms.'

Demonia grinned, running her tongue lightly over her teeth. 'Of course,' she said. 'Could it ever be any other way?'

They stood on a dimly-lit corner of the street and waited. Presently, a sleek, black limousine slid gracefully to a halt beside them and they heard the electric buzzing of a window being wound down. A small, bespectacled man's face appeared from the rear of the car.

'You girls,' he said, in a high-pitched, weak voice. 'How much for both of you?'

Demonia had no conception as to price. 'One gold sovereign,' she said after a long pause, worried that it was too much.

The man laughed; an unpleasant, cackling sound. 'Don't be fucking funny, dear,' he said, nastily. 'Look, I'll give you one hundred for the pair of you, but you stay for a full hour.'

Demonia nodded, her expression managing to hide her shock at the figure. A hundred pounds! A girl could get very rich in a single night doing this type of work!

The car door was opened and the girls climbed uncertainly into the automobile, sitting on either side of the man, whose stature turned out to be as small and insignificant as his voice implied. The vehicle pulled away quickly, speeding round a number of streets until it stopped in a darkened alleyway. The driver was hidden behind a thick, smoked-glass screen, apparently unconcerned about what his employer was up to in the back of the car.

No sooner had the engine been turned off than the man unzipped his trousers, drawing out a short, stubby erection and holding it aloft, as if for inspection. 'I want both of you to suck me at the same time, then I will fuck you in turn, and give you slags something to remember,' he commanded.

The girls looked at each other and smiled. They would certainly give *him* a time to remember.

They quickly stripped off their tight jeans and T-shirts, revealing their perfect bodies to their client for the first time. His face seemed to show some appreciation, but he said nothing and put a podgy hand behind each of their necks, pulling their faces down to his lap.

Demonia took the thick end of his penis into her soft, wet mouth and suckled the spongy tip lightly. Sinitia licked up and down the side of his stem, occasionally allowing her tongue to run over her friend's lips, then back down to his balls. She ran the tip of her tongue wetly over the wrinkled sack, drawing one, then both between the thick lips of her wide mouth in a way that she seemed to know by instinct would drive men wild with desire.

Demonia joined her in licking at the base of his stalk, then Sinitia took over the work of sucking the end of his steel-hard erection, tightening her pouting lips around the head. The man started to groan, and Demonia knew he would not last long, despite his insistence that they gave him a full hour. She knelt between his legs, raising them high into the air so that her tongue could lap greedily at his balls while Sinitia continued to suckle his raging stalk. Demonia wet her finger with her spittle and wormed it inside the man's bottom. She felt his muscles tense and he was lost. With a groan and an oath he came, his juices filling Sinitia's mouth as Demonia pushed her finger further inside him while squeezing his balls with the palm of her hand and draining him completely.

The man fell back, his tiny cock shrivelled and useless. Demonia smiled at Sinitia and pulled her friend's face towards hers until they kissed, sharing the warm seed that Sinitia had held within her mouth. The man lay, unconscious, and unlikely to recover until morning.

Demonia reached into his jacket inside-pocket and took out his wallet, gasping when she opened it. It was crammed full of strange-looking notes of high denomination. She carefully counted the hundred pounds they had been promised and stuffed the money into her jeans pocket before dressing.

The driver didn't seem disposed to take them back to where they had been picked up, sitting dumbly as he sucked on a small, foul-smelling cigar. The girls waited a few moments then opened the door, climbed out of the car and headed in the direction of the main street, their spirits high, their eyes not seeing the newspaper hoarding bearing the banner headline 'ANOTHER BLOODLESS BODY FOUND'.

'I'm still hungry,' said Sinitia, as they ambled down the busy pavement.

'I hunger also,' Demonia answered, eyeing the firm, jean-clad buttocks of a young man who was walking ahead of them. 'For me, it is because it has been so long since I drank the juices of life. But for you, dear Sinitia, that first joining becomes ever more urgent. We must find someone young and strong, someone who can give us the satisfaction that we crave.'

'Someone like him, perhaps?' said Sinitia, her eyes glinting with lust as she stared at the huge form of a nightclub doorman standing nonchalantly at the entrance to a seedy establishment. The two girls stopped walking and Demonia eyed their prospective victim hungrily, licking her lips with the tip of her tongue as she warmed to the idea of taking him. The now familiar twitching sensation began within her dampening sex.

22

The doorman stood a full six-and-a-half feet tall and was massively broad. His face was as black as ebony, even darker than Sinitia. His body, although clad in formal evening attire, was clearly firm and muscular. His expression was grim, exuding power and menace.

'Perfect,' said Demonia, huskily. 'He will suit our purposes admirably!' They walked over to the man, who regarded them casually although his eyes betrayed an obvious attraction to the two devastatingly gorgeous females clad only in skin-tight jeans and tiny T-shirts.

'Want to come in, girls?' he said, making to open the door. Demonia stroked the satin lapel of his black jacket sensuously.

'Why should we go in there,' she said, gazing sexily into his eyes, 'when we have all that we need right here?'

The doorman grinned broadly, pulling the heavy door wide open. 'Now, ladies, in you go. You'll get me the sack.'

Feigning disappointment, the girls brushed unnecessarily close against the big man and entered the gloom of the nightclub, their ears at once assailed by a cacophony of electronic sounds from within. Sinitia clasped her hands to the sides of her head.

'My ears!' she said. 'Such noise – it is a place of torture!'

Demonia ignored her complaint, walking cautiously down the steep stairs towards the source of the pandemonium. Gradually, her ears grew accustomed to the level of the volume and she was able to pick out the steady, incessant rhythm and to distinguish between the sounds. She turned to her friend.

'Come, this is merely a place of revelry!'

Sinitia followed her down the dark steps obediently, joining her as she walked through a beaded curtain into a room filled with people, their faces made anonymous by the flashing, multi-coloured lights. A few danced, their attempts at matching the time of the music with the movements of their bodies lost in alcoholic hopelessness. Others slouched drunkenly over each other, only able to remain standing because of the sheer crush of numbers.

'Hello, ladies, let me buy you a drink,' A tall, bearded

23

man of about sixty staggered over to them, pushing his way heavily through the shuffling crowd and taking advantage of a lull in the music to make himself heard. He clutched a half-empty bottle of champagne which he pushed shakily towards Demonia's face. She turned her head away.

'Come on, darling, it's the best,' he shouted, slipping an arm around her shoulders, more for support than anything else. 'Cost me a bloody fortune!'

Demonia shook her head angrily and pushed the intruder's hand from her body, causing him to lurch towards Sinitia.

'Stuck up bitch, eh? Well, never mind, I prefer your friend. I like a nice bit of black. They've always got lovely arses, black girls, and they always . . .'

His conversation was cut short by the sudden and welcome arrival of the doorman, who unceremoniously dragged him by his coat out of the door, throwing him roughly on to the stairs.

'Out, shithead, out, and don't come back!'

The bewildered drunk picked himself unsteadily to his feet and clambered up the stairway, still clutching his precious bottle and muttering angrily to himself. Demonia and Sinitia began to follow, having decided that the club was not for them.

'Don't go, ladies, he won't be back.' Their rescuer held the door for them, his grin as broad as ever and his teeth large and blindingly white against the ebony of his skin.

Demonia held up her hand. 'No, thank you, there is too much noise in this place. We wish to talk.'

The big man let the door close. 'Come up to the office,' he said, leading the way back up the stairway. 'I'll buy you a drink and you can talk as much as you like.'

He carried on climbing the stairs, not waiting for an answer. The girls followed.

'Yes,' whispered Demonia to her friend, 'he is perfect. He will teach us all we need to know.'

'And care for us, I think,' retorted Sinitia, 'and guard us whilst we sleep.'

They entered a small, sparsely-furnished room. Demonia

and Sinitia sat on the only available chairs and the door-man made himself comfortable on a rickety desk. He took a pack of cigarettes from his jacket pocket and offered them. Demonia shook her head but Sinitia sat motionless, as though unable to understand. The doorman shrugged and took one for himself, tossing the pack on to the desk and picking up a small, plastic lighter which he flicked into life. The girls both blinked, startled by the sudden flame. He looked at them curiously as he drew deeply on the cigarette and blew the smoke casually above their heads.

'Haven't seen you around here before. Where d'you usually work?'

'Work?' said Demonia. 'What do you mean?'

'You know full well what I mean. Don't come all innocent with me. Girls don't come to Hampstead dressed like you two unless they're working.'

'Hampstead? Is that where we are? I thought . . .'

'You're a strange pair, that's for sure. Where d'you live?'

'Gallows Hill.'

The big man shook his head resignedly. 'That's just a road. You probably saw it when you walked down here. Come on, where's your usual manor?'

'The manor? It's . . .' Demonia stopped herself. This con-versation was getting nowhere. 'My apologies, sir,' she said, 'we are new to the, er, work. In fact tonight is our first time.'

The big man's eyes widened. 'Really? Two little crackers like you? What are you then? Daddy's little rich girls from Purley, looking for a bit of excitement?'

'I am sorry, I do not understand. What is Purley?' Demonia was becoming impatient, but nevertheless felt that already they were learning, and this man would teach them more.

'OK, have it your way. But I tell you, it's a wicked, evil world out there, full of nasty men who would love to eat two little beauties like you for breakfast.'

Sinitia looked startled. 'Cannibals? There are cannibals here?'

Their host shook his head in bemusement. 'What's she on?'

25

'She is very young; she doesn't understand. Will you help us?'

'Help you? How can I help you? D'you want a business manager?'

'We need someone who can teach us all we need to know. We will make good and willing pupils.'

He took another long draw on his cigarette, looking at his lovely guests thoughtfully.

'OK, you got yourself a business manager.'

Sinitia jumped up from her seat, smiling gleefully, although clearly not understanding what was going on. 'Wonderful,' she said. 'Now can we fuck?'

She unbuttoned the front of his jacket and ran her hand over his muscular stomach, slipping a couple of fingers inside his shirt and running the tips over his hard flesh. 'I expect your rod is so huge that you would fill a virgin until she cried out!'

'You don't waste words, do you?' The big man's eyes were wide open, staring straight into her hypnotic gaze.

'Let us not stay in this place, it is not right,' said Demonia, pulling Sinitia's hand from the man's clothing. 'Come back with us now and we will talk some more, and show you what you must do for us.'

'Do for you? Look ladies, let's get one thing straight. You work for *me*, not the other way round.'

'Whatever you say,' said Demonia, taking his arm. 'Come, we will go back and listen to you and if you wish it you can fuck us both. We will not disappoint you.'

The doorman gulped. 'Jesus, there's something wrong here.'

'Wrong? Why wrong?'

'Well, it ain't Christmas so how come two gorgeous pieces like you are coming on to me?'

Demonia shook her head. 'I am sorry, I don't understand. Come with us. You have something we want.' She reached down and casually stroked the front of his trousers, thrilling to the feel of his hardening sex against her fingers.

'OK girls,' he said proudly, 'you got yourselves a fuck. Wait there, I'll just tell the boss I'm taking a break.'

'A break?' Demonia looked at him quizzically.

'You know, a rest.' The man was already opening the office door, his eagerness confounding his good sense.

'There will be no rest for you,' said Demonia, squeezing the rising bulge in his trousers. 'None at all.' The doorman simply grinned.

'I think he will give us what we want,' said Demonia as he left the room, 'and when we have taken it, he will serve us in other ways.'

Sinitia smiled an evil, malevolent grin, her hand trailing to between her legs and the tips of her fingers playing softly against her denim-covered sex. 'My need is great,' she implored. 'Let me take him first.'

The man returned and stood impatiently, his face a picture of eager anticipation. 'Right, lead the way,' he said, holding the door open for them. They walked down the steps to the club entrance. The doorman put his heavy arms around their slender shoulders and they slipped theirs under his jacket, hooking their thumbs into the waistband of his trousers as they headed out into the night, turning in the direction of Gallows Hill.

The big man didn't seem nonplussed as they walked into the grounds of the old manor, nor when they opened the iron gate at the entrance to the crypt. No doubt his anticipation and sexual excitement were so great that he would have accepted anything.

They entered the half-light of the main cellar, Demonia closing the heavy door firmly behind them and sliding the bolt into place. 'We don't want to be disturbed,' she said, pushing her hands under his jacket lapels and stroking his massive chest through his crisp, white shirt.

He just grinned as the two nymphets tugged off his jacket, Demonia unfastening his bow-tie as Sinitia unbuttoned the front of his shirt. He took out his gold cuff-links and put them carefully into his trouser-pocket before allowing the girls to remove his shirt completely and bare his glistening, black torso.

Demonia licked at his chest, tasting his sweat, and held

27

one of his nipples between her teeth as her hands stroked his huge pectoral muscles. Sinitia, meanwhile. unfastened his trouser-belt and tugged his zip down, anxious to get at her prize. She wrenched his trousers down to his ankles and fell to her knees, groping at his tight briefs. With one superhuman tug she ripped his pants apart, the force and strength of the operation clearly surprising him. She threw the tattered garment to one side and clamped her mouth against his hardening sex, breathing in his heavy odours lustily.

Demonia joined her friend on the floor, both girls now taking hold of his length and coaxing it quickly to full erection with the playful caresses of their expert tongues and fingers. His stiff, black manhood was long and thick and the bulbous end was weeping pre-come which glistened in the shaft of moonlight that shone through the small, barred window. Sinitia put out her long tongue and licked the delicate juice, her face a picture of delight as she tasted him and ran the wetness over her lips. She opened her mouth wide and took him in, bobbing her head back and forth and swallowing over half of his length with each forward movement.

Demonia concentrated her licking on his balls, sucking them into her mouth alternately and tickling the wrinkled sack with the tip of her tongue. He began to make involuntary thrusting movements and pushed his long stalk in and out of Sinitia's thick-lipped mouth, his breathing heavy. Without allowing his erection to leave its wet prison, she struggled out of her jeans and ripped the T-shirt from her body. She was now kneeling naked at his feet, serving him with her mouth. Demonia stood up and removed her clothes, knelt behind him and pressed her face against his bottom, her long tongue probing between the stiff, firm buttocks and reaching his tight sphincter. He stopped his movements to allow her exploration, the sensation obviously one he enjoyed.

Sinitia let his cock fall from her mouth and turned away from him, kneeling on the cold stone floor on her hands and knees, her sensuously curved bottom presented to him for his enjoyment. The sight was too much for him and despite his obvious pleasure at having his anus licked, he crouched behind the lovely girl, his prick hard and ready to impale her.

Demonia knelt at his side and took hold of his superb cock, guiding the thick, wet end to its target, opening her friend's pussy lips with her other hand. 'Now, my sister, now you will know full satisfaction.'

Sinitia let out a cry as her hymen was broken then sighed heavily, closing her eyes. The man appeared unaware that he had just deflowered a virgin and groaned as his tool sank into the soaking, spongy honey-pot. Demonia rubbed quickly at his exposed length but then let go, allowing every inch to be swallowed up by the eager, desperate cunt. Sinitia squealed with delight at the immenseness of the intrusion.

Demonia slipped her sumptuous form under her friend's body, so that her face was level with Sinitia's ravaged sex. The sight of the large black phallus sliding in and out of the thick, wet lips was incredibly stimulating. She arched her back and pushed her hips upwards, silently begging Sinitia to suckle her and gasping joyously when she felt the young girl's long tongue flutter over her engorged clitoris. She raised her head and returned the compliment on the gorgeous, hairy pussy impaled on the thick, black stalk. She flicked the tip of her tongue over the swollen bud, making Sinitia squeal and dive her head between Demonia's legs, her hands gripping firmly at her soft buttocks and her mouth greedily chewing at the pouting sex lips.

The doorman's movements became faster and faster and his pumping grew more and more urgent as he hammered his stiffness into the oozing sheath. Sinitia raised her head and shouted at him, 'That's it! Yes, fuck me, fuck me! I have waited so long for this! Sate me, saturate me! Fill me up with your delicious seed!'

'You two sure talk strange,' panted the man, 'but I ain't complaining!' The crudeness of her words seemed to drive him to thrust ever harder. He was grunting like an animal, his balls slapping against Demonia's forehead as she sucked on her friend's clitoris. With a wild and triumphant roar the man came, the throbbing of his staff vibrating against Demonia's mouth as her fluttering tongue brought Sinitia to a wild, ecstatic orgasm. She reached up and gripped his balls hard, determined to drain him of his juices and eager to taste them for herself.

He eased his slowly wilting manhood from Sinitia's warm, pulsating grip and Demonia promptly pulled it to her mouth, suckling hungrily on the remains of his ejaculation and the evidence of her friend's arousal. Sinitia lay her head gently of Demonia's wet sex, sobbing happily with the after-effects of her orgasm as she fingered and licked gently at the engorged sex lips.

As post-orgasmic tenderness began to affect him, their lover pulled his erection from Demonia's sucking mouth and sat back on his discarded clothing which afforded him some comfort on the cold stone floor. He couldn't have been ready for the sight that now met his gaze.

Sinitia raised herself up and squatted over her friend's face, inches above her mouth. Gradually, ever so slowly, the erotic cream so recently forced deep into the black girl's sheath began its inevitable journey, slipping from the pursed lips and trailing down into the open, hungry mouth below. He watched, fascinated, as Demonia drank in his fluids and swallowed with obvious pleasure the copious amounts of sperm, her face becoming flushed with excitement.

As the flow eased, she raised her head and sucked at Sinitia's sex, anxiously draining her of every precious drop. This action prompted Sinitia to ride again towards orgasm, arching her back as she ground her hips down and soaking her friend's lovely face and hair. The doorman, hard again as a result of the erotic show he had just witnessed, strode determinedly to her side, pushing his tool towards her face. Sinitia opened her mouth and gratefully accepted his offered prize, sucking hard on him and rubbing his length fiercely. Despite his recent spending he couldn't hold back, and shot another liberal amount of sperm down her throat, hearing her muffled scream as she simultaneously came on Demonia's suckling mouth.

Sinitia swallowed hard, not letting his penis leave her mouth until she was sure that he was drained. 'Oh baby, that's good,' he said. 'You sure know how to suck cock.' She took him from her mouth and licked around the now drooping monster, tasting his sweat mingled with his pubic aromas.

Wearily, the three lovers separated, the girls sat on the floor, the coldness of the stone on their bottoms helping to calm them and ease their shivering bodies back into reality.

The doorman sat on an old, upturned coffin, looking around the cellar in wonder. 'You girls have got a real nice place here,' he said with more than a hint of sarcasm as he noticed the empty caskets and profusion of cobwebs for the first time, his lust now temporarily sated.

Demonia rose and stood in front of him, her legs apart and her hand playfully pulling at her inflamed pussy lips. 'It's been our home for many years,' she said, in a serious tone. 'I am so glad you like it, as you will be here for some time.'

'Sorry, sugar,' he said, attempting to reach for his clothing, 'I gotta get back to work.' He grabbed at his trousers, but Demonia kicked them out of the way.

'But you haven't fucked me yet,' she said, her face showing an expression of genuine disappointment. 'You must sate me before we can let you go.'

He grinned, still unaware of the menace in her tone. 'I'm not sure I could raise it again, darling,' he said, making another grab for his trousers. Demonia caught hold of his penis and pulled firmly on it, digging her long fingernails into the root.

'I'm sure you can,' she said seductively, her eyes staring into his, willing his response. 'Come on, I want to see it rise once more. Come on.'

His breathing became shallow, his will completely gone. His manhood began to thicken under her grip as her hand pulled at the expanding length as though milking it. Soon, clearly to his own astonishment, he was as stiff as before; steel-hard, erect, ready. Demonia stood astride his thighs and lowered herself on to him, gasping with pleasure as the huge stalk impaled her to the hilt.

She held herself still for a moment, enjoying the mixture of fear and lust in his expression. Gradually, she started to rock her hips backwards and forwards, his length staying fully inside her. Her vaginal muscles squeezed the stiff tool, gripping the gnarled flesh like a tight, wet mouth.

Then she began to ride him, lifting herself up so that just the large bulbous head of his sex was inside her heavenly sheath, then ramming her body down hard on him, taking the entire monster into her pulsating warmth and drawing his very life into her womb.

His head fell forward heavily and his eyes closed, but still he remained hard inside her. With every thrust of her hips he slipped more and more into unconsciousness, his entire strength being sucked from him by the power of her will. Demonia moved faster now, sensing the first waves that signalled her orgasm emanating from between her legs.

'I have him, Sinitia!' she cried, panting heavily. 'He is completely at our mercy!'

She began to hump wildly, holding on to his broad shoulders, as the sensations became more and more intense.

'Oh, yes, yes,' she panted, her cries of erotic joy directed not to the prostrate figure of her lover but to Sinitia who stood eagerly watching the scene, her eyes wide and shining with lustful wonder. 'I am coming, I am coming!'

'Yes, my love,' cried Sinitia, running her hands over the smooth skin of Demonia's back, feeling the warmth of her sweat under her fingers. 'Come on that lovely big stalk! Fuck yourself insane on him! Use him as he wished to use us!'

Demonia's orgasm tore at her sex fiercely, causing her to bite into his shoulder, dangerously close to drawing blood. She fought the desire to bite harder and suck on the wound, aware of the deadly result of such an action and the fact that he would be useless to them without his life and unable to produce more of the wonderful fluids that they needed, or guide them in their studies of this new time. Instead, she raised herself from his lap, letting his erection flop noisily on to his stomach, and knelt before him, taking his thickness in her hand.

She pumped his firm penis rapidly, waiting for it to erupt again, anxious to feed on him once more. Sinitia knelt facing her, gripping him also, and the quick movements of the two, soft hands worked harmoniously in their task.

The big man fell back over the coffin, his body curved awkwardly with his head resting on the floor. The girls ignored his plight as his body now arched erotically over the casket and his erection pointed vertically under their ministrations.

They knew he wouldn't feel a thing anyway.

Suddenly, as though it had a life of its own, the end of his penis began to swell and the stem started to throb. The girls rubbed as fast as they could at the stiffening stalk until, with a sudden involuntary lunge of his hips, he shot out his seed once more. The welcome ejaculation soaked his belly. The girls licked hungrily at his juices, sliding their tongues over his wet skin and pumping him steadily until there was no more to take.

They sat back, looking in admiration at their victim as he lay across the coffin, his penis now lying harmlessly flaccid on his sweat-soaked stomach. 'I was right,' said Demonia. 'He is perfect for us. He makes copious love-fluids. I feel that my hunger is satisfied at last.'

'I agree,' said Sinitia. 'We must keep him. He will serve us well.'

'Indeed. He will provide us with occasional sustenance and will teach us about the strange ways of this time.'

Without the slightest difficulty, they raised the huge unconscious man to his feet and dragged him by his upper arms to a wall, fixing his arms and legs to the ancient iron manacles that hung there, a testament to past indiscretions. He hung forward slightly under the restraints, his head bowed to his chest as if in subordination. The girls stood back and surveyed their captive, looking greedily at his firm, ebony body and his long, drooping manhood.

'Yes,' said Demonia, 'Perfect. When he has prepared and clothed us we shall again go out into this world and seek to draw others into the sisterhood, and to share the knowledge of the many joys and deviations of sexual conquest that have been learned over the centuries!'

Sinitia smiled a broad, gleaming grin of sheer excitement. 'And for my part there will be nothing I will not experience, nothing I will refuse!'

Demonia glanced at the small window, seeing the faint light of dawn appearing. 'Indeed, you will learn much, and soon be ready to teach others. But come now, we must sleep.'

They walked steadily to their eerie resting places and climbed within the reassuring surrounds of the old wood. They closed their eyes to the increasing daylight outside, awaiting their reawakening with the onset of the beautiful night.

Two

The ancient notebook sat on the edge of the desk where Doctor Alex Tankard had left it while he busied himself marking the pile of students' submissions before him. He was becoming increasingly exasperated; the keenness of the undergraduates to participate in the studies of erotic psychology was matched only by their apparent inability to write coherent sentences.

He took off his reading glasses and pinched the bridge of his nose, rubbing his eyes with the back of his hand. He glanced at the book and the yellowing, curled leaves beckoning for his attention, and thought of the strange character who had delivered it to him the previous evening. Hardly a word had been exchanged between them. The dusty package had merely been thrust into his hand at the door, the old man mumbling something about it being the work of an ancestor of his and that he had strict instructions to give it to him personally.

Apart from taking a cursory glance at the faded sheets of notepaper, pressures of work had served to stem his curiosity so far. He had studied his undergraduates' vain attempts at clarity well into the night and throughout most of that morning, but now he was rapidly becoming weary of trying to make sense of the pages of misunderstandings and incompetence that barely warranted his concentration.

Sarah, his lover of three years, sat in an armchair on the far side of the office, deep in thought. As head of occult studies at Cowden University, she could often be found apparently daydreaming when in reality her sharp mind would be mulling over the latest thesis on the mysteries of the earth and beyond. Married to Professor Fox, one of

35

the most senior and certainly the dullest of dons, she had taken to wiling away the hours in Alex's company, their intellects and sexual libidos ideally suited.

The studies of Doctor Tankard's class had recently been centred on the history of polygamy, a rather dusty subject which clearly, from the standard of their submissions, had not inspired his students. Next week the discussions would cover anal sex; perhaps they might respond better to a more basic topic.

He pondered to himself that it had been only two years previously, at the age of thirty-one that he had had his first ever experience of anal sex, the first of many wonderfully mind-blowing sessions with the beautiful Sarah. He looked at her affectionately and smiled as he remembered how he had once thought of her as a witch. Her long blonde hair was perpetually tied severely in a tight bun on her head, thin-rimmed glasses perched precariously on the end of her nose and she insisted on wearing shapeless clothes to classes.

How differently she had appeared that first evening in his room, her shining hair falling softly over her slender shoulders and the spectacles kept in their case. She had called to discuss her thesis on erotica and the occult and the conversation had become more and more sensuous as they talked well into the night. Eventually they had both surrendered to the inevitable, tearing at each other's clothing and falling to the thinly-carpeted floor in a frenzy of uncontrollable lust. There had been no passion or affection in this first coupling; he had fucked her, and she had fucked him. It was as simple as that.

The sight of her perfect bottom presented to him as she had begged him to enter that sweet forbidden orifice had nearly made him lose control there and then, but he had somehow managed to contain his burning desire for release, sinking deep within her tightness until his cock was embedded to the hilt, his groin pressed against the soft curves of her buttocks while his balls lightly touched the warm wetness of her pussy.

He had come then, a powerfully explosive orgasm that had caused him to collapse over her kneeling body, groaning with the sheer joy of the moment. If Sarah had been disappointed at the speed of his release she hadn't shown it, visiting him almost nightly thereafter to teach and prove to him that the wonders of erotic encounters were not only to be found within the dusty, leather-bound covers of his old psychology books.

From that moment on, Alex had partly concentrated his studies on anal erotica, even writing a thesis on the subject which, unusual in the world of academia, had become an instant bestseller. In truth, Sarah had co-written the book with him, but her desire to maintain an aura of respectability among her studious colleagues had caused her to beg him to keep her name off the credits.

As Alex sat looking at her now – the long legs curled under her lovely bottom, her baggy clothing all but concealing the perfection of her lithe physique – he began to feel a familiar stirring within his loins.

'I've had enough,' he exclaimed brusquely, the sudden break in the silence startling Sarah back to reality. He threw yet another file of badly-scrawled notes on to the growing pile and sat back in his chair, picking up the old book as he did so.

'What's that?' asked Sarah.

'A strange old guy brought it to me yesterday. He said it belonged to an ancestor of mine, and that it was imperative that I should read it. Weird chap. Looked as old as the book itself.'

'Have you read any of it?' Sarah walked over to his desk, as usual interested in anything hinging on the mysterious.

'A little. It appears that I'm descended from a vampire hunter!'

Sarah looked astonished. 'You're joking!' she exclaimed, grabbing the book from his hand and swiftly sifting through the parchment-like pages, 'Professor Stanley Tankard . . . he's your ancestor?'

'You know of him?'

'Of course. He was one of the most celebrated of demon exorcists in the eighteenth century. I can't believe you're descended from him!'

'It's possible, I suppose,' said Alex, barely interested, 'Tankard isn't a particularly common name. Does it matter?'

Sarah was already absorbed in reading, flicking the pages excitedly. 'May I borrow this? I promise I'll take great care of it.'

'Keep it,' said Alex, reluctantly picking up another file. Without another word, Sarah gathered up her coat and left the room. Alex glanced after her, shrugged his shoulders as the door closed and went back to his work.

'You *must* read it! Alex, it's incredible!' Sarah burst into his room, loudly interrupting his early evening nap. He regarded her through dozy eyes.

'What do you mean? Read what?'

'The notebook! Professor Tankard's notes! You won't believe what he says!'

'The man was clearly mad,' said Alex, taking the book from Sarah's hand. 'Anybody who believed in vampires no doubt spent most of his spare time dancing with fairies.'

Sarah scowled. 'I've told you before. There's a lot more . . .'

'I know,' he said impatiently, 'there's a lot more to life than can ever be supposed by mere mortal man. OK, I'll read it, I promise.' He set the book down on a table. Sarah picked it up and thrust it back into his hand.

'Now! Read it now!' she demanded. Alex was a little taken aback by her enthusiasm for this tatty epistle. He'd never seen her so excited, apart, of course, from the numerous occasions when she squirmed her luscious body against his during their regular bouts of exquisite lovemaking.

He sat down and opened the book, taking up his reading-glasses. 'I'll leave you to it,' said Sarah, opening the door. 'I'll call back in an hour or so.'

Alex nodded irritably, and began to read.

The content of most of the notes served to confirm Alex's initial inclinations; that they were the ramblings of a severely deluded mind. Tales of vampires stalking the streets of London, the good professor's encounters with the living dead, and the final purge when victory seemed to be within his grasp were all the stuff of Victorian horror novels. It wasn't until he started to read the last few pages that his opinion began to change.

Scrawled in a hand, albeit similar to his illustrious ancestor's copper-plate, the words had clearly been hastily scribed. Gone were the dusty historical references and the academic style of prose. There was a sudden urgency; a clarity that begged attention.

'May God in His Heaven forgive me,' the section began, 'I have made a terrible mistake! For years I have hunted them down, the evil that plagues humanity, vampires that feed from the very life-blood of their victims; and I was so wrong!

'Were it not for that sweet child who visited me last night I would have gone to my grave believing that all such entities are evil, but it is not so!

'I had taken to my bed early, suffering from a slight fever and awoke in the depth of the night to find her standing at my bedside, a gentle waif of a girl barely in her twenties, the most sensuous of visions. She was naked, save for a sliver of gossamer about her waist, her body slender, her breasts small, and her face, oh her face! Such perfection belongs in heaven itself!

'She spoke, in the gentlest of tones. "Professor," she said, pleadingly, her eyes filling up with tears, "you must stop. We are not all evil. Only the males of my creed present any threat to humankind. We, the sisters, obtain our sustenance in a far more pleasurable way."

'I pleaded with her, telling her that I did not understand her words, my mind still heavy with sleep. She approached me, resting her hand on the counterpane and pulling it slowly back, revealing my nakedness.

'I lay in terror, fearing that my last moment had come. I wanted to pull myself from the bed and run, to escape what I saw as certain death but was rooted to the spot, mesmerised by her sheer beauty and an unexplainable aura of erotic sensuality.

'I closed my eyes and waited for the sharp kiss of her teeth on my neck. Instead, I felt her take my manhood within her grasp and gently rub it before closing her mouth around the rapidly stiffening stalk. For one terrible moment I thought that she might bite into it, a truly ghastly way to die but instead she continued her oral caress, coaxing my member into an incredible hardness. Clearly, she merely wished to give me pleasure.

'As she suckled on my raging weapon she rubbed it steadily until, with a certainty that can be imagined, I ejaculated, my seed filling her sweet mouth. She stood up and smiled, pointedly swallowing my fluids, a truly arousing spectacle. "This is our way," she said. "We mean you no harm."

' "How can I believe you?" I asked, my voice weak from my illness and from the ultimate pleasure I had just enjoyed. She smiled and turned to look at the window. I followed her gaze, to be greeted by the most wondrous of sights. Standing in the portal, their naked frames silhouetted against the brightness of the full moon, stood three more maidens, the perfection of their young bodies accentuated by the sheen of silver light.

' "Let us convince you," my first nocturnal visitor said, in a voice that rang with the sounds of angels. She bent over my body and took my penis once more into her mouth, while at the same time removing the tiny wisp of material from around her waist. Despite my release I felt my stalk rising within the warmth of her suckling mouth, the rapid movement of her hand around my shaft speedily forcing my member once more to the fiercest of erections.

'The three newcomers seemed to drift to my side, standing around me, their hands delicately caressing my sweating body. One by one they kissed me, full on the mouth, their tongues snaking between my lips, exploring, probing. I reached up and put my fingers to the hairless mound of one, finding it wet with her arousal. My other hand was taken by another maid and pressed to her joyous prize, my fingers delving deep into the slippery lips. The third girl clambered on to my bed and squatting over my head, lowered her broad hips until her cunt touched my mouth.

'I slid my tongue between the sweetly-scented sex lips, the taste as enchanting as anything that heaven could provide.

'I felt the angel who had been sucking my raging tool raise herself; my next sensation being that of her divine, tight sheath enveloping my stalk to the hilt. She held still for a moment, then began her erotic dance, moving her hips in a circular motion, absorbing me within her sublime pulchritude.

'On and on, as the night wore on they moved around me, each allowing me to taste the delights of their excitement, each lowering her perfect body upon my throbbing shaft. At one time my legs were raised and two of these enchanting nymphs licked at my balls and anus, a third fucking herself on my cock, the fourth sating her lust on my probing tongue.

'At length I could take no more, and my lovers seemed to sense my imminent climax. Allowing me to fall from within the confines of her soaked sheath, one of the maidens took hold of my tool and rubbed it furiously, my seed copiously spraying across my chest and stomach, the sheer joyous pain of my climax tearing at my very soul. Then, with an almost manic delight, they licked at my fluids, sharing them, their tongues sliding all over my upper body. This sensation, as I slowly recovered from my release, is one that can barely be imagined.

'Then my first visitor spoke again. "If we had meant you harm," she said, a small droplet of sperm slipping erotically from her pouted lips, "we could have bitten into your flesh at any time." She licked her lips and swallowed hard. "This is all we need, I swear."

'Then they were gone, vanishing into the night from whence they had come. I considered her words at length, imagining that there was trickery here or that my fever had been more severe than I had supposed but, perhaps as a result of her hypnotic persuasion, I somehow *knew* that the words that she had spoken were the truth.

'I fear that their resting place will soon be uncovered by one of my colleagues, and that their mortal remains will be

41

destroyed. I am an old man; I cannot imagine that God has left me enough time to right the awful wrong I have committed. I pray, therefore, that a brave and trustworthy descendant of mine will uncover these hurried scribblings and believe the truth of my words, and implore him to discover whether any of these unfortunate maidens survived and beg their forgiveness.'

Alex pondered the old professor's last jottings quietly. When Sarah returned he was deep in thought, re-reading the last passages of the notebook over and over again carefully.

'Isn't it fantastic?' she said, almost gleefully. 'What a discovery!'

'But no one believes in vampires any more. What good will it do to publish this? It'll be dismissed as nonsense.'

'We must study the accounts of the professor's purges some more, look at his records and those of his colleagues in depth. There's got to be further clues somewhere!'

'But where do we start?'

'Hampstead! That was where he lived and died. Church records, anything, we must honour your ancestor's last wishes! And who knows, perhaps some of them have indeed survived. Perhaps there are female vampires in London today!'

Doctor Alex Tankard eyed the throng of young men and girls which packed the cramped hall with a mixture of suspicion and apprehension. It was certainly true that as senior tutor of erotic psychology his lectures were always well patronised by eager students anxious to further their libidinous education, but today's attendance was by all accounts exceptional.

The subject matter of this week's programme of discourses clearly had something to do with the heightened interest in the studies amongst the bright-eyed, chattering undergraduates. The hardly innocuous title 'The History and Folklore of Anal Sex' appearing among the dry and dusty subjects on the week's roster had attracted many a wet-lipped and dry-throated youngster to this stuffy room on a hot, June day.

Alex walked to the podium and stood quietly, surveying the scene before him. For once there seemed to be far more women than men which was unusual for his classes and confirmed his theory that the erstwhile taboo practice of anal penetration was becoming of great interest to the females in the community while the males still tended to be overly cautious of even suggesting such a thing to their partners. Today's lecture was to be the first drawn from his thesis. His decision to introduce the work into the course was clearly the right one.

He coughed, nervously shuffling the papers on the desk before him. The room fell into immediate silence, all eyes turned towards him. He coughed again, clumsily stacking the papers on the side of the desk, only to have them fall to the floor. The room erupted into laughter and Alex cursed under his breath as he stooped to retrieve the scattered notes. Why was he so nervous? He had given countless talks containing the most explicit of material in the past and yet, for some reason, the old taboos were affecting even him.

He stood up, regaining his composure as he stacked the papers untidily in the centre of the desk. He coughed again and the laughter died away.

'I am going to ask you a question,' he began, his voice barely concealing a tremble. 'A question that many of you will consider to be deeply personal, even offensive.' He paused for effect, the students eagerly awaiting his next words. 'I want you to raise your hand if you have ever experienced anal penetration.' The silence in the room was almost intoxicating, broken only by the distant cries of footballers playing on the green outside. The students looked at each other nervously, none of them presumably possessing the courage to be the first to admit such a fact. Alex had expected just this level of response. Even in these modern times and despite standing before such an enlightened audience, he knew there would be a marked reluctance to own up to what was after all a perfectly normal sexual practice.

'Come now,' he said, with feigned impatience. 'Is there nobody here who will admit to it?'

A small, oriental-looking girl at the front of the hall began to raise her arm then, looking about her and realising that she was on her own, quickly withdrew it. Somebody giggled childishly. Alex scowled.

'Throughout history,' he said, in a deliberately tutorial tone, 'anal intercourse has been considered normal and, indeed often the preferred method of sexual enjoyment amongst all races and classes. In Victorian times it was seen as a perfectly acceptable method of contraception, especially amongst landed gentry and noble lords when taking the favours of their unfortunate serving wenches.' The students laughed; the ice was broken.

'I am going to show you some slides,' he said, signalling for the blinds to be drawn across the brightness of the summer sunlight, 'but I warn you, they are erotic in the extreme and, if any of you feel that you are likely to take offence I would ask you to leave the lecture hall now.'

He paused. As he had expected, nobody moved to the door as the room was gradually eased into semi-darkness. Alex nodded to one of the students at the back of the room, who flicked on the projector.

The slides were of ancient icons of Egyptian, Greek and Roman origin, all depicting various methods and positions enabling anal penetration. One in particular, that of a handsomely endowed young stud impaling a frail nymph drew gasps from some of the young ladies present, the act seemingly made impossible by the sheer size of the youth's appendage. Another, a beautifully drawn picture of a voluptuous goddess accommodating two fine erections between her ample buttocks simultaneously brought a wave of applause. Other, equally explicit icons and drawings followed, the images arousing both laughter and gasps from the increasingly attentive group.

The show came to an end, and the shades were drawn back. Alex looked into the sea of flushed, excited young faces. 'Those icons are over two thousand years old,' he said profoundly, as though in an attempt to keep the discourse on an academic level, 'and prove that there is nothing new in matters of the flesh. It was only at the turn of the century, when the garotte of Victorian suppression was at its greatest strength that such practices were driven underground and even today the inhibitions remain, as I consider was proven earlier.'

A murmur of agreement filled the room. 'Those of you who have taken the trouble to drag yourselves from the implicit attractions of the students' bar and read my thesis on the subject will know that, according to some very reliable research over fifty per cent of females and sixty per cent of males regularly indulge in anal sex. Buggery, sodomy, call it what you will, it is a pleasure to be enjoyed, provided both parties agree. Now, let us discuss the matter further . . .'

Alex relaxed on his sofa, gently stroking Sarah's long, golden tresses as she lay her head in his lap. They were both naked, exhausted from yet another bout of sexual excess, his own performance inspired by the memory of the mass of female undergraduates who had gathered around his desk at the end of the class, excitedly asking questions of the most personal nature. They would have to bolt the doors tomorrow, he mused, to stop the hall becoming dangerously overcrowded. The lecture had been a great success, of that there was no doubt.

He leant forward and kissed Sarah lightly on the head. She sat up sleepily and wrapped her arms around him, drawing his face to hers. They kissed again, deeply and passionately; an embrace of lovers.

'I must go,' she mewed, 'it's getting late.'

'Can't you stay just a little longer?' he asked, knowing her response.

'I have a husband,' she chided. 'He may suspect about us, but there's no need to throw it in his face.' She stood up, clasping her suspender belt around her slim waist. Alex watched hungrily as she drew on her black stockings, smoothing the sheer material over her long, slender legs. His erection began to grow once more. Sarah noticed his predicament and smiled.

'Don't you ever get enough?' she laughed.

Alex responded by leaping to his feet and grabbing her around the waist, pulling her lithe body to his. Their mouths met and they kissed with a wild fervour, their tongues playfully lapping around each other, their crotches rubbing sensuously together. He felt the familiar wetness of her pussy against his cock, now fully erect and he knew that Sarah's husband was going to have to wait a while.

He ran his hands over the silky-smooth skin of her back and down to cup the pert globes of her buttocks, his fingernails digging into the soft, plump flesh. She groaned into his mouth as he eased a finger between them, teasing the tight, puckered orifice, the instant effect being to cause her to press her mound against him even harder. Gradually, he eased the finger inside her, his other hand slipping down over her stomach, sliding between their bodies and squeezing the soaking softness of her sex-flesh.

'Oh, no, Alex,' she pleaded between hungry, demanding kisses, 'not again! I must go!'

Ignoring her protests, he moved his mouth downwards, kissing her throat, licking around the shape of her large firm breasts and sucking her hard, pink nipples. He traced a snail-like track over the gentle curve of her stomach to the damp warmth of her crotch. He parted the lips of her pussy with his thumbs, slid his tongue between them and tasted his own juices along with the scent of her arousal, savouring the succulence and the sensuality.

He drank thirstily from her heavenly chalice, moving his tongue in a circular motion within the open, welcoming lips of her cunt before allowing the tip to flutter over the erect bud of her clitoris. He felt her legs trembling and her knees shaking as she crouched slightly to offer him easier access. His finger once more wormed its way into the tight confines of her anus.

'Oh, all right, Alex,' she breathed, 'once more, but please be quick. No marathons this time.'

He moved back, allowing her to slip to the floor where she lay, her legs wide open, her sex lips red and engorged with her arousal. He leant forward on his hands and knees, his cock finding its target immediately, the length slipping effortlessly into the soaked sheath. He began to pump into her steadily and expertly, his years of study giving him the knowledge to sate the most ardent of lovers. Wriggling his hips he probed her very depths, stretching her and fulfilling her every need.

'God, you're the best fuck I've ever had,' she groaned, moving her hips in time with his quickening thrusts. 'Give it to me, hard, harder . . .'

Alex obeyed, pumping into her more and more rapidly. He manoeuvred their bodies so that they lay on their sides, facing each other and drew her upper leg over his shoulder, slipping his hand to her soft mound, his fingertips quickly finding her clitoris. Rubbing it steadily, he fucked her as hard as he could, the full length of his hard shaft sinking deep into her shuddering body.

'I'm coming, I'm coming!' she yelled, clawing at his back with her long fingernails. 'Come with me, now!'

He stiffened his buttocks and tried to force his orgasm as Sarah squealed with the sheer joy of her own climax. 'Oh, God, oh yes!' she babbled, kissing and biting his neck, the movement of her hips becoming steadily easier.

He hadn't come – he couldn't – but the pleasure of his lover's release was enough. They lay quietly for a moment, their bodies entwined, his cock still firmly ensnared inside her warm prison, their breathing heavy but steady. He felt the beating of her heart against his chest and for a moment felt closer to her than he had been to anyone before.

The knock on the door came suddenly and without warning, causing the two lovers to pull apart quickly. 'My husband!' exclaimed Sarah, struggling to her feet.

'Nonsense!' whispered Alex, standing a little shakily, his long cock jutting ludicrously from his slim, athletic body. 'How would he know you were here?'

Sarah nevertheless looked at him in panic, then ran into the bathroom. Alex grabbed a dressing-gown as a second knock sounded. 'Just a minute!' he called, struggling to conceal his wilting erection within the folds of the garment. He unlocked the door and opened it.

In the hallway stood two young Asian girls whom he

instantly recognised as members of his study group. He also remembered thinking it strange that two such innocent and unworldly students should choose erotic psychology as their principal subject. Nevertheless, they had participated well during the previous year, always keen to learn and ready to play their part in debate, and he had been glad to see them back in his lectures.

'Suzi, Jamina, what brings you here so late?'

'We must see you, Doctor. It is so very important.' The girl who spoke was Jamina, the taller of the two, slender with waist-length black hair and olive skin. Her large, brown eyes were brimming with tears.

'I . . . I'm sorry,' spluttered Alex, vainly attempting to think of a good excuse, 'I'm very busy, I . . .'

'Oh, *please*, Doctor Tankard,' begged the smaller girl, her eyes and complexion almost identical to her companion. Her hair was cut short and her figure was somewhat fuller. 'Please. We are very worried.'

'Can't it wait till tomorrow? I . . .'

'It's all right, let them come in.' Alex turned round. Sarah stood behind him and to his relief was now fully dressed. Without waiting for an invitation the two students brushed past him and sat themselves awkwardly on the sofa, their hands clasped nervously between their knees like naughty schoolgirls.

'Would you like something to drink? Coffee?' asked Sarah gently.

'No thank you,' said Jamina. 'We are sorry to disturb you, Mrs Fox, we didn't know.'

'It's OK,' said Suzi quickly, 'we won't say anything.'

Alex slumped on to a dining chair, resting his head resignedly in his hands. Sarah sat in an armchair opposite the two girls. 'Now, what's troubling you?' she asked softly.

There was a short pause, as though the girls were summoning up the courage to speak. Then Jamina took a deep breath. 'It was the lecture this afternoon,' she began. 'The things Doctor Tankard told us, or rather *showed* us.'

'Have you been corrupting the minds of your students again, Alex?' asked Sarah, with mock severity.

Alex ignored her, getting to his feet. 'The title of the course made it clear as to the content . . .' he began.

'Oh, yes, we know,' interrupted Suzi. 'We want to learn. It's just that we didn't realise the, well, the mechanics of it.'

'It is the tradition of our caste,' Jamina continued, 'that when we marry we will be expected to enjoy sex in the way you have described. Other forms of contraception are forbidden.'

'Do you object to the prospect?' asked Alex, sitting down again and crossing his legs in an attempt to control his erection which was threatening to rise once more.

'No, no,' said Suzi, 'it's simply that we've never really thought about it, not until today, and it doesn't seem possible.'

'We are so small,' said her friend, 'and men, well, they are so large!'

Sarah smiled. 'Believe me, it is possible,' she said. Alex shuffled uncomfortably in his seat.

'But doesn't it hurt?'

'Not if your man is considerate. It really is very, very nice.'

'I wish I could believe you,' said Jamina, looking down at the floor. 'It is so frightening.'

Sarah sighed, stood up, and walked over to where Alex was seated, a bemused expression on his face. 'Shall we show them, darling? Prove to them that there is nothing to worry about?'

Alex looked up, startled. 'What . . . what . . .' was all he could manage to say.

'A practical demonstration for two of your top students,' said Sarah, matter of factly. 'Come on, it'll ease their concerns and besides, you know you'd enjoy it.'

Alex pondered for a moment, his common sense deserting him as fast as his erection stiffened. Having only recently been brought close to the point of orgasm the thought of impaling Sarah's perfect bottom filled him with intense desire, and the idea of his performance being closely observed by two lovely young girls made the notion even more attractive. But his job . . . his career . . .

'You're surely not serious?' he said, resting his arm on

49

his lap to conceal his fierce erection from the excited gaze of their two guests. Sarah answered by untying the cord holding his dressing-gown together and pushing the garment from his shoulders. The two girls gasped. Their tutor now sat, virtually naked, his cock standing upright like a flagpole. Sarah bent over, took it in her mouth and sucked it gently for a moment. Then, still clutching his hard stalk with one hand, she looked him directly in the eyes.

'I'm serious,' she said huskily. Alex sighed resignedly, sitting back to watch as Sarah undressed quickly in front of the avid gaze of the two students, obviously proud of her perfect form. She reached into her handbag and took out a small bottle of baby oil. 'You'll need something like this,' she said, showing it to them with an unmistakably suggestive gleam in her eye before walking slowly over to Alex and taking his hand.

He rose from the chair obediently, the dressing-gown falling from his body. Sarah coaxed him to walk in front of the sofa, displaying him like an animal in a fair. The students' eyes were firmly fixed on his rampant erection. Sarah knelt in front of him and took hold of his cock with both of her hands, rubbing it carefully. 'He has a fine prick,' she said to the girls. 'You will be unlikely to find one bigger.' Jamina and Suzi nodded in unison, licking their lips. Alex noticed that the smaller girl had allowed her hand to stray to her crotch, her fingers almost nonchalantly stroking her mound through the thick material of her tight jeans. He began to get the worrying feeling that he might come before the demonstration had even begun, and bit his lower lip in order to control his yearnings.

Sarah turned and crouched on the floor, resting her forearms on the carpet, her sumptuous bottom presented to him in the most erotic fashion. Alex was lost. Whatever the circumstances, whatever the effect upon his career, he knew he would have to go through with it. His body would not allow him to refuse.

He knelt behind his lover and kissed her bottom lovingly, then ran his tongue slowly down the cleft between the pert globes until the tip touched her anus. Pushing forward, he slid his tongue inside as far as he could, moving it in and out, thrilling to Sarah's groans of pleasure. She loved to have her arse tongue-fucked, as she would often so delicately say. He reached under her body and squeezed her breast, the other hand snaking to her warm, wet pussy, his fingers probing inside the soft, yielding flesh. He sensed that the girls were watching closely, and he shifted his position so that they could get a good view, like an actor in a pornographic movie posing for the cameras.

Deliberately, he licked Sarah's sex lips and anus with long, slow strokes of his tongue, thrilling to her scent and taste and his cock throbbing in anticipation of things to come. He smiled inwardly as he sensed Jamina and Suzi leaning forward even further, their eyes no doubt wide in lustful wonder as he licked some more and probed the tip of his tongue into the tight, puckered orifice before sitting back and taking up the bottle of baby oil. He poured the oil carefully on to the top of the cleft between Sarah's lovely buttocks, letting it run slowly down to her anus, smoothing it with his forefinger and then slipping his finger inside, as far as it would go.

Sarah groaned as he moved his finger in and out of her bottom, then sighed loudly as he allowed two fingers to move inside her after carefully pouring more oil over them to prepare her. Then he withdrew his fingers slowly and positioned himself between her legs, resting his big cock against her bottom. He smoothed yet more oil over his thick stalk. Suzi was now brazenly rubbing herself, her eyes glassy. Jamina just stared, her mouth open. Alex had a momentary urge to turn and push his cock between her pouted lips but no, a far greater prize beckoned to him.

Carefully but confidently he pressed the bulbous end of his stalk against Sarah's anus and pushed forward. She moaned and arched her back as he slid into her tightness, cautiously moving inch by inch, slowly in and out, her bottom accepting more and more of him with each forward thrust. At last, she held his full length within her divine sheath and he held still, allowing her to become accustomed to the intrusion.

51

'OK?' he asked, with genuine concern.

'Wonderful,' she breathed. 'Wonderful.'

Alex began to steadily fuck her bottom, sliding his long cock slowly in and out, allowing her to savour the full length with each movement. Gradually, his pace increased and Sarah groaned in time with the constant rhythm of his thrusts and the quickening caress of his fingers between her legs.

Alex looked at Suzi who now sat with her legs wide open, one foot resting on the sofa, the other on the floor. Her fingers were rubbing her pussy through her jeans at an alarming rate. He looked pointedly at her crotch, then into her eyes. Her face betrayed only one expression; that of total lust. Jamina continued to stare at his cock as it plundered Sarah's beautiful backside.

'Why don't you take your clothes off?' he said to Suzi, regretting it immediately. Luckily, his student didn't take offence, and stood up instead to peel off her T-shirt. She revealed a pair of large, brown breasts, the nipples proudly erect. Alex continued his steady pace, the tight grip of Sarah's anus driving him to distraction as Suzi stepped out of her jeans and panties in one movement. She stood next to him, as though waiting for instructions.

Sarah looked round and grinned at Jamina. 'You too,' she said, simply. Jamina obeyed as though in a trance and was quickly as naked as her companion. Her tall, slender frame was a contrast to Suzi's voluptuous body, but her boyish figure and small breasts were no less exciting to Alex's eyes. He slipped his hand around Suzi's waist, then moved it down to caress her plump bottom, reaching out with his other hand and delving his fingers into the luxuriant bush of hair between Jamina's legs to find her sex lips soaked.

To his surprise and delight, Sarah pulled his hand away and replaced it with her own. She slipped her fingers inside the young girl's pussy and turned and twisted her hand, making Jamina moan softly, her eyes closed. Alex speeded up the thrusting of his long, thick cock into his lover's perfect bottom, his heart thumping as he watched the slim Asian girl slip to the floor and lie prone on her back with

52

her heels tucked under her backside and her hips bucking in response to the incessant probing of Sarah's fingers. Despite his lover's virtually insatiable salaciousness, this was a side to her that he had never suspected, and it thrilled him immensely.

Suzi ran her hand down the front of Alex's body, gripping his hard shaft at the root to hold him still. 'I want it,' she breathed, her eyes sultry with lust. Alex was not inclined to refuse her. He slowly eased his cock from the tight sheath of Sarah's bottom and turned to wrap his arms around the plump voluptuousness of Suzi's body while Sarah moved forward and buried her head between the outstretched legs of the suppliant Jamina. He watched for a moment as the lovely blonde bobbed her head up and down, kissing and licking her succulent prize, then he turned his attentions to Suzi and moved her over to the sofa.

She lay down with one leg resting over the back of the settee and the other on the floor so that her pussy lips were open and inviting within the down-like, wetly matted hair. 'Fuck me, Doctor Tankard,' she pleaded, pinching her nipples and moving her hips up and down in a brazen display of submission. 'Fuck me.'

Alex knelt on the sofa and leant over the young girl's supine nakedness, his cock throbbing as the end touched the soaked lips of her sex. 'Are you a virgin?' he asked cautiously. Suzi smiled and shook her head, as though his question was the most ridiculous ever posed. He pushed forward and the soft, hot flesh moulded itself around his aching length until he filled her completely.

'Oh, Doctor, it's wonderful,' Suzi breathed, wrapping her arms and legs around his body. 'It's so big, so hard.'

Alex pumped steadily in and out of her sumptuous body, anxious to hold back so that he wouldn't come. The need for release tore at his loins and his cock was harder than he had ever known it before. He put his forefinger between his teeth and bit hard, his shaft throbbing heavily as a jet of pre-come shot deep into the wriggling student's soaked sheath. He held still for a second and the urgency passed.

53

Feeling more relaxed, Alex assumed a steady rhythm of ecstasy, gripping Suzi by the ankles and pushing her legs back until her knees rested against her large breasts. He pounded heavily against the soft flesh of her buttocks, his ears filled with the sounds of her gasps of joy and the cries of mutual elation coming from the two girls writhing together on the floor beside him.

'Harder, Doctor, harder,' cried Suzi, her fingernails digging into his back. 'I'm coming, I'm coming!' Alex fucked her as hard as he could manage, the full length of his long cock slipping in and out of her as she cried out in joyous climax. Suddenly, she pushed her crotch up to meet his and held him still, her eyes wide as though in terror, and then sighed heavily as the climax passed. Her fingers clawed at the tender skin of his back.

Suzi fell back on to the sofa, sobbing gently as her entire body trembled. Alex moved from her and sat at her feet, his cock rigid and ready for more. He looked at Sarah and Jamina. They lay on the floor with their legs entwined around each other's head, licking and fingering their pussies, oblivious to what was going on around them. They clearly had no need for his attentions, at least for the moment.

'Doctor . . .' The voice was soft, seductive. He looked at Suzi, who was moving to sit up and holding the bottle of baby oil. Alex sighed happily and took the bottle from her, pouring a little of the warm liquid into the palm of his hand. Suzi turned and knelt on the floor, her upper body resting on the sofa with her plump, brown bottom presented to his delighted gaze. He smoothed the oil gently between her buttocks, slipping one, then two fingers into the tight, virgin hole. Suzi groaned.

With his free hand, Alex poured more of the oil directly on to the shaft of his eager cock before setting the bottle down and rubbing the sensuous fluid over his stiffness. He carefully eased his fingers from the grip of her anus and pressed the thick, bulbous head to the tiny orifice, pushing forward slowly.

'It hurts, Doctor, it's too big,' pleaded Suzi as the tight sheath closed over his ridge. Parting her buttocks with his thumbs to ease his movements he slowly pushed forward again. The inches entered steadily, and he felt the muscles of her anus quickly relax as though in acquiescence to his demands.

Sarah and Jamina had ceased their cavorting and were watching him closely as he sank his full length deep inside Suzi's bum. 'He's got the whole thing inside you,' said Jamina, excitedly. 'What's it like?'

'It's incredible,' moaned her friend, pushing her bottom back and forth to meet his steady thrusts. 'It's not the same as normal fucking, but it's just as wonderful.'

Alex looked at Jamina, a grin on his face. 'Would you like to try it?' he panted. She nodded sheepishly and knelt next to Suzi in the same position, her slim, pert bottom awaiting his pleasure. He felt he would explode as he watched Sarah oiling and fingering Jamina's hole to prepare her. He pumped rapidly into Suzi, pausing occasionally to stay his own orgasm and his fingers digging into her lovely, big bottom.

'I think she's ready,' mewed Sarah, slipping her fingers from within Jamina's anus. Alex pulled himself slowly from within the tight grip of Suzi and shuffled across to the kneeling form of her friend. Sarah took a firm grip of his cock and directed it to its ultimate target. He eased into her easily; Sarah had done her work well. Reaching over, he stroked Suzi's bottom as she knelt where he had left her, then slipped two fingers easily into her bottom while his thumb found the warmth of her sex lips. At the same time, Sarah lay on her back on the floor and moved her head between his legs to lick his balls. He was lost.

With a roar that must have been heard throughout the hallowed halls of the university building he came, thrusting rapidly in and out of Jamina's tight hole, his seed at last jetting inside her. His orgasm seemed to last for an age and the throbbing was almost painful, unbearable. The muscles of Jamina's anus seemed to be purposely gripping him tightly, as though draining him of all he could give, as he finally slowed his movements and collapsed across her lovely back.

55

Gradually he withdrew and sat back on the floor, exhausted. Sarah squatted next to him, stroking his tender sex-flesh softly. Suzi and Jamina turned and knelt silently next to them, their breathing heavy, their olive-coloured skin soaked with sweat.

'Well,' said Sarah mischievously, 'are there any further questions?'

Despite its red-brick façade, the occult studies section of the library of Cowden University maintained an aura of sanctuary, the modern, technical tomes of the main reference area giving way to aged, dusty works of long dead authors. Alex found Sarah sitting at an incongruously modern desk avidly perusing the ancient pages of a giant, hide-bound volume, with the professor's notes scattered about the surface of an adjacent table in apparent disarray.

Opposite her sat a group of four young people; two males and two females. Alex recognised them as members of Sarah's study group, now in their final year. The girls were also occasional participants in his own classes, and he knew them well. Karen, a small, innocent-looking waif with closely cropped, dark hair looked up as he walked over to them. The other students were too engrossed in their work to notice him.

'Morning, Doctor Tankard,' piped Karen cheerfully. Belinda, the other girl, glanced up and smiled, then gathered up a number of books and walked over to the stacked shelves to replace them. Alex immediately felt a familiar warmth within his loins as he regarded the voluptuous shape of her young body, the tight jeans and T-shirt serving to emphasise her perfection.

He tore his gaze away from her sumptuous backside and sat on a vacant chair next to Sarah. 'Any luck?' he asked.

'I think we may have found something,' she replied, turning back a few pages of her book. 'Andrew, let me have that map.'

Andrew, a bespectacled and shy individual who was rarely to be found without the company of an open book passed a roll of parchment across the desk. 'D'you want the modern version as well?' said the other young man.

56

'Please, Stuart,' said Sarah as she unrolled the old chart, placing a book at each corner to hold it flat on the desk. Alex put on his spectacles and regarded the detail.

'This is Hampstead towards the end of the eighteenth century,' said Sarah, smoothing the surface of the old map and circling a small part of it with her finger, 'and this is Gallows Hill, the locality where the professor concentrated his purge. His notes make it very clear; I've even been able to identify some of the streets.

'The area was very different in those days, of course. It was a neighbourhood of very rich people, court and government officials mainly, and a few legal types. All the houses were big, set in extensive grounds. Most are long demolished now, but one or two still remain. Now, look at this . . .'

Sarah took hold of the contemporary chart and pointed at the maze-like design of the modern city. 'Look there!' Alex peered at the map, Sarah's fingertip indicating a small street close to the centre of the town. The legend 'Gallows Hill Road' was clear enough for him to see.

'Is that where he lived?'

'No, his home was on the other side of town. Gallows Hill was where he and his colleagues hunted the vampires. The descriptions of the houses in his notes are very detailed; if any of them still stand they will be pretty easy to pick out, and there's one of them, next to a graveyard, which is where he cornered Baron Mansola.'

Alex recalled the name from his initial brief reading of the notes. 'Oh, yes, the governor,' he said, sombrely.

'Head vampire, a sort of Dracula character, I suppose. He actually lived on that road! Can you believe it?'

'So, what now?' said Alex, virtually certain of her answer.

'We must go there, to Gallows Hill Road, to see if the house is still standing. Perhaps the present owners are descended from the baron. You never know . . .'

'Or perhaps the house will be filled with gorgeous vampire females, desperate to have their evil way with unsuspecting young men,' said Alex, with more than a hint of exasperation. 'To be honest, I expect you'll find it's all been turned into an office block or shopping complex.'

'We won't know if we don't try,' said Sarah, angrily closing a book with a bang. 'Are you coming or not?'

Alex looked across at Belinda, who was perched on the end of the desk leaning over Stuart. The two of them were studying the maps carefully. Her large breasts hung freely within the loose confines of her cotton T-shirt and her long blonde hair flowed sensuously across her face. He looked away.

'I still don't see what this is going to achieve,' he said. 'Even if what the professor said is true, it was over two hundred years ago.'

'Oh, come on, Alex,' said Sarah, encouragingly. 'You can't say that you're not just the least bit curious. He was your ancestor, after all.'

Alex had to admit to himself that his curiosity was getting the better of him, despite his busy schedule. But there were lectures to prepare and endless evaluations to perform . . . 'Do you need me to tag along? I mean, you've got four able assistants here.'

'The notes make it clear,' said Sarah earnestly. 'It must be a descendant of the professor's who is to right the wrong he committed. Please, Alex, stop being a pain!'

'Please, Doctor Tankard,' said Karen softly, placing her small hand on the back of his as it rested on the desk, 'it'll be fun.'

'Fun,' he muttered to himself, fully aware that his cause was lost. He looked across at Belinda, her mouth formed into a sensuous pout. 'All right,' he said finally, 'when do we set off for Gallows Hill Road?'

Three

The long, hot Hampstead day was finally mellowing into a humid evening and the reddening sun cast long, eerie shadows across the overgrown lawns of the house on Gallows Hill Road. Inside, Demonia sat in the relative darkness of the musty sitting-room, the heavy curtains drawn across the large window. About her, the remains of ancient furniture reeked of dampness and putrefaction, the thick dust and cobwebs adding to the overall scene of decay.

The atmosphere suited her mood as she impatiently waited for the welcoming shafts of moonlight to appear through the gaps in the loosely hanging drapery, giving her the sign that she and Sinitia could once more venture into the outside world.

Her need for sustenance was once more overpowering, the nourishment she had received as a result of the previous night's pleasures having long since lost its potency. Sinitia would awake soon, and she knew that the young girl's desires would be even stronger than her own, all the more so now that she had savoured the wondrous feeling of a long, hard shaft thrusting within her lithe body. How her sweet sister had enjoyed her first experience! How they had drained that poor, unsuspecting doorman, sucking the very strength from his mountainous body into their own!

He would suffice to act as their protector while they became used to the ways of this strange, new existence. But Demonia knew that they needed more; someone who could guide and teach them; someone who understood and sympathised with their plight and their unearthly destiny.

The sisterhood must be reborn, of that she was certain. Whether the evil Baron Mansola again walked the wicked streets of the city or whether he still lay hidden in some ungodly refuge awaiting the chance to rise once more, she was fully aware that this time she must be prepared and ready to do battle with the malevolence that he would inevitably unleash on the unsuspecting citizens of this great metropolis.

'Sister, our captive awakes.' Sinitia stood in the doorway, her naked perfection all but hidden in the shadows. Demonia glanced at the curtain. The red hue of sunset had given way to soft, delicate shards of the rising moonlight, the air around them already becoming fresh with the scents of the night. The young girl glided over to her and knelt at her feet, stroking the cool skin of her thighs tenderly.

Demonia rose and took Sinitia by the hand, drawing her to her feet. 'Come,' she breathed, 'let us return to our resting place and arouse our mentor. We will sate ourselves on his fine body, preparing us for a night of adventure!'

She led the way out of the room to a small door under the crumbling staircase that would take them down to their dank sanctuary. They moved gingerly down the creaking, wooden steps. Sounds of verminous rustling in the darkness broke the otherwise total silence.

The cellar was pleasurably cool and the moonlight now clearly illuminated the shackled form of their prisoner. His ebony nakedness glistened with sweat and his eyes were wide open, his facial expression incongruously fearful. He watched his two, delicate captors as they moved slowly towards him, his whole body visibly trembling.

'Let me down,' he growled, vainly tugging at the stiff, iron braces that dug into the flesh of his wrists. 'Let me down, or ...'

'Or?' queried Demonia querulously, a malevolent smile playing across her pouted lips. 'What will you do? Have you not already tasted enough of our strength, both of will and body, to know that you are completely at our behest?'

The big man struggled again, furiously writhing in his chains. Demonia reached out and caught hold of his long, drooping phallus and he held still. 'Stay, friend, stay your efforts. Your resistance is worthless.'

He looked down at her gripping hand, more in terror than delight. 'What are you going to do to me?' he asked, his voice shaking.

Demonia rubbed his stalk gently. 'We mean you no harm,' she said, her voice once more soft in tone. 'We merely need you to pleasure us once more. We must feed.'

The doorman raised his eyes and glared at her. 'You're fucking weird, you two,' he snarled. 'Let me down now!'

Demonia responded to his anger by gripping his stiffening erection firmly, causing him to wince. 'Would you disobey your mistresses?' she asked menacingly. The man shook his head quickly, tears beginning to sparkle in the corners of his eyes, and she relaxed her grip and let his manhood fall from her hand.

'Did you not delight in enjoying our favours last night?' asked Sinitia, stroking his muscular arm with unconcealed lust. He nodded, his eyes darting between the sumptuous forms of the two naked females before him.

'We only ask for more of the same,' said Demonia lightly, bending forward and kissing his massive chest.

'I . . . I'm not sure I could,' he pleaded. 'I feel like I've been fucking for a month without a break!'

Demonia took on a pained expression, kissed her fingertip and put it to his parched lips. 'Oh,' she cooed, 'I'm sure you *could*, if you really tried. Come, let us see if we can raise your magnificent weapon.'

'Well, at least unfasten these chains so I can get my hands on you.'

She looked at him meaningfully, then grinned at Sinitia. 'No,' she said, sensuously, 'I don't think so, do you?'

Sinitia smiled, licking her lips with delight at the prospect of continuing the erotic torture of their captive, then shook her head, running her hands over his steel-like torso. His body stiffened momentarily then relaxed as she began to trace her tongue around the shape of his sharply-defined pectoral muscles, pausing to nibble quite harshly at each nipple in turn. Her hands continued to roam over his flesh and she caressed and coaxed him while carefully avoiding his long cock, which was already showing definite signs of response and thickening steadily before Demonia's excited gaze.

He groaned as Sinitia ran her tongue down to his stomach and wormed the tip into his navel, her pouted lips sucking at his flesh. Slowly but persistently his huge phallus hardened until the purple-black, plum-sized end touched her wet lips. Still she ignored his plight, teasingly moving her face away and biting the flesh of his torso.

Demonia watched her colleague quietly, happily surprised at the young girl's instinctive, oral expertise. Then she turned and bent over to retrieve the doorman's jacket, her movements slow and deliberate, ensuring that he had a good view of her perfect bottom and long, widely-spaced legs. Searching through the pockets, she at last retrieved the cigarette lighter which had so fascinated them the night before and with some effort managed to light the flame, holding it close to his face.

His eyes resumed their fearful expression. Demonia licked her lips and grinned wickedly. 'What ... what are you gonna do with that?' he asked.

Demonia looked at him with feigned confusion. 'Just lighting a candle,' she said, after a moment which must have been an agonising wait for their captive. 'Just lighting a candle, so we can examine your fine form more closely.'

Casually, she took up one of the long, black candles that rested on a nearby bench and lit the tapered end, the damp wick sparkling into life. Sinitia stood back as Demonia held the flame close to his face, then moved it down, her eyes feasting on his superb physique. 'A truly magnificent body,' she mewed. 'So strong and powerful.'

She moved the flame up again, the flickering light reflecting in his dark, wide eyes. Carefully, she tipped the candle slightly and the hot wax dripped slowly on to his chest, hardening immediately into a soft, jet-black trail down his body. She moved further down, allowing more of the wax to slip sensuously on to him, her eyes feasting on the sight of his erection, now fully stiff and eager.

'Such a monstrous weapon,' she sighed, tipping the candle further, the flame sparking brightly as it touched the cold grease. Holding his cock firmly in her hand she ran a line of the wax along the full length of his throbbing stalk.

'Jesus!' he groaned, closing his eyes and gritting his teeth, the sensation clearly pleasurable. Demonia let go of his cock and watched it spring upwards almost vertically, the tip in line with his navel. His stomach was still wet from Sinitia's kisses.

She picked up another candle, ignited it from the first and handed it to Sinitia. The young girl held it still and watched quietly, savouring the sight of Demonia's ivory-white nakedness bathed in the shimmering glow of the flame. The doorman tugged at his restraints. 'For Christ's sake, let me get hold of you!' he begged. 'I'll do anything you want, anything!'

Demonia smiled seductively and licked the fingertips of her free hand before pinching out the flame and smoothing the cooling wax over the thick stem of the candle. She moved it to her face, licked the end and then put it into her mouth, sucking it suggestively between her wet lips.

'Oh, God, please, please,' he implored. His hugely erect cock was throbbing visibly and a trail of glistening pre-come slipped down the full length of his shaft. Demonia knelt before him, gazing hungrily at his juices then, linger-ingly, she moved the candle between his legs, pushing the soft tip against his anus. Twisting the saliva-soaked phallus carefully, she gradually eased it inside his tight hole, mov-ing it backwards and forwards. The thick stem steadily penetrated him deeper and deeper.

She looked up at him, querulously. 'This is how a girl feels,' she breathed, 'when you invade her most precious prize. How is it for you?'

The big man merely groaned, his hips bucking in re-sponse to the movements of the hard shaft within his loins, his answer crystalline. Demonia cautiously removed the candle, hearing him sigh with abject pleasure as it was re-leased from the confines of his anus, and stood before him, holding the phallus triumphantly in her hand. She put it to her mouth and ran her tongue along the long stem. She tasted his scent, her eyes fixed on his.

63

'Oh, God! Oh, no!' he cried, his body stiffening and the chains straining at their clasps to hold his writhing form. His cock seemed to jump as though trying to pull itself from his body, then a long jet of sperm shot from the angry head into the air, spraying across the damp floor. Demonia threw herself to the ground at his knees, allowing him to soak her face and breasts as she held them, cupped in her hands, like a pagan offering. Sinitia dived to her friend's side and began to lick the copious fluids from the soft skin of the huge globes, then ran her tongue over Demonia's face, swallowing greedily. Demonia pushed her own face forward, raised her breast further and licked the traces of white sustenance from her milky flesh until there was no more.

Finally, the two girls kissed, a long, passionate and deep delving of tongues within mouths, their hands roaming tenderly over their nakedness, their muffled groans echoing around the dark chamber.

Eventually they separated and gazed lovingly into each other's eyes. 'It is beautiful,' whimpered Sinitia, 'but it is not enough. I need more!'

Demonia looked at the doorman, now hanging heavily in his chains, his breathing stilted. 'He has no more to give, at least for the present,' she said, standing. Sinitia reached out and held the drooping cock, vainly attempting to coax it into life. The man remained still. His eyes were closed and he was drifting into unconsciousness. Demonia took hold of her wrist and pulled her hand away. 'Come, sister, we must venture into the night and hunt.'

The underground train lurched noisily along the Northern Line, the carriage empty at this relatively late hour apart from the two figures of Sarah and Alex. They sat opposite each other, their thoughts their own. Conversation was virtually impossible in the circumstances.

Sarah stared through the window into the rushing blackness, pensive as ever. Alex read his copy of the *Evening Standard* thoughtfully, their recent discoveries making the headline story all the more pertinent. He reached over and tapped Sarah on the knee. 'Look at this,' he said loudly.

Sarah took up the paper and glanced at the banner print. 'VAMPIRE KILLER STALKS LONDON' screamed the headline. She gripped the paper, her eyes widening with each word that she read. Alex moved across the carriage and sat next to her to re-read the article. 'I was thinking,' he said. 'The old man who delivered the professor's notes. D'you think there might be a connection?'

Sarah looked at him. 'Oh, surely not,' she said, turning back to continue reading. 'It must be a coincidence. Newspapers are always sensationalising this sort of thing.'

'Bloodless,' stressed Alex, pointing at the word. '*Bloodless*. It says they've found four bodies within the last week in the Hampstead area, all of them completely drained of blood. It takes a hell of a lot, you know, to do something like that.'

Sarah folded the paper and laid it on the seat next to her. 'You know my feelings on the matter,' she said cautiously. 'I really believe that such entities as vampires existed in the past, and there's no reason why they should have suddenly disappeared with the onset of the twentieth century.'

'I'm still not convinced. It's just that it seems remarkable that such a thing should happen now.'

'If there *is* a link,' said Sarah, her complexion becoming pallid, 'then we must tread very, very carefully.'

Alex nodded and sat back. The train screeched into Belsize Park. 'Next stop,' he said, feeling suddenly anxious.

'Here it is,' said Sarah apprehensively. 'Gallows Hill Road.' Alex regarded the two rows of ancient houses, many of them all but concealed by equally old trees and bushes. Light from the occasional street-lamp served only to heighten the gloom. They walked slowly into the street, sharply conscious of the echo of their footsteps on the paving slabs.

'If there *are* vampires in London, then this is where they'd live,' said Alex, trying to lighten their mood. Sarah said nothing, glancing both fearfully and excitedly from side to side at the old buildings. Behind them, the hum of evening traffic seemed to be fading into the night, the ensuing silence unsettling.

'There's the graveyard,' Alex said suddenly.

'Then the house must be there, behind those trees. Oh, I do hope that it's still standing.'

'I can't understand why the road hasn't been re-developed, or, at the very least the houses refurbished. This is a very expensive area. It must all be owned by the same person, or some faceless corporation waiting for the right moment to make a killing.'

'I wish you wouldn't use words like that,' said Sarah, resting her hand on the rusting gate to the manor. She paused, looking nervously at Alex. 'Well, do we go in?'

'We've come this far,' he replied, unsure of the prudence of his decision. 'Come on.'

Sarah tugged the old gate open, surprised at the ease with which it swung back on its grating hinges. They walked slowly along the barely discernible path, treading through the thick carpet of weeds and overgrown lawn that covered the crumbling stonework and pushing back the branches of dense foliage that seemed to be attempting to bar their way. The moon disappeared behind a heavy cloud and the sudden and silent blackness that enveloped them was almost unendurable.

'Oh, come on, this is absurd,' said Alex, gripping Sarah's shoulder. 'God knows what we'll find in this place. We should have brought the others.'

Sarah looked at him and grinned like an excited child. The relatively comforting moonlight returned, basking her lovely face with its silver glow. 'There it is! The house, it's still standing!'

Alex peered into the darkness through the thick cloak of foliage. The old manor stood blackly, defying them. They pushed their way through the bushes and got closer to the grim edifice that seemed to be regarding them through its dead windows. Something screeched in the distance. Alex jumped and caught his breath.

'What the hell was that?' he whispered loudly, sensing the coldness of sweat on his brow.

'It's only a fox,' she mocked. 'You're really scared, aren't you?'

'Yes I am, I admit it. Not of vampires or ghoulies or anything like that; I'm more terrified of the living than the dead. This is not the sort of place to be at night. Let's come back tomorrow, in the daylight.'

There was a sudden crack of a branch breaking in the blackness ahead of them. Sarah jumped and clutched Alex's arm. 'Perhaps you're right,' she said, to Alex's profound relief. 'Let's come back tomorrow.'

Sarah and Alex walked slowly towards the front door of her house, purposely keeping well apart. The evening was warm, much warmer than it had felt when they had ventured along the eerie path on Gallows Hill Road, and the sounds of traffic in the distance and the discordant music emanating from various open windows in the student's block was somehow comforting.

'What an incredible atmosphere that place had,' said Sarah presently.

'It was like something out of Edgar Allan Poe,' muttered Alex, still feeling rather foolish at his sudden panic. 'I can't imagine that it'll be much better in broad daylight.'

Sarah wrapped her arms around her body, as though hugging herself. 'It was wonderful,' she breathed. 'Frightening, yes, but incredibly exciting. Arousing even.'

'Arousing?'

'Yes, but I don't expect you to understand. I felt so *near* to something really ethereal, I could actually sense an aura of evil there.'

'You're letting your imagination get the better of you again.'

Sarah scowled at him and looked up at her house, the windows in darkness. 'He's asleep,' she said. 'Come on. Let's go into the garage.'

'Garage? Now?' queried Alex, but she was already heading for the large door, fumbling with her keys. 'Come on,' she repeated. 'I want you.'

Alex glanced tensely at the house. There was no movement; no sign of life. Shrugging his shoulders he followed Sarah to the garage as she silently lifted the heavy door.

Once inside, she closed it again before clicking on the light-switch. Her husband's old Daimler was there, its lovingly cared-for paintwork gleaming in the fluorescence. Sarah tested a rear door and it opened, the inner light flickering into life.

'Good,' she murmured. 'Switch the lights off.'

Alex did as instructed, so that the garage was illuminated only by the small light shining from within the car. Sarah wriggled inside and lay on the back seat as he followed. He saw her hurriedly reach under her long skirt and pull her panties down over her stocking-covered legs.

'God,' he whispered as he closed the car door behind him, the area falling once more into complete darkness, 'what's brought this on?'

'I told you, it was that place. I've been feeling like this ever since we set off for home.' He felt her grab his hand and force it between her legs. She was soaked.

'Christ, you're in a state,' he said, his fingers delving within the engorged lips of her pussy. Her hips bucked in response.

'I know, I know,' she panted. 'I need it so bad. Don't mess around, just fuck me, fuck me hard!'

'What about your husband?' Alex asked, beginning not to care as all four fingers of his hand slipped in and out of her soaking honey-pot.

'He won't hear a thing. Come on, Alex, for God's sake fuck me!'

Alex struggled with his belt and the zip of his trousers with his free hand, reluctant to cease his erotic caress of his writhing lover. He had never known her so excited or so fired in her passion for sex. Whatever the magic was that emanated from the ancient walls of the house on Gallows Hill Road, he wasn't complaining.

He wrenched his trousers and pants to his ankles in one swift movement then pulled his hand from within her, parting her legs wide and pushing her skirt up about her waist. He leant forward and kissed her inner thigh above the top of her stocking, then moved his tongue upwards. Sarah grabbed his head and lifted him roughly.

68

'Alex! I said fuck me, just *fuck me*!'

Happy to comply, he manoeuvred himself so that the tip of his raging erection touched the silky-smoothness of her wet sex lips. Sarah grabbed him by the hips and pulled him towards her, his long cock sliding effortlessly into her creamy sheath, in one almost ferocious thrust. Sarah groaned loudly.

'That's it, yes, harder, yes,' she babbled, her fingernails clawing at his naked buttocks. 'Oh, Alex, yes, ram it in hard, you know how I like it. Harder, harder . . .'

He began to pump into her like a man demented, the old car shaking heavily on its superb suspension, the springs of the leather seat groaning under the strain of their heaving bodies. Harder and harder, faster and faster he thrust into her as her cries and obscenities rang in his ears.

'Alex! Darling, I'm coming, I'm coming! Come with me, please!' Sarah had her legs raised as high as possible within the tight confines of the car and her heels dug into the plush covering of the roof. Alex pounded into her, sliding his full and not inconsiderable length in and out of the succulent but gripping folds of her cunt and thrilling to her sudden shout of ecstasy as she orgasmed and thrust her hips hard against his, matching his every movement.

With a guttural groan he joined her in orgasmic bliss. The thumping of his release tearing at his loins was almost painful. He shuddered, she cried out once more, and they fell together, sated.

In the sudden silence that followed the near cacophony of their passion they heard the scratching sound of a key against the lock on the garage door. Still embedded deep inside his lover's body, Alex pulled Sarah over and fell with her on to the carpeted area between the front and back seats, holding her down. The hump on the floor pressed into his back, arching it painfully, but he held still.

The garage lights flickered into life. 'Who's there?' called a voice Alex instantly recognised as that of Professor Fox, senior don of the university, and Sarah's husband. He hardly dared to breath despite his exhaustion and his heart thumped so loudly he wished to silence it forever. He felt Sarah's body trembling against his.

He heard the soft padding of slippered feet as Professor Fox walked slowly around the large garage interior, then bit his lip as he felt the car tip slightly as it was peered into. He thanked God for Sarah's dark mode of dress: They lay unseen in the deep well behind the high-backed front seats of the vehicle.

'Damn cats,' muttered the voice and after an agonising few moments the lights were switched off, the garage door closed noisily, and the car once more plunged into darkness.

Sarah breathed a long sigh of relief, then struggled to the seat. Alex followed with difficulty, his back aching and his whole body trembling.

'Wow, that was close,' Sarah sighed, leaning back and closing her eyes. Alex said nothing and the two of them sat in silence for some minutes.

Presently, he felt Sarah catch hold of his hand and draw it to her oozing sex lips once more. 'You can lick me now, if you like,' she cooed.

Demonia sat in the drab sitting-room of the manor, staring blankly through the tattered curtains into the darkness outside, the taste of male release still on her lips. Sinitia lay across the prone, unconscious forms of the two young men that they had lured from the street with their brazen nakedness. Her eyes were closed in half-sleep and she still held the limp manhood of one of their conquests in her mouth.

It had been easy; perhaps too easy. The youths had followed them without a word through the thick undergrowth that surrounded the house. Their erections threatened to burst from their jeans and their simple minds did not question for a second the sudden appearance of two, naked nymphets begging for their favours. Now they were finished, their bodies drained of strength and will, lying on the filthy, damp carpet.

Demonia felt at once both nourished in body and empty within her soul. There had to be more to their new existence than prowling aimlessly through the night streets and feeding on compliant but unsuspecting mortals merely to satisfy an ever-more demanding thirst.

She looked solemnly at the garden, the moonlight high-lighting the stark, twisted shapes of the old trees which mocked her with the gentle swaying of their branches. She remembered the old days; times of gaiety and merriment, of parties and dances. She closed her eyes and *willed* it were again so.

She shivered. There was a sudden, strange aura about her, as though a presence had entered her very soul and possessed her with a will far stronger than her own. She held her eyes closed, sensing an inner heat or perhaps a comforting warmth. She didn't fight the feeling; it was too strong, too all-pervasive. Then she knew she had taken complete control of her senses once more, and with this new power came a fresh certainty.

Someone would come, someone of intellect and honesty who would guide, teach and help her in her quest and somehow she felt that she would know this person from the past, although that was impossible. No mortal being could have lived so long.

An owl hooted in the darkness.

Demonia looked again at the garden, her eyes widening in amazement. As though in a dream, the landscape was changing and as the ugly, overgrown foliage receded, the lawns reappeared magically, as fresh and crisp as in years gone by. She blinked and shook her head, trying to make sense of it. The path was clearly defined now, meandering through an avenue of strong, young trees to the tall, iron gate which gleamed newly silver in the moonlight.

Suddenly, the room was bright, as though lit by a thou-sand candles. She turned quickly and regarded the scene of opulence behind her. The fine, wooden furniture shone as she remembered it and the chairs and sofas were soft and invit-ing. The carpet was thickly-piled and warm. Sinitia lay on the floor alone, their visitors having disappeared, as though into thin air. The lovely black girl was no longer naked, but clothed in a long white dress of the sheerest silk, accentuating the perfection of her lithe form as she lay asleep.

71

Demonia put her hands to her own body and looked down, more with expectation than surprise. She, too, found that her nakedness was covered, clothed in a dress of delicate, clinging lace which moulded itself to her form. She stood up and smoothed the garment over her sumptuous shape, thrilling to the sensuous touch of the material. What had happened in those few, magical seconds she couldn't imagine; whether it had been her will that had caused this wondrous transformation or whether some other, unknown force had been involved, it didn't seem to matter. At last she felt completely alive.

She walked over to Sinitia and knelt at her side, gently stroking the smooth, flawless skin of her face. The eyes opened slowly; deep brown pools of emotion blinking in the brightness of the light. Sinitia smiled. 'Have they gone?' she asked huskily.

'They are not important. See, look about you.'

Sinitia sat up suddenly as the mantle of sleep fell away from her sated body. 'What's happened? Where are we?'

Demonia slipped a calming arm around her shoulder. 'Shhh,' she said, putting a fingertip to the young girl's lips, 'we are home. Everything has been returned to us, just as it was.'

Sinitia struggled to her feet, then clasped her hands to her stomach, smoothing the soft material. 'This dress!' she exclaimed. 'I remember wearing it! How can this be?'

Demonia shook her head kindly. 'Do not question, sister, just be happy. Now we can live as others do. Now we can welcome guests into our home to join us. We are fulfilled!'

'And what of the day?' asked Sinitia as she walked to the window. 'Will I again feel the warmth of the sun?'

Demonia frowned. 'Sadly, I fear not. We are children of the darkness; it was ever so. We must shelter from the daylight within the sanctuary of our lonely caskets below, but it is a small price to pay for eternal life!'

Sinitia smiled cheerlessly. 'Come!' continued Demonia, brightening her tone purposely. 'Let us visit the other rooms of the house!'

72

She took hold of the young girl's hand and led her from the room, her steps light and her heart filled with happiness.

Alex and Sarah walked briskly down the long high street leading to Gallows Hill Road, the warmth of the sun already beginning to recede with the onset of early evening. He cursed his luck; the one day when he had wanted to get away from classes quickly he had been called to the administrator's office to sort out some petty paperwork mix-up.

He had suggested to Sarah that they leave it until the following day but she had been adamant. She wanted to re-visit the old house before darkness fell that evening, and she wouldn't be put off.

'I hardly slept a wink last night,' she chattered as they turned the corner into the dreary road that signalled their destination.

'Nor I,' he replied, his memories of the previous evening's close call still fresh in his mind. He knew that wasn't what had deprived Sarah of her sleep, however. Her single-minded approach to this vampire nonsense was typical of her.

But was it nonsense? he mused. Certainly the aura surrounding the old manor had affected even him, filling him with inexplicable feelings of both dread and enthusiasm.

'This really is an odd area,' said Sarah, gripping his arm for the first time on their journey. 'Any one of these houses could be full of vampires; and listen, no birds singing . . . just like in the films.'

'It's very difficult to hear birds singing in London; coughing, yes.'

She ignored his poor attempt at humour. They were getting close to the manor and despite it being over an hour until sunset the shadows cast by the lines of gnarled trees along the sides of the road ominously predicted the rapidly approaching gloom.

'I've been studying more of Professor Tankard's theories and discoveries. He used to write regular articles in an old publication called *Occult Truths*; there's stacks of copies in the library. I've never really bothered to examine them too closely before. It seems that Bram Stoker's writings in *Dracula* were pretty accurate in a lot of respects. The vampire is a supremely powerful and malevolent creature, driven by incredible sexual urges, not just a thirst for blood.

'In fact, that adds a certain credence to the professor's later findings, about the female of the species. For all vampires, sex is everything, the *raison d'être* for their existence. The males merely take the blood of their victims for sustenance, the females preferring the fluids of human release.'

Alex shook his head benignly. 'You really do believe they existed, don't you?'

Sarah looked at him coldly. 'They *exist*, Alex, I am sure of it.'

'I remain unconvinced, I know there are . . .'

'Alex! Look!' Sarah was suddenly still, both hands gripping his arm tightly, her eyes staring ahead of her. He followed the line of her startled gaze and gasped.

The manor stood before them, clearly visible behind young, lush trees. The walls were pristine in white stone and the windows were gleaming. The window frames and the massive front door were glossed in black as though freshly painted. Alex looked quickly about him, assuring himself that they were at the right place. They were.

'I don't understand,' said Sarah. 'What's going on?'

'Maybe because it was so dark last night, maybe . . .'

'Oh, come on! The place was a ruin! And I suppose the fairies tended the garden?'

'Perhaps . . . oh, I don't bloody know,' said Alex, his frustration becoming swiftly overwhelmed by his curiosity.

'Come on, let's go and see who lives here,' said Sarah, already opening the gate and stepping on to the meticulously weeded path.

Alex paused for a little more than a second, then followed his lover towards the great house. Even in its pristine condition the building still seemed to exude an atmosphere of foreboding, and there was something else; an ambience he found difficult to comprehend.

'Do you feel it?' asked Sarah, her face flushed with excitement, echoing his thoughts.

'Feel what?'

'It's sex; the place just shouts sex!'

He knew exactly what she meant. In his mind there were feelings of trepidation, but his body was possessed by an unmistakable sensation of arousal and his cock was thickening quickly within the confines of his tight briefs. 'Yes,' he said, simply.

Sarah ran her hand over the increasingly prominent bulge in his trousers. 'I could do it here, now,' she breathed.

Alex tried vainly to force some common sense into his clouded mind. He looked across at the gate; they were only yards from the road. They would be seen. 'No, no, we're here to do a job of work,' he struggled. 'Perhaps later, later.'

There was nothing he could do. All sense and all willpower was drained from him. Sarah fell to her knees, right there in the open, and tugged almost manically at his zip. She pulled down the front of his briefs and hauled his thick prick into view, gripping it immediately at the root and clamping her suckling mouth over the wet end. He glanced again at the road as a car sped past.

'Sarah, look, let's go over to the bushes. It's a bit too public here,' he begged. She merely shook her head without allowing his raging stalk to leave her mouth, rubbing the shaft rapidly with one hand, the other snaking up her skirt to pleasure herself.

A double-decker bus drew up and the occupants of the upper saloon were afforded a clear view of the proceedings. Instead of struggling to escape, Alex arched his back and stiffened his buttocks, proud to display his hugeness to the goggle-eyed commuters who stared back at him. The bus pulled away, and he actually felt disappointed.

He looked over to the house, wondering whether their performance was being witnessed by the occupants. There was no sign of life. Then he looked down at Sarah, her head bobbing back and forth as she sucked his cock. He felt his stalk thicken rigidly within her wet mouth, and an unmistakable urgency throbbed within his loins. 'Oh, fuck!' he muttered under his breath as he felt the sperm surge along his pulsating shaft into her mouth. Sarah grabbed him with both hands and rubbed furiously, sucking and swallowing until he could take no more.

She leant back and let him fall from her, looking up into his eyes, as a trickle of his fluids slipped from the corner of her mouth. She smiled, licked the traces of his pleasure from her lips and stood up. Alex stood bemused, the trembling in his thigh muscles slowly abating. Sarah breathed quickly. There was nothing to be said.

As they approached the massive door to the manor Alex felt his sensations of fear and apprehension returning to his mind, his body temporarily sated. Sarah reached for the bell-chain and tugged it. Alex started as a heavy, clanging sound resounded from within the house. He began to hope that there was no one home but the rattling of chains and turning of locks from behind the door dispelled any such optimism.

The heavy door swung open. He half expected to find a twisted dwarf standing behind it but no, quite the reverse. A huge man, black as the formal suit he wore, towered above them. Alex looked at his face. The eyes were expressionless.

Sarah and Alex stood in uncomfortable silence, each waiting for the other to speak. The man said nothing, his stone-like features not moving.

'May we speak with the owner?' Sarah said at last, her voice sounding very small. The big man stepped back a pace, opening the door further. 'Come,' he grunted. 'You are expected.'

Sarah and Alex exchanged puzzled glances as they were led through the large hallway to another door. Opening it, the man motioned silently for them to enter.

They found themselves in a substantial and lavishly-furnished sitting-room illuminated by hundreds of red and black candles. Heavy curtains were drawn across the windows. A log fire burned unnecessarily in the huge grate and the heat of the room was stifling. 'Please sit,' said the man gruffly.

The two guests did as they were bid, perching nervously on the edge of a massive settee. They watched as the servant walked over to a window and carefully held back the thick drapes to peer outside. 'My mistresses will be here presently,' he said, in a vague, distant tone before letting the curtain fall back to cover the glass.

Alex found his voice. 'You said we were expected. How . . .'

The man ignored him, walked back towards the hallway and left the room, closing the door behind him.

They sat in silence for a moment, both absorbing the intense and sensuous aura of their surroundings. The heat was unbearable. Sarah took off her short jacket and put it on the back of the settee. Alex's gaze was drawn immediately to the soft mounds of her breasts. She noticed his glance.

'Are you still feeling horny?' she asked huskily.

'It must be the heat,' he replied, removing his own jacket.

'No, it's more than the heat. As I said, it's *sex*. It seems to radiate from the walls. I just *know* we've found them.'

'Them?'

'The vampires. I told you, sexuality is their driving force. It fills this house. I know you can sense it. We have them.'

'I just hope that the professor was right,' said Alex, absently allowing his hand to touch himself between the legs, his erection already beginning to stretch once more, 'and that it *is* just sex. I don't fancy becoming one of the undead.'

Sarah smiled at him weakly. 'We can go if you like.'

He pondered her words for a moment, the temptation to flee the overpowering atmosphere of sensuality suddenly appearing very judicious. He reached for his jacket.

'Welcome!' The voice was strong but calming. They looked up at the door, unsure of what to expect.

Framed by the tall portal stood two females. One was

77

tall and commanding in her appearance, and the other was shorter but confidently statuesque and no less imposing. Alex felt his throat become dry as he regarded the newcomers. The bright light emanating from the hall shone through the sheer fabric of the long white gowns they both wore, the contrasting perfection of their bodies clearly visible to his eye.

The taller girl was the more voluptuous and her hugely rounded breasts strained against the material of her dress while her narrow waist and broad, receptive hips were complemented by her long, shapely legs. Her skin appeared alabaster white, its sensuous pallor accentuated by the blackness of the long, silken tresses of her hair.

Her companion's dusky skin shone in the candlelight and her large brown eyes gleamed as her face formed into a perfect, seductive smile. Her figure was lithe, and her firm breasts pert, the black nipples clearly visible through the gossamer of the fabric.

He stood and moved towards them. The taller girl's face took on an expression of horror, the suddenness of the change taking him aback. 'Professor,' she gasped, her voice trembling, 'how can it be? How can you still live?'

Her meaning was at once clear to Alex. He smiled as kindly as he could and shook his head. 'Not *Professor*,' he said. 'I am *Doctor* Alex Tankard. It appears that the illustrious professor was an ancestor of mine.'

Demonia regarded him suspiciously for a moment, then visibly relaxed. 'Welcome, Doctor Tankard,' she said, the two of them gliding into the room, 'and forgive my mistake. You bear an uncanny resemblance to your distinguished forbear.'

'So it would seem,' said Alex, taking her hand in greeting. It felt surprisingly warm; somehow he had expected her touch to be icy. 'May I know your names?'

'I am called Demonia, and this is my dear sister Sinitia.'

'Sister?' he queried, regarding the deep black of the younger girl's complexion.

'We are sisters of the soul,' Demonia answered, her voice hushed. 'And your companion?'

78

Sarah stood up nervously. 'I am Sarah Fox; we have been learning about the history of this house, and we . . .'

'You have been sent to help us,' interrupted Sinitia, stepping forward. Alex looked at her hungrily. She was truly beautiful; a black nymphet, a vision of perfection.

'Help you?' he asked.

'We knew you would come,' continued Demonia. 'We have been waiting.'

'The house,' asked Sarah. 'How did it, how did you . . .'

'Our will is strong, and we need comfort, just like any mortal.'

The use of the word 'mortal' reminded Alex suddenly that these were no ordinary females. 'What do you want from us?' he asked. 'How can we help you?'

Demonia regarded him with a serious expression, still apparently shaken from the shock of his similarity to the professor. 'I am uneasy,' she said, presently. 'All is not well. If we have awakened then possibly so have others.'

'The men?' asked Sarah. 'The real vampires?'

'We are all of the same creation, but the men, they have different needs.'

'Blood?'

Demonia looked hard at her. 'There is one who is all-powerful. He is the embodiment of evil, and I sense his presence.'

'Baron Mansola?' asked Sarah.

Demonia nodded slowly. 'You have studied well. If he has risen there is great danger here.'

Sarah looked suddenly shocked. 'The murders?' she exclaimed. 'Bloodless bodies; four or five of them recently!'

Demonia turned and looked at Sinitia sadly. 'Then he has returned,' she breathed.

'But how can we be of help?' asked Sarah anxiously. 'We know little of such matters other than what is held in dusty books and the folklore of the ages.'

Demonia walked over to an ornate, high-backed chair and sat down. Sinitia stood at her side. 'You must join with us, and help us gather others into the sisterhood. Only in numbers do we have a chance of defeating the evil.'

79

'But how do we join you?' said Alex, already fairly certain of the answer.

Demonia smiled. 'I sense your arousal, that of you both. Such is the power of these walls. And I feel the yearning that you have for my sweet sister.'

Alex coughed. 'You are both very beautiful . . .' he began.

Demonia rose from the chair and took him by the hand, taking her companion's arm and drawing them together. 'Take Sinitia,' she said in a soft but commanding tone. 'Take this dear child. She is young but eager, and she will make a willing pupil.' She smiled again, broadly. Sinitia stood silently, her head bowed coyly. It was true that the lust that Alex felt for this delicate, ebony nymphet was tearing at his heart. He held out his hand and Sinitia slipped her fingers through his with the nervousness of a virgin bride. They began to walk slowly from the room, Alex turning momentarily to glance at Sarah, who was already slipping into the welcoming arms of their serene hostess.

The opulence of the great hall and the sitting-room was, if anything, exceeded by the sheer luxuriance of the bedroom. The deep red carpet supported elegant, antique furniture and the centre-piece of the room – a huge bed – manifestly beckoned to them as they walked into the room.

Everywhere there were mirrors. On the walls and on the ceiling above the bed were giant, gilt-framed reflections of the grandeur of their surroundings. The room had been designed for hedonistic pursuits and the bed was large enough to accommodate many who sought such pleasures.

Alex turned and looked at Sinitia, her deep brown eyes burning into his. The urge within his loins was all-consuming, as was his need to possess this vision of erotic mystery. He kissed her lightly on the mouth, the fullness of her thick lips thrilling him. Running his hand slowly down her back he stroked the pertness of her bottom, the curves far more pronounced than any he had touched before. The firm globes were uncovered save for the sheer silk of her gown. He kissed her again, cupping her buttocks with both hands, and Sinitia responded by pressing her body hard

80

against his and smoothly rubbing the firm mound of her sex against the hardening bulge within his trousers.

Their tongues met, playfully sliding around each other. The thought of slipping his cock within the heavenly confines of this sumptuous mouth filled his mind as he pressed himself harder against her. The knowledge that he would soon possess her lithe, superb body made his head swim.

Without breaking off from his delightful embrace, he unclasped the small brooch on her shoulder and stepped back slightly, allowing the soft material of her dress to slip to the floor. He glanced at the mirror behind her. She was naked, save for a pair of elegant, silver white shoes. Her flawless skin appeared to be even blacker in her nakedness, and her bottom, oh, her bottom! Such total, erotic quintessence! He ran his hands over the magnificent orbs, running his fingers delicately between them and thrilling to the murmur of pleasure she made at the back of her throat as he touched her tiny, puckered orifice. It would be so unfair, he thought, if she were to deny the ultimate pleasure of the sweet sphincter he now teased with his fingertips.

Alex pulled his face away reluctantly from hers and smiled gently. 'Are you a virgin?' he asked quietly.

Sinitia looked to the floor, as though ashamed. 'No, my lord,' she said in a faint tone that was almost a whisper, 'but I have much to learn.'

She walked slowly away from him and slipped on to the bed, lying on her back in the centre of its great expanse so that she looked small and vulnerable. He stood for a moment, drinking in the sight before him: the beautiful features of her young face, her firm breasts with their long, black nipples, her flat stomach, her legs, and between.

The thick bush of luxuriant hair that nestled between her rounded thighs shone wetly, a testament to her extreme arousal. Alex began to undress, not taking his eyes off her for a moment as she lay with her legs parted slightly to reveal the puffy, red flesh of her pussy. She ran a finger suggestively between her sex lips as he removed his briefs, and as he stood naked before her, his erection was harder than at any other time he could remember.

'It is big, so very big,' she mewed, opening her legs wider and pushing her fingers deep inside her welcoming sheath. Alex clambered on the bed beside her, taking her hand away from her cunt and replacing it with his own. She was soaked, soft and suppliant with lust.

Sinitia reached over, gripped his long, thick stalk and rubbed it with practised delicacy. Alex lay back, savouring the sensation and the scene reflected in the mirror above his bed. He gazed up and watched as she first leant across his body, then knelt as she kissed his chest, her bottom presented in the most concupiscent way to his avid stare.

Slowly, agonisingly slowly, she moved her kisses ever downward over his chest, across his trembling stomach and round to his thighs, her tongue licking his hot skin and her teeth nibbling his aching flesh. She gripped his cock again, rubbing her hand up and down the full length to draw the loose skin back and forth over the rigid stalk.

Alex felt that he would explode as he sensed her hot breath on his throbbing erection and then, as her soft, full lips closed around the end he shut his eyes tightly and dug his fingernails into the palms of his hands. 'Please, God, please,' he prayed, silently. 'Let me hold back!'

His prayers were miraculously answered and the desperate need for release passed as quickly as it had come. He opened his eyes and looked down at his beautiful lover, now kneeling between his thighs as she ran her tongue up and down his long shaft and over his balls. She sucked one, then the other, into her wide mouth, all the time caressing his length with the incessant pumping of her hand.

Sinitia stopped her oral touch and looked at him, her eyes filled with innocence and wonder. 'Do I do well, my lord?' she asked meekly.

'Please call me Alex,' he said, 'and yes, you do very well.' He sat up and moved her to lie on her back, positioning his body between her long legs, his face level with her stomach. He kissed the firm flesh tenderly, then moved slowly downwards, his senses rejoicing in the scent of her womanhood as his mouth neared her ultimate prize. He licked around the thick, black hair, teasing her as she had teased him, then flicked the tip of his tongue lightly over her bush, barely touching her flesh. She groaned, her hips moving. Delicately he pushed his long tongue forward, tasting her sex lips and slipping inside their warm wetness. His tongue probed inside her, suckling her juices.

Never had he felt such ecstasy as he drank from her and the warmth emanating from her body filled his very soul. His mind became addled; his thoughts blissfully confused. He was being possessed, he knew it. He was consumed by her lust. He raised her legs high into the air, gripping her ankles with one, strong hand, and parted and delved into the lips of her pussy with the fingers of the other. He licked round and round the soft, engorged flesh, suckling and absorbing her and burying his face in the saturated heat of her cunt.

He took a breath, then returned his tongue to her, this time allowing the tip to trail slowly to the puckered sphincter of her anus. Sinitia reached up, gripped her own legs and pulled them right back, tucking her arms behind her knees. The calves of her legs pressed close to the sides of her enchanting face.

She was offering it to him; giving that sweet orifice to his pleasure, to do with as he wished. Alex parted the cheeks of her bottom with his thumbs and lapped at the hole, probing into it with his tongue in the way he knew Sarah loved.

'Mmmm,' was Sinitia's only response. It was sufficient. Curling his tongue at the sides he pushed it forward, deeper and deeper into her anus, and moved it in and out like a small, wet cock. 'Oh, my lord, Alex, that is so good,' she sighed. He carried on, with his face pressed against her delightful bottom and his nose soaked with the wetness of her pussy.

Presently, she lowered her legs and Alex pulled away from her. He knelt and looked into her eyes, their hypnotic gaze absorbing him. 'Fuck me, Alex,' was all she said.

He leant over her body, supporting himself with one hand, while the other guided his cock to the bloated, receptive lips between her legs. He slid into her easily, so aroused was she by this time. Sinitia raised her legs again, pulling them back as far as she could to let her take every inch of him inside her. He began to pump slowly, moving his full length in and out; the wet sounds of their love-making filling his ears. He pushed harder so that the tip of his long cock touched her cervix with each forward thrust, causing her to groan with satisfaction. He bent his head and took the nipple of one of her breasts between his teeth, nibbling on it as he moved his free hand to her crotch. His fingers rubbed rapidly at the swollen bud of her clitoris.

'I'm coming, my lord, I'm coming!' she groaned. 'Rub harder, rub harder!'

He did as ordered, stiffening his legs and ramming his huge cock deep into her trembling body as violently as he could. She let out a scream as he hammered into her, any concern that he might hurt her delicate body dismissed from his mind in his lust.

He felt the muscles of her cunt contract around his stalk and he bit into his lower lip. He wasn't ready to come yet – not yet. He pulled from her and lay at her side, his breathing heavy as he ran his hand wearily over her sweat-covered skin. She held his cock gently, hardly moving her hand, and turned her smiling face to his.

He looked at the mirrors around the room, each reflecting a different view of their passion and each vision better than the last. His prick looked huge in her tiny hand. He was a happy man.

She knelt again at his side, kissing him warmly over the face and neck. Alex moved himself to a sitting position and stroked her lovely bottom, planting occasional kisses on the sensuous curves before moving behind her and licking her once more along the deep cleft between her buttocks. Wetting his fingers with the copious juices soaking the matted hair around her pussy he eased two of them inside her anus, carefully turning and pushing until they were fully accepted into the tight hole.

Sinitia turned and looked at him meaningfully. 'You want to fuck me there, don't you?' she breathed enticingly. Alex nodded, slowly withdrawing his fingers from within her. She rested her arms on the small pillow and pushed her bottom further upwards, the sight filling him with almost uncontrollable salaciousness. He knelt between her legs, gripping the base of his stalk with one hand and rubbing the stem over the soft skin of her bottom, then positioned himself to impale her. The thick end of his prick pressed against the tiny hole.

'You are very big,' she implored. 'Take care not to hurt me.'

Alex said nothing but moved his hips forward steadily, the bulbous end of his rigid sex slipping, with some difficulty, into the tightly-muscled grip of her anus. He held still for a moment, fondling the pert, black globes lovingly, then gradually eased a couple more inches into the relaxing sheath. He pulled back a little then pushed forward again, this time sinking virtually his full length inside her.

She groaned; a moan of joy. Steadily, Alex increased the pace of his movements, glancing at the magnetic images held within the myriad of mirrors. The sight of his long, thick stalk invading the sumptuousness of her pert, dark orbs thrilled him. Her muscles had relaxed completely now, becoming used to the intrusion though the concupiscent sheath still gripped his rigid erection tightly. He pumped steadily, his breathing becoming heavier and heavier and sweat dripping from his brow on to the glistening skin of Sinitia's back.

He felt her reach between her legs and grip his balls. She squeezed the sack gently then the middle finger of her hand reached up to press against his own anus and the tip wriggled inside. He held still again, his cock throbbing inside her bottom and the exquisite feeling of her finger moving in and out of him driving him to distraction. Then he thrust in and out of her once more, her rhythmic moans assuring him that she shared his delight.

'Oh, sweet Jesus, I'm coming!' he said. As suddenly as he had spoken these words, Sinitia threw herself from him, quickly turned around and grabbed his cock and almost wrenched it from his body as she pulled it to her mouth. As her thick lips closed around it he came; a searing, explosive climax that tore at his body with a vengeance. His seed shot to the back of her throat. She gulped and swallowed quickly, sucking greedily on his wilting stalk. Alex felt his vision clouding, his senses deserting him. He fell forward on the bed, and knew no more.

Alex woke slowly from an exhausted sleep and the first sight that met his eyes as they focused in the glare of daylight was the reflected image in the ceiling mirror of Sarah and himself, lying naked on the bed. He sat up suddenly, regretting it immediately. His head was pounding; his throat dry and parched.

Sarah stirred at his side and her eyes opened blearily. He waited as she came to, suppressing a slight feeling of nausea within his stomach.

'Are you all right?' he asked finally.

'Mmm, what about you? Did you enjoy yourself with the lovely Sinitia?'

'Very much. And you?'

'I don't think I've come as many times in my life as I did last night,' she croaked, stretching her arms above her head. 'I dread to think what we've let ourselves in for.'

'I passed out,' said Alex. 'I actually passed out when I came!'

'So did I, the first time. It's the initiation, or whatever you like to call it.'

'Initiation?'

Sarah grinned, leaning back on a pillow. 'You still don't get it, do you? I am to become a fully-fledged member of the sisterhood and you, well, you are one of our trusted servants, at our command whenever we need you.'

'You mean I'm a vampire?'

'No, Demonia told me that would only happen if you were bitten by one – if one actually sucked your blood. We have both merely tasted the sex-fluids of the sisters.'

She paused and took a long, deep breath. 'We have the chance to become immortal.'

Alex tried hard to focus on her words, his head swimming. 'You mean,' he said, cautiously, 'that we could turn into vampires, the undead, cursed to have to avoid daylight and sleep in a coffin?' As he said them, his words seemed more and more ridiculous.

Sarah shook her head. 'Demonia has explained everything. We have 28 days, a full cycle of the moon, to make our decision. During that time we can live as we do now, although we will develop an incredible appetite for sexual fulfilment or, as Demonia put it, we will thirst.

'If we then decide not to join them we will be free to return to our drab lives but, should we drink from Demonia or Sinitia's lovely bodies after 28 days then we will become as they are. The choice is entirely ours.'

Alex stood and walked unsteadily to the window, peering out at the large, well-tended garden. 'How do you feel about the prospect?' he said, turning to face Sarah who lay back enticingly on the huge bed.

'Excited and apprehensive. In one respect it seems to be the culmination of everything I have worked and studied for – the thought that I could be in a position to unravel the mysteries of the occult forever. But I am also very scared.'

Alex moved over to the bed and sat next to her, cradling her head in his hands and running his fingers through her soft, blonde tresses. He felt her hand playing across his thigh and the fingers delicately encircle his stiffening erection. Sarah moved her head down quickly, taking it in her mouth.

'As Demonia said,' he breathed, laying back contentedly, 'we thirst.'

Four

Sarah sat quietly in her lounge, absently turning the pages of an irrelevant magazine, reading nothing. Professor Fox, her husband, was dozing in an armchair opposite with his mouth open and his legs spread-eagled untidily. She glanced up and regarded the prone form then looked back at the glossy pages, more in disinterest than dislike.

She began to wonder, not for the first time, how she had found herself to be in this situation. She was still young and attractive – very much so if Alex was to be believed – and yet when in her husband's company she felt decidedly middle-aged. She closed the magazine and dropped it on to the low table in front of her, leaning back in her seat and closing her eyes. The only sound in the room apart from the occasional snort from the direction of the armchair was the loudly incessant ticking of the clock, steadily eating away at her life.

So much had happened in such a short time. There was so much to think about; so many decisions to be made. Just two short days ago, the future had been plain: years of steady decline into the oblivion of a loveless marriage, her only release from the torment of drudgery being the occasional (although admittedly highly pleasurable) clandestine meetings with Alex. Now, though, things were very different. Now she had the chance to escape the meaningless travail of her existence. Now there was the prospect of eternal life.

The ache within her loins was powerful, far more so than she had ever known it before. Alex had usually been on hand to relieve it, to sate her ever-more demanding libido, but he would be in class now. She mused how he would be coping today; how he would be managing to concentrate on the prattling of his students after the events of the previous night. She let her hand fall to the mound of her sex, warm through the silk of her robe, and remembered Demonia's taste and her exquisite tongue. She moved her fingers gently and the lips of her pussy softened in response. She was wet already and the salaciousness of her needs began to cloud her mind.

Sarah opened her eyes and looked again at the reclining form of her husband. He's still handsome, she thought, despite the spreading paunch and thinning hair. Perhaps . . .

She stood up and walked from the lounge, heading for the bedroom. Her movements were slow and deliberate and she concentrated on every step, occasionally steadying herself by resting her hand on the wall. She felt drunk and stupefied by the feelings within her body. Strange, alien sensations seemed to be fighting to control her.

She opened a drawer in the heavy, antique dressing-table. Her underwear, plain and functional, looked back at her. She reached under the carefully folded garments, her fingertips touching the unmistakable lace of her black basque, a costume rarely worn except perhaps for Alex. She pulled the garment free and held it to her body. The raging, hungry animal between her legs seemed to throb.

She shrugged the robe from her shoulders and stood naked in front of the long mirror. Her body was good – she knew that. Alex had told her often enough, as had students who chatted amiably to her as she worked out in the campus gym, her skimpy leotard or lycra shorts worn for effect as well as comfort. She stepped into the flimsy basque and moulded the diaphanous lace over her sumptuous breasts, pinching her nipples into immediate response. Reaching into another drawer, she found a pair of seamed black stockings, smoothed them over her long legs and fixed them to the suspenders that were attached to her lacy garment, before stepping into a pair of black, high-heeled shoes.

She looked again at the mirror, delighting in the image that faced her. The basque was small and clinging, unforgivingly forcing her large breasts forward and making her long nipples clearly visible. The delicate lace hemmed well above her crotch and the prominent lips of her pussy were brazenly exposed. The tanned flesh of her thighs contrasted sharply with the blackness of her stockings. She put her hand to herself again and her fingers sank into the warmth.

She thought again of Demonia, and of Alex, and imagined his strong, lithe physique and long cock slipping effortlessly into the ebony perfection of Sinitia's body. Her loins ached again as she thought of his impaling length held deep within her own body; filling her, stretching her, satisfying her every need.

God, she needed a fuck.

She walked slowly back to the lounge, her breathing heavy, if stilted. Professor Fox remained as she had left him; dead to the world. Kneeling at his feet, she ran her hand along his inner thigh and cupped the unresponsive bulge between his legs. He stirred, a small sliver of saliva dripping from the corner of his mouth. Sarah closed her eyes in disgust. This would not do. This would definitely not do.

Returning to the bedroom, she quickly dressed herself in a comfortable tracksuit, concealing her erotic underwear within the loose folds of thick cotton. Replacing her shoes with a pair of brightly-coloured trainers she slipped out of the house and into the warmth of the mid-morning sunlight.

The sun seemed unusually hot and the brightness of the daylight burned into her eyes. She wished she had dressed in shorts and a T-shirt and remembered to bring her sunglasses, but the restraining caress of the basque made her discomfort bearable. Her husband would sleep on, probably into the afternoon when the demands of his classes would force him into activity.

Sarah ambled along the path towards the tennis nets and the running track, dragging her feet through the dusty gravel. Professor Fox hadn't seemed in the slightest bit concerned over her absences during the previous night; her lame excuse, forgotten already, had been enough to suffice.

The exalted cries of labouring athletes filled her ears as she neared the track, causing her to quicken her step. She would often sit on one of the weather-beaten wooden benches, savouring the sights of the wiry, exercise-honed bodies of the students as they engaged in the pointless pursuit of chasing each other around the circuit. Little did they know that they were the objects of their tutor's fantasies. Some would wear plain running wear, their unfettered manhoods swinging flaccidly within thin, cotton shorts, while others would appear to intentionally display the shape of their genitals within the sheaths of tight, stretch material which moulded itself around their forms and accentuated the muscular lines of strong, young buttocks.

Her bench was empty. A small group of female undergraduates were standing close to the edge of the track, half-heartedly cheering the running men on, the strains of competitiveness showing in the grimacing faces of the athletes. There were six of them; six tall, fit young men. She wanted them all, all at the same time, plunging their long cocks into her cunt, her mouth, her bottom. Sarah sat back to enjoy the spectacle, slipping a hand into the trouser-pocket of her tracksuit so that her fingers could find the comfort of her yearning pussy. The weather was hot. She began to perspire.

'Mrs Fox?' The voice was young and seemed reticent. She snatched her hand from her pocket like a child who had been caught with her fingers in the sweet-jar and looked at the newcomer. He stood with his back to the sun, the glare of the light forcing her to shield her eyes. The young man appeared unaware of her plight. 'Are you Mrs Fox?' he repeated.

'Yes,' she replied brusquely. 'Look, sit down, the sun's in my eyes.'

'Oh, sorry,' he said, swiftly obeying her order and joining her on the small bench. She peered at him, her eyes still dazzled, regarding him with the attitude of a teacher to an errant student. He said nothing, but sat nervously, as though waiting for her next command.

'Well, I'm Mrs Fox. What do you want?' she said, immediately feeling guilty about her apparent impatience. She didn't know him so he was obviously relatively new to the campus. He was young, fresh-faced and innocent, looking as all first-year students did as they trod the long path towards learning, untouched as yet by the vagaries and corruptions of university life. The year was nearly complete and yet she couldn't recall his face which, at the moment, was distinctly crestfallen.

She smiled kindly. 'I'm sorry,' she said, 'my mind was elsewhere. How can I help you?'

The young man visibly relaxed. 'My name is Colin,' he said quietly, 'Colin Morris. I'm a student of Doctor Tankard.'

'Oh?' said Sarah casually, concealing the irritating pang of guilt that always surged through her body whenever Alex's name was mentioned.

'I was talking to him the other day about, well, er, vampires, and he said I should talk to you.'

'Vampires? What have vampires got to do with the study of erotic psychology?'

'Oh, nothing. I've always been interested in the subject; a hobby, I suppose, ever since I was a kid.'

'And you want to know more,' said Sarah, unintentionally patronising.

'Oh no,' he said quickly, taking her aback with his sudden arrogance of tone. 'I've made a few discoveries, and the doctor felt that you'd like to know about them.'

'Discoveries? What d'you mean?'

'It's difficult to explain.' He looked uncomfortable and stared down at the ground.

'Try,' said Sarah gently, resting her hand on his arm. The young man looked directly into her eyes. She felt a sudden twinge; an electricity that seemed to fill her body. She shivered, despite the heat.

'I feel a sort of affinity with vampires, as though I *know* they exist. The more I've studied, the more certain I am that the old stories were based on true facts.'

'You say you know they exist; you mean here and now?'

He nodded solemnly. 'I'm sure of it,' he said.

93

'What makes you so sure? I mean, I'm not doubting your sincerity, but what proof have you?'

He looked disappointed. 'You, above all people, should know that proof isn't everything. You're head of occult studies; don't you believe in anything you teach?'

'It's not a case of belief, it's a case of understanding others' beliefs.' Sarah was astonished at the way the conversation was developing in such a short time. She was also curious about this young man. Something inside her told her that he was not all he appeared to be.

'Come with me, back to my flat,' he said, presently. 'I've got some documents you might be interested in seeing.'

'Can't you bring them to my study?' she asked, her heart thumping inexplicably.

'No, there's too much. Come on, it's not far; I can give you a lift.' He stood and began to walk away, leaving Sarah with little choice but to follow.

As they walked down the stony path to the car park he chattered continuously about his beloved subject, telling her nothing that she didn't know already, but his enthusiasm making up for the lack of substance in his information. Finally, he steered her to his transportation – a battered and decidedly unroadworthy motor scooter of considerable antiquity.

'You want me to ride on *that*?' she said, unhappily aware of his answer.

'Come on, it's not far. I'm afraid that I haven't got a spare helmet, so you'll have to cling to me tightly.'

As Colin put his legs astride the machine, Sarah noticed his pert, jean-clad bottom. The ache returned. She sat, rather reluctantly, on the rear of the small seat as he donned his helmet and kicked the engine into life. The bike roared with the desperation of a dying bull, clouds of acrid fumes filling the space around them, and they moved slowly off.

Never having ridden on such a mode of transport before, Sarah hadn't realised just how rough and pot-holed the road to town was. She clung desperately to Colin, her legs gripping the sides of the uncomfortable seat. Suddenly, the bike hit a particularly large obstruction and lurched violently, throwing her forward to grasp at Colin's clothing. Her fingers dug into the harsh material of his denims. She found something she recognised immediately but hadn't expected. He had an erection. He had a bloody hard-on!

Sarah pulled her hand quickly away from the rod-like bulge, slipping her thumbs into the belt-loops of his jeans for safety. The scooter continued to battle against the road and the thumping of the machine caused the muscles of her lower body to ache.

He's got a bloody hard-on, she thought to herself. A fucking great stonker! What the hell have I let myself in for?

Despite her misgivings, she felt relieved when he pulled the bike up outside a large, Victorian terrace in the centre of the town. She clambered awkwardly from her steed and waited as he reined the brute in on its precarious stand. She glanced at the front of his jeans as he turned to her. The erection was still there; firm and prominent.

Colin merely smiled and guided her in the direction of the front door. She felt nervous but the hunger within her loins had returned with a vengeance. If this was just a trick, a come on, and all he wanted was to get inside her pants, well, why not? She needed a fuck, of that she was certain.

He opened the door and led her into a dark, damp hallway. The three flights of stairs they ascended were equally cheerless and the small room he finally introduced her to as his home little better. Attempts had been made to brighten the interior by festooning the walls with an interesting mixture of magazine photographs of motorbikes and naked women; some of them an amalgamation of the two.

'You like motorbikes?' she asked, deliberately ignoring the other subject of the displays.

'I share the room with another student,' he replied apologetically. 'Most of these are his idea.'

'I'm sure they are. Where are the documents?'

There was a long pause. Sarah sat on one of the two small beds, the only form of seating in the room. Colin sat opposite her on the other. 'There are no documents,' he said quietly.

'What d'you mean? Why are we here?' Sarah was angry, and beginning to feel a little afraid. The youth said nothing, merely staring at her with nervous eyes. She stood up and made for the door. 'This is no joke,' she snapped. 'I'm leaving. You're in a lot of trouble, young man!'

Colin stood and grasped her arm firmly. 'Please, Mrs Fox, please, I mean you no harm. I just had to talk to you privately.'

Sarah looked into his eyes, their expression one of fearful sincerity. 'What was wrong with the track? Nobody was listening to us there.'

He relaxed his grip of her arm and sat down again. Sarah followed suit, her fear lost in her curiosity. Colin took a deep breath.

'You remember I told you that I feel a sort of affinity with vampires,' he began, carefully judging each word before he spoke, 'there's something within me; a gift, or maybe a curse. Whatever it is, I *know* they exist, and I believe I can find them.'

Sarah listened with silent intensity. Her recent experiences had made her fully aware that he was likely to be telling the truth, but where was this leading?

'There's a great power,' he continued, leaning forward to stress the enormity of his words. 'Something has been unleashed into the world recently, as though a malevolent evil has been reborn.'

'Why do you say that?' she said, her tone subdued.

He paused again, looking her steadily in the eye. Sarah felt uncomfortable and looked away, her mouth becoming dry.

'You're one of them, aren't you?' His words pierced her brain like a dagger.

'What do you mean?'

Colin stood up and walked across the room, sitting next to her and resting his hand on her shoulder. 'Mrs Fox,' he said soothingly, 'I lied when I said I'd spoken to Doctor Tankard. I knew the instant that I saw you, on that bench, that you were a vampire. Like I said, I have this affinity.'

'What are you going to do?' asked Sarah realising that denial was pointless but uncertain as to whether his knowledge was a threat.

'Nothing, I mean, it's just that . . .' He paused, as though summoning up an inner courage. 'I want to learn, to discover everything I can about you, but most of all, I need to make love to a vampire.'

From the moment she had accidentally touched his erection, or even before that, Sarah had wanted him not to make love to her but to *fuck* her. She looked at the floor, as though considering his proposal, then raised her head, her face inches from his. 'Kiss me, Colin,' she breathed.

She moved her head forward and their lips met, her tongue darting forward to gently slide against his. She savoured the taste of his mouth and curled both her arms around his neck as their embrace surrendered further and further into the deepest of passions. She felt his hands exploring underneath her tracksuit top, running over the lacy material of her basque before tugging the garment upwards. She raised her arms to let him remove it altogether, then pulled off her training shoes before lying back and lifting her bottom to allow him to pull down her trousers. He threw the pants on to the floor and gazed at her, his face a picture of delight.

'Do you always wear sexy underwear like that?' he asked, stroking the stocking-covered surface of her inner thigh.

'I must have known,' she pouted, opening her legs wide to afford him the most delectable view of her engorged pussy lips. He ran his hand up her leg slowly until his fingertips brushed against her wetness, the tenderness of his touch causing her to shiver. 'Don't think of me as a vampire, Colin, think of me as a woman.'

'You *are* a woman,' he said, leaning forward and kissing her lightly on the mouth as his fingers delved deeper into her soaking sheath, 'and a very beautiful one.'

Sarah could feel the damp trickle of her juices running down the cleft between her buttocks as he turned and twisted his hand. Four fingers were held within the soft grip of her pussy lips while his thumb playfully rubbed against the erect bud of her clitoris. He may be young, she thought, but he certainly knows what he's doing. She drew her knees back to her shoulders and gripped her ankles in a wanton display of total submission as he fondled and caressed her. She groaned as he leant forward and took her nipple between his teeth, suckling it gently with his lips.

He withdrew his hand from her slowly, the emptiness inside her demanding to be sated. Still holding her legs high, she watched as he knelt between them and gazed at her pussy like a worshipper at an altar. He stroked the outer lips again with his fingertips. 'So beautiful,' he sighed, 'so beautiful.'

He bent his head forward and Sarah closed her eyes, waiting for the sensation of his tongue lapping at her hot cunt. She felt the warmth of his breath between her thighs and the touch of a kiss on the matted, wet hair, then the ultimate joy of his tongue slipping inside her; a long, curling, stimulating invasion of her most sensitive treasure. He slid it in and out of her, like a soft, wet prick, and her hips rose from the damp bedcover to meet his suckling mouth. She pulled her legs back further, the soles of her feet touching the wall behind the bed as Colin moved his tongue down to her anus, the tip pushing at the tight orifice.

She felt him part her buttocks with his fingers, his tongue probing ever deeper into her. She ran her hand down to her aching pussy to pleasure herself, and pulled at the soft lips before fucking herself with her slim fingers. His tongue seemed incredibly long as it slid in and out of her bottom, the sweet sensation causing her to gasp for breath.

'Oh, God, that's fantastic,' she moaned. 'More, more, suck it, lick my arse!'

Spurred on by her obscenities, Colin moved his tongue rapidly inside her, his lips pressed hard against her bottom, the fingers of one hand meeting with hers inside the soaked lips of her pussy. Sarah felt the inevitable rise to her first climax; the tingling of the nerves along her legs and the intensifying build up within her loins. She rubbed herself rapidly over her clitoris and stiffened her buttocks. Colin's

98

tongue was gripped within the tight sphincter of her anus as his fingers pumped deep inside her.

'Oh, God, I'm coming, I'm coming!' she wailed, lifting her lower body from the bed as her thighs gripped her lover's head. The explosion of pleasure that surged through her body tore at her senses. Every nerve ending between her legs was alive with electricity. 'Yes, yes!' she shouted through gritted teeth. 'I'm coming!'

The suddenness of her orgasmic release hit her brain like a shaft of lightning, causing her to gasp for air. Her fingers gripped Colin's head tightly and pulled at his hair, the uncontrollable thrusting movements of her thighs soaking his face with her juices. He lapped hungrily, and she knew, even in her state of ecstatic oblivion, that he had become one of them; that he too would serve Demonia.

Sarah relaxed at last, her heart pounding and her blood thumping in her veins. Never before had she experienced an orgasm of such magnificent intensity. If this is what it's like to be a vampire, she thought, then I will surely sell them my soul.

Colin sat back and gazed at her, his eyes filled with a mixture of wonder and lust. Sarah slowly lowered her legs to the bed, her back stiff from holding such an awkward position for so long. Nothing was said for a long while; he knew that he had reaped the consequences of his desperate thirst.

Presently, he smiled. 'You have much to teach me,' he whispered, casually stroking her heaving breasts. 'I must know everything, and you must introduce me to the others.'

'You know of them?' Sarah's throat was dry and her voice cracked. Colin nodded.

'I know they exist, that's all.'

Sarah looked at him through glazed eyes. 'Fuck me, Colin,' she whimpered. 'Please fuck me.'

He stood and quickly removed his clothing, scattering the garments haphazardly over the floor. Then he was naked, and the sight of his lean, muscular body filled her with expectation. His cock stood proudly erect. She sat up and took hold of his stalk, put it to her mouth and drew it between her pouting lips, her tongue circling the hard shaft. Then she pulled her head back and stared up at him, clutching his stiff phallus tightly.

'Please,' she sighed. '*Please* fuck me now.'

Colin knelt on the bed between her outstretched legs, Sarah clutching his cock as though unwilling to set it free. She drew him towards her, pressing the thick, bulbous knob against the suppliant lips of her pussy. He slid into her easily, her arousal so extreme that she hardly felt his movements until he was deep inside her. Their mouths met and their loins crushed together, unmoving. She felt him throb within her then slowly he began to move gently in and out of her burning sheath. Gradually his pace quickened, his hips circling and his cock probing the very depths of her cunt; exploring her and filling her completely. She raised her legs high and gripped her ankles, pulling them back until her toes once more touched the wall. Colin stiffened his body, gripping the headboard to steady himself, and pounded down into her with ever-increasing force.

She knew she wouldn't come again – her orgasm had been too powerful; too all-pervading. She was happy to feel him inside her, delighting in the abject joy betrayed by his expression as he fucked her steadily, his breathing sharp and rhythmic in unison with the deep thrusts of his long shaft within her. She tensed the muscles of her vagina, gripping his plundering stalk tightly. Colin threw his head back and gritted his teeth, pumping rapidly.

'In my mouth!' she cried. 'Come in my mouth!'

Colin didn't need telling twice. He pulled quickly from her and presented his purple-ended stalk to her face. Sarah took it within her mouth and sucked and rubbed his length quickly, desperate to taste his seed. He groaned, and she felt him throb between her pouted lips. She rubbed his stem faster until the throbbing became incessant, the heavenly texture of his release filling her mouth. She sucked harder and drained him, unwilling to free him until she was sated.

Eventually, he could give no more and he fell, exhausted, into unconscious oblivion to the floor at her side. Sarah licked her lips and swallowed hard, the warmth of his sustenance filling her body. She slipped her fingers into the warm wetness of her sex and then put them to her mouth, tasting the intoxicating perfume of her own scent, then fell into a deep sleep.

Alex sat beside the blazing fire, his eyes heavy with sleep. He was gradually becoming used to the need for extreme heat that seemed to be an incongruous requisite of the vampire's vitality although strangely, the midday sun had borne down on him heavily, sapping his strength.

Demonia sat facing him, regarding him closely. The flickering of the flames illuminated her ashen pallor, her eyes sparkling with new life as the late evening gave way to the short, summer night. She wore a simple, clinging gown of black silk and a heavy chain of gold around her neck, encrusted with blood-red rubies. Sinitia knelt at her feet, resting her arm on her sister's leg and staring absently into the fire.

A crack of burning wood broke the silence, causing Alex to start. He sat up straight, took a deep breath and rubbed his eyes. Little had been said since his arrival, and the girls seemed content with their own thoughts. He glanced at Sinitia and pondered on the events of the previous night; her mouth, her breasts, her sumptuous bottom. He felt a familiar stirring in his loins.

'Sinitia tells me that you pleasured her well,' said Demonia, her hushed tone blending with the calm atmosphere of their surroundings. Alex beamed immodestly, looking fondly at the dark features of his lover. Sinitia smiled coyly.

'Are you pleased to be one of us?' Demonia continued.

'I think so,' said Alex genuinely, 'but there is still much I need to know. I am a male vampire, I suppose, and yet I don't seek the taste of blood but the delicate scent of a woman's arousal. Will that change? I pray that it will not.'

'A man will only become a leech if bitten by another vampire, whether it be male or female. You will be safe if you remember and guard against this.'

101

'Another thing,' said Alex, now fully awake, 'this character you call Baron Mansola worries me. Can we really have a hope of defeating him? It seems to me that one bite from him and I'll be on his team.'

'Team? Oh, yes, I see. You are right to be concerned. We need to draw more into our company – people of strength, both of body and intellect and, above all likely to become sensitive to and supportive of our cause.'

Alex considered her words for a moment. 'There are members of Sarah's classes that may well be willing,' he said, after some thought. The waif-like Karen with her sensuous mouth and innocent look and the voluptuous Belinda with her superb body; they would be sympathetic, he felt sure. And the two male students; what were their names? The academic interest was certainly there; they would be easy conscripts.

'Where is Sarah?' asked Demonia.

'I don't know. I haven't seen her since lunchtime, and then only briefly.'

'She is safe. We would sense it if she had come to any harm.'

'Would I know?'

Demonia nodded. 'Slowly, gradually, the gifts that you have received will become more and more apparent. We are as one, a binding of souls together. Where there are many of us there is strength. Go, Alex, and seek out Sarah. Ask her to introduce us to her students. We have very little time to prepare, I feel it.'

Sarah walked slowly but purposefully down the long, grim passageway. She was naked but felt nothing; not the damp, dankness of the air nor the cold of the stone beneath her feet. Around her swirled a thin mist tinged with green, illuminated by the phosphorescent lichen that clung to the black walls, the only sounds being the steady dripping of water and the scurrying of rats.

She didn't know where she was or why she was there, but knew that she must go forward and that somehow her destiny lay hidden in the darkness ahead. There was no fear, just acceptance.

Her path became steadily steeper, descending as though into the bowels of Hades itself. She did not slip; in fact she hardly felt the need to move her legs as she drifted ever downwards. She felt a hand reach out and touch her, then another, caressing her breasts and stroking her between her legs, but she fixed her stare before her. More hands, and the wetness of a tongue across her backside. She closed her eyes, holding herself motionless, but still she glided forward.

She opened her eyes again. The mist had cleared, her passage now lit by flaming torches. She glanced at the walls as they drifted past, etched with drawings of nameless creatures and ethereal landscapes, glistening with a sheen of dampness.

The unseen hands became more insistent, caressing every inch of her nakedness simultaneously. Then the touch of the tongue, then another and another, wetly worshipping her body, licking her pussy, her nipples, her anus. Sarah shut her eyes again, fearful that if she opened them the sensations would disappear into the ether. Down, down, she seemed to float, her legs moving slightly, but her feet barely touching the ground. Her pussy ran with her juices, the ache for fulfilment within her loins gnawing at her consciousness. Down, descending into the very depths of the unknown.

The ghostly caresses stopped suddenly, and she opened her eyes. She was in a great cavern, its sheer, cliff-like walls festooned with hundreds of black-stemmed candles, the burning, flickering sheen of light filling every crevice of the unearthly grotto. At the far end of the cave stood an altar of stone carved from the rock, at the centre of which stood a large, gold chalice which seemed to be somehow drawing her towards it. There was a silence; unnerving and unreal, but Sarah knew that she must go forward and that she must approach the altar. She began to regain her senses as the cool dampness of the atmosphere enveloped her aroused body and caused her to shiver. She felt the cold hardness of the stone floor against her bare feet and her breath drifted from her mouth like small clouds of steam.

The unseen hands were back, this time gripping her tightly and clawing at her wrists and ankles to pull her to the altar. Though they tugged her she moved willingly forward; there was no terror, only extreme excitement. They laid her submissively at the foot of the altar, her legs splayed apart obscenely. Ghostly fingers pulled apart her soaking sex lips, and fingertips rubbed sensuously at her hard bud, as if preparing her.

Then she was alone again. No force gripped her limbs but she remained acquiescent, looking around her at the eerie shadows cast by the shimmering candlelight. The constant drip of water seemed to be measuring the time that she waited. The unyielding stone floor became warmer to her back and the air was now not so icy.

From the deepest of the shadows stepped four figures wearing hooded robes, their faces completely hidden. They moved silently over to the prone figure of Sarah and stood regarding her from the blackness beneath their cowls. She waited, her heart beating loudly. Her nipples were painfully erect and her cunt was aching to be touched.

As though at a given signal the four pulled back their robes, revealing their manhoods proudly erect before her eager gaze. The first visitor moved forward and knelt at her side, presenting the thick, bulbous head of his cock to her mouth. Sarah parted her lips and accepted him, sucking lightly on his engorged member. Two others crouched at her sides, their demands clear. She reached out and gripped each prick firmly, her fingers circling the hard shafts, rubbing them up and down instinctively. The final hooded figure knelt between her legs and reached under her buttocks, raising them from the floor before guiding his stiff cock into her in one swift movement. The suddenness of his intrusion caused her to cry out, her voice shattering the silence with an unending echo.

She was fucked without emotion or passion; steadily and mechanically. The four silent strangers moved ceaselessly around her, each savouring the rhythmic caress of her hands, her suckling mouth and her cunt. Then, as though sensing her arousal was complete, they withdrew back into the darkness from where they had appeared.

104

The dripping of water from the menacing stalactites above her head grew louder and the atmosphere suddenly became cold once more. There was a noise. Sarah peered into the blackness behind the altar, conscious that she was not alone. Something moved. The flickering candlelight caught the image of a man, hugely tall, and as naked as she was. He moved forward silently and his face came into view. He was malevolently handsome, grinning without kindness, and his dark eyes were filled with lust.

Sarah heard his voice but his lips didn't move. 'Welcome, sister,' it boomed, 'you have come to place yourself at the feet of your master.' He moved further towards her and she saw his phallus for the first time. It was monstrously erect, thick, gnarled and far larger than anything that she'd ever seen or imagined. He held it within his grip like a weapon and the huge end pressed between the slab-like pectoral muscles of his chest. 'Look, my child, and worship!' the voice said.

For the first time, Sarah was afraid. It was too big; no woman could accommodate such a monster. She tried to move but couldn't. He leant forward over her trembling body, the arm-thick stalk sliding into her insistently. The pleasure was instant, but her terror remained. 'No, no, it's too big!' she protested. The man merely widened his grin and revealed the needle-sharpness of fang-like teeth as he moved his face towards her neck.

'Nooooo!' Sarah's scream could have been heard throughout the entirety of the university buildings as she woke, shivering in the calm of the library. Karen and Andrew rushed over and gripped her by the arms as she looked around wildly, scarcely believing the reality of her surroundings. She held her eyes wide open, as though afraid to blink, even for an instant.

'What's the matter? What's up?' asked Karen, relaxing her grip and allowing Sarah to settle back in the chair. She suddenly felt very foolish. A dream; nothing but a dream.

'I'm sorry,' she said after a moment, regaining her composure. 'I . . . I must have dozed off. I had this incredible nightmare. You wouldn't believe . . .'

'You've been acting very strangely these past couple of days,' said Andrew, picking up a book on the history of vampires that lay on the desk before her. 'I think you've been over-working.'

'Nonsense,' said Sarah, snatching the volume from her student impatiently, 'it was just a dream. Everybody dreams.'

'True, but they don't wake up screaming in the middle of the library,' smiled Karen, perching on the end of the desk. Sarah looked at her and smiled resignedly.

'Perhaps you're right,' she said. 'Perhaps I need a little time off.' She gathered up a small pile of old books and pushed them into her briefcase, looking again at Karen. Demonia would love to meet this young lady, she thought to herself, and Belinda, too. Perhaps I should speak to Alex . . .

Sarah lay quietly in the hot, stuffy room, the heavy curtains drawn against the searing brightness of the afternoon sun. Alex dozed next to her, the bed damp with the sweat of their love-making. Her bottom ached; it had been good, very good.

Sex with Alex had become even more intense since their fateful meeting with the two beautiful vampires in the house on Gallows Hill Road. They would snatch every opportunity, day or night, to be together. They had fucked in his bed, in cars, in the library, in empty lecture halls; little caring whether they might be discovered. Their common sense was utterly blinded by the power of their mutual lasciviousness.

It would always end in the same manner – she suckling on his long, thick cock, draining his seed into her hungry mouth and he almost devouring her soaked pussy lips until they were both fully sated. Then they would sleep, always dreaming strange, sensuous nightmares as real as daylight itself.

They talked of their dreams, at first astounded at their similarity, then gradually realising that it was all part of the game, and the unearthly transformation that their bodies were undertaking.

They had spoken to Karen and Belinda, and to Andrew and Stuart, and were not surprised at their students' eager excitement at the prospect of meeting with two genuine vampires. Indeed, it seemed that their young charges had almost expected the invitation, as Sarah's talk was of nothing else in class or general conversation. The meeting was to be that night, and the prospect of tasting Demonia's wonderful juices once more and possibly those of her four students filled Sarah's mind with delight.

'What time is it?' muttered Alex in his half-sleep. She glanced at the illuminated display on the radio-alarm.

'Three-forty,' she replied, 'I thought you didn't have a class this afternoon.'

'I don't,' said Alex, struggling to sit up, 'but I've a stack of work to mark. I've still got to make a living, you know.' He slid himself over Sarah's naked body, pausing to kiss her tenderly on the mouth, then stood up unsteadily. 'God, that was a good one,' he said, stroking his flaccid cock suggestively.

'Just gets better and better.'

He grinned and pulled back the blind, squinting in the sudden light. 'It won't be long before we become creatures of the night ourselves,' he said, letting the curtain fall back into place.

'Won't it be wonderful?' said Sarah warmly, stretching herself to reach out and grip his cock, thrilling as she felt it thicken within her grasp. He watched as she teased it into full erection, her fingers barely encircling its girth.

'I just can't seem to get enough,' he breathed as Sarah steadily moved her hand up and down his long shaft, her eyes staring hungrily at the monster and her tongue wetting her lips. 'I came close to fucking Belinda in the library this morning when she bent over to pick up those books. Such a pretty little arse.'

'You should have done,' cooed Sarah, kissing the swollen knob in front of her face. 'She's not exactly a virgin, you know.'

'It was tempting, I can assure you, but like I said, I still have a living to make. What about Karen, though?'

'What d'you mean?' asked Sarah, now rubbing him with both hands and occasionally licking the end to savour the texture and taste of his pre-come.

'Well, everyone knows that Belinda is a bit of a tramp but Karen, she's so quiet, so innocent-looking.'

'Looks can be deceiving,' said Sarah, pumping rapidly on his engorged cock, her intention clear. 'When you first saw me in the staff restroom, I bet you never imagined you'd end up with your dick up my bum within 24 hours.'

Alex laughed, the sound turning to a groan as Sarah clamped her wet mouth over the end of his tool, sucking in over half of his length. He came for the fourth time that day, his sperm rushing to the back of her throat in a momentarily endless stream of sustenance for his lover. Sarah drew in her cheeks and sucked hard as her tongue encircled his thumping flesh and her neck muscles swallowed quickly. Alex gripped the thick, blonde tresses of her hair to steady himself, his cock softening rapidly within the heavenly succulence of her mouth, then pulled himself from her. Sarah made a last grasp at his wet phallus, putting her fingers to her lips like a child savouring the forbidden taste of cream from a cake.

Alex quickly pulled on his trousers. Sarah feigned a look of disappointment and watched with pouted lips as he finished dressing and made for the door. 'I'll call for you at eight,' he said, grinning.

The two black cabs pulled up at the house on Gallows Hill Road as the sun began to dip behind the nearby office-blocks. The students clambered out of their taxi and waited at the gate like a group of excited youngsters on a school outing, while Alex and Sarah paid the two drivers.

'It doesn't look much like a haunted house to me,' said Karen in a tone of abject disappointment.

'You should have seen it a few days ago,' said Alex. 'It's amazing what a little magic can do.'

'Magic?' asked Belinda querulously. He looked at her and smiled. Unlike the other students, who wore the regulation tight jeans and T-shirts, Belinda had chosen to dress in a remarkably short, skin-tight black dress that moulded itself round the sumptuous curves of her young body like a second skin. The smooth lines of the garment emphasised the fact that she plainly wasn't wearing anything under-neath – of that he was certain. A surreptitious glance be-tween her legs when she sat facing him on the train from Kent had proven the fact: a delicious glimpse of the prob-able joys to come.

'No, more than magic,' he attempted. 'It's difficult to ex-plain. Come on, our hostesses will be waking soon.' He opened the gate and ushered them in.

'Waking?' whispered Stuart. 'Where are they – lying in coffins in the cellar?' Alex and Sarah ignored him, quickly leading the way to the main door of the house.

As ever, the huge unsmiling figure of the doorman waited to greet them. 'I'll bet he's called Igor,' chuckled Karen under her breath. Alex pondered that despite the fact that he and Sarah had become regular visitors to the house over the past few nights they hadn't learned the man's name. Igor would suffice; at least out of the big man's earshot.

The party was led silently into the plush sitting-room, Igor leaving them immediately and closing the door behind him. The large log fire blazed with its customary fierceness and the flames cracked loudly as they devoured the newly-laid wood, casting eerie, flickering shadows across the lux-urious furniture. The four students sat nervously together on the long settee, looking for all the world like errant schoolchildren waiting to see their headmaster.

Alex took up two large black candles and lit them from the flames, totally oblivious to the searing heat that roared from the grate. He placed them carefully in sturdy silver candlesticks at each end of the high, ornate mantelpiece, the extra light serving to illuminate a massive oil painting depicting the images of Demonia and Sinitia.

The painting had appeared two evenings previously; Alex didn't know from where, and hadn't asked. So many inexplicable things had occurred over the past few nights that such an occurrence was hardly worth a thought.

'Is that them?' said Andrew, rising from his seat. Alex nodded.

'It doesn't do them justice,' he said.

Andrew walked slowly towards the fire, staring reverently at the images in the painting. 'They are beautiful,' he breathed, his eyes transfixed by the hypnotic essence of the portrait, 'beautiful.' He ran his fingertips over its surface, as though expecting the texture to be other than mere canvas.

'You will come to worship them, as we do,' said Alex quietly.

'Worship? What do you mean?'

'Their power is all-consuming; divine. They have conquered us with their infinite perfection, Sarah and I. We are little more than their slaves, albeit willing slaves.'

Andrew gazed into the depths of the portrait, clearly besotted. The fire spat.

'Wow, it's hot in here.' It was Belinda who spoke, fanning herself with a cushion. Karen and Stuart got up and joined Andrew, who continued to gaze.

'They are so different and yet so gorgeous,' said Karen wistfully.

'It's just a painting,' snorted Belinda, walking over to the curtain-covered window. She pulled back a heavy drape and looked outside. 'It's dark already,' she said, letting it fall back into place. 'When are these spooks of yours going to appear?'

'Belinda!' blazed Sarah.

'Don't talk that way, young lady,' said Alex, angrily. 'You were invited here because you believed.'

'Believed?' said Belinda, patronisingly. 'I don't believe in vampires, or werewolves or anything. I just came along for the laugh.'

Sarah strode over to her and raised her arm, as if to strike her, then seemed to think better of it. 'Please, Belinda, take care what you say.'

The young student turned away and sighed with exasperation. 'What's the matter with you?' she asked, swinging round suddenly, waving her arm in the direction of the

110

painting. 'You're supposed to be highly educated people and here you are, saying you're slaves to these two, er, females and expect us to sit here waiting for them to rise from the dead! It's just too ridiculous for words.'

She sat down heavily on an armchair like the petulant teenager she was, folding her arms and crossing her legs simultaneously. Alex walked over to her and rested a hand on her bare shoulder, unable to avoid noticing the way her large breasts heaved within the tight dress. 'You *must* believe, Belinda, you must.'

The young girl shrugged his hand from her shoulder. 'If she wants to go, then let her,' said Sarah angrily.

'She will believe.' Demonia stood behind them, her long white translucent gown shimmering in the half-light. Alex rushed over to her, a look of abject apology on his face.

'I'm sorry, Demonia, we thought ...' he began. She smiled, gripping his hand and putting it to her lips. She kissed his fingers lightly.

'Don't worry, Alex,' she said calmly. 'I will speak with her.' She walked over to the seated girl, who regarded her with more than a hint of fear. Her colleagues simply stood and gazed in awed silence at the beauty who seemed to glide across the room. Demonia caught hold of Belinda's hands and helped her to her feet. 'Look at me, Belinda,' she breathed.

The young girl's eyes seemed to be drawn magnetically to Demonia's piercing gaze. There was a long silence while the two stood motionless in the flickering shadows. Alex felt his mouth go dry. Sarah moved to his side, gripping his arm nervously.

'Do you still feel hot?' asked Demonia in a sultry, hushed tone. Belinda nodded slowly. Demonia relaxed her grip on the young student's fingers, letting her hands fall to her sides. Alex licked his lips as he watched Belinda reach for the hem of her dress and begin to draw it upwards, revealing her long shapely legs, the sensuous curve of her plump bottom and the wispy, white-blonde curls between her legs.

Slowly, the garment was pulled over her head and fell to

111

the floor so that she stood before them completely naked, her body trembling and her large breasts heaving rhythmically. Demonia reached forward and cupped the firm mounds of flesh, her gaze not leaving Belinda's for a moment. The young girl's nipples grew quickly erect under the expert, delicate touch of Demonia's fingertips. Slowly, as if responding to some silent command, she bent her legs and fell to her knees, staring up at the tall form before her. Her face was a picture of submissive serenity.

Demonia unclasped her own dress at the shoulder and the diaphanous material drifted to the floor. Andrew and Stuart gasped audibly at the sight of her statuesque perfection and Alex finally lost the battle that was raging within his loins. His erection rose rapidly.

'Kiss me,' whispered Demonia to the kneeling figure. Belinda moved her head forward to obey, pressing her mouth against the glistening lips of Demonia's pussy. 'Taste it, drink, and you will believe.'

Alex watched hungrily as Belinda's tongue lapped around the wet, puffy flesh. Demonia parted her thighs slightly to allow the young girl even deeper access and Belinda gripped the standing woman's calves and pressed her face hard against the soaked mound of her pussy. The room was filled with the erotic sounds of her oral caress.

Demonia reached down, took hold of her arms and raised her once more to her feet. She kissed her lightly on the mouth, running her fingers through the silky, blonde tresses of her hair. 'Now you believe,' she said confidently. Belinda nodded.

Demonia turned to Alex and smiled benignly. 'Take her, Alex,' she said. 'Welcome her fully into the sisterhood.'

He moved quickly forward and took the young girl immediately into his arms, running his hands over the firm globes of her sumptuous bottom. He put his mouth to hers and his tongue darted forward to taste the delicate but distinctive scent of Demonia on her fleshy lips. He moved a hand around her body, over her soft stomach and down to the welcoming wetness of her pussy, his fingers slipping between the velvety folds. She moved her hips in response to his touch, her arousal total.

'Fuck me, Doctor Tankard,' she whispered, hoarsely. 'Fuck me, please.'

Alex reluctantly freed her from his embrace and tore at his clothes, stripping himself completely. His cock jutted forward hugely, the tip wet. Belinda turned her back to him and bent forward, resting the palms of her hands on her thighs. Her legs were held straight, and splayed apart. Alex moved forward and rested his hand on her plump bottom, while he guided the angry head of his stiff cock within the silken folds of her sex-flesh. Then he drove his length deep into her hot little pussy.

He fucked her for a while with long, deliberate strokes, thrilling to her moans of ecstasy with each deep thrust. Then he started to pump harder with an urgency that made his knees tremble.

Demonia stepped forward, resting her hand on his shoulder. 'Her mouth, Alex,' she whispered, 'she must take it in her mouth.'

Alex pulled reluctantly from within the enchanting grip of the young student's pussy and stood back. Belinda fell again to her knees, taking hold of his monstrous erection and put it immediately to her mouth, her tongue licking around the swollen head while she rubbed his hard stalk slowly. He throbbed involuntarily, a small trickle of sperm seeping out of the tiny slit on to her pouted lips. She ran her tongue over the damp fluid, drawing it into her mouth and swallowing. Then she pushed her head forward and took his length between her suckling lips, her tongue lapping and slithering against his tortured flesh. She arched herself slightly and moved further forward, gradually easing his full size inside her mouth, so that his cock was gripped within the undulating sheath of her throat.

Alex looked across at the other students and watched as Karen slowly stripped off her T-shirt to reveal small, pert breasts and then began to slip off her tight jeans and panties. The house was clearly working its magic.

He looked back at Belinda crouched before him, and

113

marvelled at the way his large cock disappeared completely within her beautiful mouth and down her gently undulating throat; an experience that he'd only previously dreamt about. He heard Sarah groan and looked over towards her. She was lying naked on the carpet and Demonia was kneeling between her widely-splayed legs, hungrily lapping at her cunt with her perfect bottom presented to his excited gaze in the most erotic fashion. His cock throbbed again at the sight and Belinda's expert sucking brought him dangerously close to the edge. He desperately wanted to impale his beautiful queen – to sink his long shaft between the flawless globes of her arse – a joy as yet denied to him.

Belinda moved her head back, slowly allowing his penis to slip from inside her mouth, inch by hard inch, until she held just the thick, bulbous head within her pouted, fleshy lips. He sensed her running the tip of her tongue round and round it as she gripped his steel-like shaft with both hands. Then she pulled her face away and held his cock vertically, pressing it against his stomach. She ran her tongue slowly upwards along his thick stalk, kissed the tip lightly then licked all the way down again to his balls, taking one then the other into her mouth, and sucking them like plump, ripe strawberries soaked in cream.

Belinda rubbed his raging erection steadily with one hand, as she held both of his balls inside her mouth, her tongue tracing their shape wetly. Then, without altering the delightful pumping rhythm of her hand, she slid her lips back up to the tip of his cock and took it once more inside her warm mouth.

Alex was desperate to stop himself coming; the exquisite sensations caused by Belinda's succulent mouth were just too astounding to end. He looked across at the other three students, more to take his mind off the deep-throated caress of Belinda's mouth than anything else, but carefully avoiding a glance at Demonia's magnificent bottom. Karen now knelt on the floor with Stuart's cock firmly grasped in one hand and Andrew's in the other, and the two male students were struggling to divest themselves of their clothing without allowing her to loosen her grip. She looked tiny

114

and frail, but somehow totally in command. But it was the sight of Andrew's cock that took his attention. Alex had always been proud of his own size, which was certainly well above average, if books were to be believed. But the monster that jutted from the thick mass of black hair below Andrew's belly exceeded the length of Alex's pride and joy by at least three inches, and looked as thick as Karen's wrist. She seemed untroubled by its immense size, however, as she happily opened her mouth wide to accommodate the beast.

The sight of her innocent, elfin face being impaled by such a monstrous prick, coupled with the fact that she continued to pump the not inconsiderable offering from Stuart was too much for Alex. He groaned, the surging from within his loins out of control, and the sperm rushed along his throbbing shaft and down Belinda's throat. She clamped her lips against the groin and dug her fingernails into his taut backside as she suckled and swallowed, the sensation of her throat muscles undulating against his swollen cock making his head swim. His orgasm seemed never-ending, a constant stream of cream draining from his body into the incessantly demanding mouth of the sensuous young temptress at his feet. Belinda will make a good vampire, he thought. A natural.

Gradually the sensations of extreme pleasure gave way to ones of sensitivity, and he slowly withdrew his cock from her mouth. She looked up at him and smiled sweetly, running the tip of her tongue over her lips as though unwilling to allow a drop of his seed to escape her. Alex knelt quickly at her side before his legs could give way and kissed her with genuine, post-orgasmic affection. Belinda pushed her tongue into his mouth and shared the unmistakable texture of his juices with him. He savoured the moment, his lust hardly abated as he looked into Belinda's lovely young face and saw her wide eyes and her smooth skin flushed with excitement.

'D'you feel OK now?' he asked.

'Yes,' she replied.

'And do you believe?'

She looked at him curiously. 'Of course,' she said. 'Of course I believe.'

Alex grinned, stroking her hair tenderly. She smiled a sweet, happy smile of contentment. 'I love the taste of cock,' she said presently. 'I love to swallow it deep down inside me.'

Alex sat back on the carpet and rested against an armchair to watch the others at play. 'You'd never get that one down your throat,' he said, indicating Andrew with a nod of his head. Belinda laughed, watching as Karen sucked steadily on the thick end of the proffered monster. Stuart's cock was deeply embedded into her cute, shaven little pussy from behind.

'You'd be surprised,' she said.

'Have you sucked it?' he asked, with more than a twinge of jealousy.

Belinda nodded, grinning. 'It nearly choked me; it's just too big for that type of thing. Stuart's is much nicer.'

'Stuart as well, eh?'

'I'm afraid I've got a bit of a name for myself in that respect,' she said, wiping the back of her hand across her mouth. 'Like I said, I love to suck cock.'

'You're very good.'

'Thank you doctor,' she said mischievously, getting up and walking over to join her three colleagues. Alex watched her go, knowing that soon she would share her juices with her friends and that they would all be willing slaves to Demonia and Sinitia, just as he and Sarah had become.

He looked across at Sarah and their beautiful hostess, still happily engaged in suckling each other's pussies. Sarah was lying on her back with her legs wrapped around Demonia's neck, the beautiful vampire's bottom held high, vulnerable and inviting. Alex let his hand fall to his crotch, feeling his cock harden within his gently moving grasp. He glanced again at the four students and watched as Belinda licked the cleft between Andrew's buttocks. Andrew's huge prick was still being orally worshipped by Karen, and Stuart was steadily fucking Karen from behind.

Alex's erection rose to its full magnificence as he

116

savoured the scenes of copulative excesses before him. His throat felt dry; his lips parched. He needed to taste the fluids of ecstasy – he needed to suckle at the warm, wet flesh of a dripping pussy. He looked again at Demonia, watching as Sarah lapped at the widely-splayed lips of her cunt, and noticed that the welcoming pink slit glistened with come and saliva. He would take her now; she would not object. He would quench his rabid thirst from this chalice of joy.

He shuffled over to the couple and knelt with his face close to Demonia's bottom, savouring the delicious aroma of sexual arousal. He pushed his tongue forward and the tip touched the silken lips then lapped greedily around the engorged sex-flesh, meeting Sarah's fluttering tongue occasionally in a perfect, erotic kiss. The scent was heady and the taste one he could never have imagined, and it filled his entire body with a delightful warmth. He suckled voraciously, filling his mouth with the copious fluids of love then sensing an inner strength surging through every part of his body. His cock stretched painfully. He had to fuck her; he had to fuck the stunning Demonia *now*.

He raised himself up and squatted on the balls of his feet, holding on to her back for support with one hand, the other guiding his aching cock towards her enticing cunt. Sarah flicked her tongue rapidly over her clitoris. His thick knob touched the lustrous wetness and a sensation like a charge of electricity shot through his brain. He plunged forward, the tight sheath welcoming his full length and gripping him within her depths. She drew him inside her like a sucking mouth.

He gritted his teeth and held himself still, his cock throbbing heavily. Despite so recently sating himself within Belinda's delightful mouth he already felt the desperate need to release his seed within this succulent envelope. He felt Sarah licking his balls and bit his lip, tasting blood. Gradually the urgency subsided and he began to move carefully in and out of Demonia's pussy, drawing the full length of his engorged cock to the very tip then driving it back into the hot flesh firmly while Demonia suckled at Sarah's cunt as though oblivious to his efforts.

117

Harder and harder he fucked her, pounding down on the two submissive bodies. Sarah had now returned her tongue to Demonia's pussy, lapping at his length as it moved swiftly in and out. Suddenly he was coming, and he knew what he had to do. He pulled himself from within the pulpy flesh and dragged himself quickly around the two women, pushing his cock towards Demonia's face. She took him inside her mouth immediately and drained him as he came, his thighs trembling uncontrollably with the searing sensation of total pleasure. He roared, the sound filling the room. Demonia finally took his hard stalk from her mouth and put it to Sarah's soaked sex lips. He slid into his lover to the hilt then pumped furiously, ramming his cock into her as deep as it would go until he could thrust no more and thrilling to her cries as she came.

He fell back, exhausted. It had been quick, perhaps too quick, but he had no more to give. He lay back on the floor and closed his eyes, the sounds of ecstatic pleasure filling his ears as he drifted off into sleep – the now customary sleep of exhaustion.

Sarah woke to find herself alone in a large bed. How she had got there she couldn't remember. Her loins ached and her legs felt stiff. She glanced at her watch. It was still early but the sun would be rising soon. Demonia would have returned to her nameless resting place. Perhaps Alex would still be downstairs with the others.

Memories of the previous night began to fight their way into her half-conscious mind. She smiled inwardly at the thought of her excesses: the taste of Karen on Stuart's cock as she sucked him and the incredible fullness she had experienced when Andrew impaled her with his huge prick. She put her hand to her sex, then quickly drew it away. No more; not today. For the first time in many days she actually felt sated.

She heard a noise. Struggling to sit up, her eyes focused on the form of Sinitia, standing in the gloom by the open door. 'I need you,' said the lovely black girl, a pleading look in her eyes. 'I need you to lie with me.'

Sarah rubbed her eyes wearily. Her body ached but the sight of the nubile girl approaching her – the flawless skin glistening in the candle-light, the firm, pert breasts, the round, thrusting buttocks and the soft, inviting cushion of her pouting sex lips – was impossible to resist.

She put her fingers between her own legs again; she was wet and ready. She lay back and parted her thighs widely as Sinitia moved her head between them and her mouth quickly touched Sarah's tender pussy, her tongue darting forward and lapping rapidly over her hardening bud.

They shifted their positions, and Sarah found herself once more gazing at the exquisite sight of Sinitia's delightful bottom as the pink gash of the wet flesh of her cunt was gently lowered to her hungry mouth.

Five

Demonia walked slowly along the winding, gravel path of the garden, the cooling air of the late evening breathing gently across her nakedness. Overhead the leaves rustled and branches of strong, young trees swayed in the light breeze.

The long summer days drained her. The need to take refuge from the unforgiving sun within the cold confines of her coffin was strongest at this time of year; her only comfort being the bed of unconsecrated earth beneath her body. She yearned for the winter; neverending nights and dismal, gloomy days when she and her sisters would be free to walk for hours in the open, sating their lust for the sweet juices of sexual release.

Sinitia had remained in the house, content for the moment to suckle on their ever-faithful servant's thick, black cock. Demonia had thought about joining her – the sight of his huge, ebony tool being drawn between the full, wet lips of her young companion and the vision of her delicious, rounded bottom as she sat astride his face was strongly tempting – but instead she had chosen the solitude of the garden and her thoughts.

She sat on a small mound beneath a tree. The grass was already damp with the evening air and soothingly cool against her buttocks. She parted her legs, feeling the breeze waft through the hairs between her legs, and lay her back against the gnarled trunk, remembering the joys of the previous night. Alex and Sarah had served her well; their four young students, with the athleticism and insatiable libidos of youth and their demanding curiosity, had provided the most wonderful entertainment. She thought of Andrew's superb cock, almost as long and undeniably as thick as that of the evil Baron Mansola himself.

Mansola. She cursed herself for bringing his vile existence into her thoughts. A branch cracked above her head, followed by an urgent hiss of leaf on bark as it landed heavily at her side, the foliage spraying across the grass before her. She jumped to her feet and listened hard, her eyes keenly attempting to penetrate the near-darkness. The breeze had stopped and the silence was unnerving. He was near; she was certain.

She felt her heart thumping beneath her large, heaving breasts; her nipples standing erect in the sudden coldness of the atmosphere around her. Almost unconsciously, she put her hand between her legs, as though seeking comfort in the touch of her warm sex-flesh.

'You need more than the caress of your own hand to satisfy your cravings, my lady.' The voice was deep and unearthly, surrounding her with its malevolence. She knew the voice well.

'Where are you?' she demanded. 'Come out of the shadows and show yourself to me.'

'Demonia.' The voice came from behind her now, quieter and yet even more menacing than before in its venomous tone. She swung round. He stood before her, the moonlight playing across his massive form. He stepped forward a pace and the light caught his leering features as he drew back his long, black cloak to reveal his body. Her eyes were drawn immediately to his phallus – obscenely swollen and erect – and a trickle of white fluid slipped slowly from the plum-sized end to slide down the heavily-veined stalk. She felt her mouth go dry and her knees threatened to buckle as she stared at the monster.

'It is for this that you crave, my lady Demonia, he hissed. 'You yearn to be impaled once more on my fine rod; to have your tight sheath stretched to the limits of joyous pain.'

Demonia tried to speak but the words remained locked within her throat. Mansola moved forward and caught hold of her breasts, gripping them tightly until she winced.

Then he cushioned them around his massive cock, putting the thickly-rounded end close to her lips.

'Suck, my lady,' he snarled. 'Take your sustenance and return to me.'

Demonia closed her eyes to the sight of the huge, weeping temptation, knowing well that just the touch of her tongue to his fluids would be enough to force her to surrender her soul to his control.

With a sudden, desperate surge of will she pulled her body from his grasp and flung herself against the tree, her eyes blazing, her teeth bared. 'No!' she screamed. 'I will never return to your evil coven! The years of death-sleep to which you condemned me have allowed me to understand the truth. You are foul; the lowest of depravity and corruption! I am well rid of you!'

The baron moved over to her and pinned her against the rough bark by one arm, his fingernails digging painfully into her soft flesh. Demonia turned her head and waited for the pain of a fierce blow. It didn't come. Instead, Mansola released his grip and drew back.

'And your companion,' he said. 'That delicate black nymphet whose virgin charms you denied me. Does she feel as you do?'

Demonia looked at him directly in the face, her fear gone. His power had clearly not yet returned; not enough innocent blood had quenched his rabid thirst. She narrowed her eyes contemptuously. 'Sinitia thinks as I, as do the sisters that I have already brought into my fold, and as will the many who are yet to follow. I will teach them to defy you and to seek out and destroy your foul iniquity!'

The baron drew himself to his full height, gripping his cock menacingly in his hand. 'I *will* fuck you, my lady,' he growled. 'I shall fill you with my seed, and we will become as one.'

Demonia stared at the proffered monster, her loins beginning to ache for invasion. Suddenly, her eyes widened as a startling realisation filled her mind. 'You *need* me!' she cried triumphantly. 'You *need* to sate yourself with one of the sisterhood before you can regain your power! Be gone,

123

you loathsome creature, back to the folds of Satan where you belong!'

'There are many females within my coven,' he snarled. 'You will be but one more.'

Demonia shook her head. 'No, you are lying. You have needs which only I can provide.'

The baron moved closer, his monstrous erection barely inches from her naked flesh. She shuddered with a mixture of revulsion and maddeningly powerful lust. 'You are wrong, fair Demonia,' he said, his voice softening slightly, 'but here, take it within your grasp. You know you ache for it to sink within your tight sheath.'

Demonia closed her eyes to the sight of the weeping, purple head. 'No, Baron, you have cast me into the arms of death once; you will never again have the opportunity.'

Mansola's leer became a glare of the most heinous malevolence and his lips drew back over yellowing fangs as his strikingly handsome features twisted with rage. He began to rub his stalk furiously, the end quickly becoming swollen and engorged. Demonia suddenly understood. She dived to one side, falling heavily on to the ground and narrowly avoiding the spray of the copious ejaculation that spat from his massive cock. His seed soaked the tree, hissing as it burnt into the bark. The baron threw back his head and roared in his fury, vainly attempting to direct the stream on to her twisting body until there was no more. He quickly drew his cloak back over his nakedness as though unwilling to allow her the sight of his wilting manhood.

'I will return, my lady Demonia, be assured of that,' he snarled. 'I will regain my power and vanquish you and your kind. You will come to regret this night's work!'

He was gone as suddenly as he had appeared, fading into the shadows like a rat into a sewer. Demonia lay quietly for a moment, her body shaking and her breathing heavy. The breeze returned. She shivered as she pulled herself to her feet and began to walk back to the house.

Darkness had already fallen as Alex walked briskly across the quadrangle, his thoughts as ever occupied by the delights of his new existence. He didn't see the sleek, black limousine draw up beside him, nor did he hear the purring of the motor as it kept pace with his stride.

'Professor Tankard?' The voice was strong and distinctly feminine. Slightly startled, Alex peered into the semi-darkness of the interior of the vehicle through an open window. A face appeared, features of such infinite beauty that he gasped audibly. The woman smiled.

'It *is* Professor Tankard, isn't it?' she said softly, leaning further out of the car.

'*Doctor* Tankard, actually,' he replied, trying to maintain some form of dignity as he gazed upon this vision of perfection. Her long hair was flame-red and her flawless complexion as white as Demonia's. Her mouth was full, the lips pouting voluptuously. But it was her eyes. They were the deepest blue and wide with a curiously sad sensuality, looking for all the world as though they were about to fill with tears. The driver halted the car and the woman opened the rear door slightly.

'Can I give you a lift, Prof . . . er, Doctor?'

'I'm just off to catch the train to London,' said Alex, 'but thank you anyway.'

The woman opened the door wider. 'That's all right, Doctor. I'm going to London. Come on, the car's much more comfortable than the train.'

'Look, I'm sorry,' said Alex, regaining his senses, 'do I know you?'

'We have a common acquaintance,' she purred. 'I believe you know the lady Demonia?'

'Oh, I see,' he said. 'Has she sent you for me?'

The woman said nothing and Alex decided, perhaps unwisely, that Demonia had indeed arranged this luxurious transport. The woman was astoundingly stunning and he needed to know more about her. She leant back in the car, smiling coquettishly as Alex clambered in. He sat awkwardly on a small seat facing her in the roomy interior, still more than a little uncertain of the prudence of his action. She closed the door and Alex noted the click of the lock. He regarded her closely.

125

If her face was one of abject loveliness her body seemed even more so. Despite being covered almost entirely by a sheer, diaphanous gown of fine black silk he could discern her form perfectly. Her breasts were superbly large, more so even than Demonia's magnificently erotic mounds and her long, thick nipples were clearly outlined through the tight-fitting material. Her waist was slender, her hips were invitingly broad and her legs were long and shapely. He licked his lips involuntarily. The woman smiled again as his eyes met hers. Her perfume filled his senses; exotic, intoxicating.

'I have to stop at my home to change,' she said in a tone that Alex hoped contained an element of promise. 'I trust you don't mind a slight delay in your journey?'

'No, no,' he replied. Already he felt his penis hardening within the tight confines of his trousers as the car pulled away into the night. His libidinous urges were difficult to control of late.

They sat in silence for some moments, Alex vainly attempting not to stare at the sumptuous form so erotically sheathed in the magnificent gown. She moved her position in the seat, her large breasts shifting heavily. He gazed at the monstrous globes and the prominent nipples. His erection grew to full length and his lack of underwear ensured that his discomfort was clearly plain, should she choose to glance down.

He looked at her face. She was regarding him intently; staring into his eyes as though searching for some hidden truth. Her gaze was hypnotic and incredibly arousing. He began to sweat.

'Are you unwell, Doctor Tankard?' she asked softly.

Alex shook his head. 'It's just a little warm, that's all,' he lied, clearing his throat. 'Tell me, you know my name; may I know what you are called?'

'I am Lady Harman,' she said proudly, 'but you may address me as Melissa.'

'Lady, eh?' said Alex, raising an eyebrow. 'And how do you come to know Demonia?'

Melissa grinned and sat forward in her seat, her pendulous breasts swinging freely within the black silk. 'I have known Demonia for many years,' she said. 'We are old friends.'

Alex regarded her suspiciously. She was clearly lying but there was something in her manner that made him want to know more about her. And, of course, there were her breasts. Unfettered and unencumbered by the luxurious material of her gown they would surely be something to behold. He wanted to touch, hold, lick and suck them; to bury his face in their warmth. His cock throbbed, a slight dampness on his thigh causing him to cross his legs in embarrassment. Melissa sat back again, her eyes fixed on his. He looked away and peered out of the window, watching the dark shapes of the trees that lined the winding country lane scurry past the speeding car like nameless creatures in the darkness.

'We are here,' said Melissa presently as the vehicle drew up outside a large, gothic-styled mansion. Alex looked out of the car window at the grim, stone edifice, its presence remarkably similar to that of the house on Gallows Hill Road. Three of the central windows were illuminated but the remainder of the building was in darkness.

The rear door of the car was opened by the chauffeur who stood impassively as Melissa and Alex stepped out into the cool night air. They walked slowly towards the pillared entrance, the only sounds being the crunching of gravel as the limousine was driven away. He knew then that his delay would be longer than just a few minutes.

Alex stood alone in the large sitting-room, cradling a glass of fine brandy in his hands as he studied the paintings displayed on the ornately-decorated walls. Melissa had excused herself and disappeared upstairs to change, the seductive sway of her broad hips as she left the room seeming to hold a promise of joys to come. The lust that he felt for this divinely erotic epitome of womanhood was far stronger than anything he'd experienced before. She seemed to ooze sexuality through every pore, through

127

every breath she took and through every gliding, sensual movement she made. His erection had remained solid from the moment they had stepped from the car, the prominent bulge in his trousers an obvious testament to his excitement.

The portraits were very old and the sheen of the oil had long faded. One in particular took his interest; a centrepiece of the array of shadowy ancestors and melancholy landscape. It was a likeness of Melissa, Lady Harman herself, and the eyes stared from the canvas as though alive in an expression of both accusation and deep sensuality. His loins ached with desperation. He needed to fuck her. It was as simple as that.

Like the others, this painting was ancient and the surface was cracked with age. She said she'd known Demonia for years; Alex understood now what she had meant. He also realised why she had addressed him as *Professor*. She had known his long dead ancestor.

He drained his glass quickly, the warmth of the spirit if anything sharpening his desire to possess her. He walked across the room a little unsteadily and looked at another painting. This one was a large gloomy landscape depicting an unearthly place and the artist had captured the sinister aspect with astounding mastery.

He felt hot; uncomfortably so. The twisted shapes of the painted trees appeared to sway before his blurring vision and then the clouds moved across the dead moon, plunging the scene suddenly into total darkness.

Alex drifted back into consciousness slowly, his first sensations being of extreme coldness. His head ached, the blood surged in his temples and the pain behind his eyes caused him to wince. Something was resting heavily on his stomach, and he felt hair brushing gently across his skin. He opened his eyes and raised his head. A large black rat stared back at him, squatting on his belly like a pet animal. He made to throw the creature from its comfortable resting place but found himself restrained, his wrists and ankles clasped by metal manacles attached to thick chains which stretched his limbs widely. He was naked and his body was splayed obscenely on a cold stone block like a victim awaiting sacrifice.

He shook himself; the rat merely turned its body slightly and sat down again, its backside resting on his genitals. He felt his mouth go dry and he hardly dared to breathe, as thoughts of the vile creature gnawing at his tender flesh filled his mind. Straining painfully against his shackles he bucked his hips sharply and the animal jumped from him and quickly scurried into the darkness.

Alex lay back, his heart thumping. Over his head the stone ceiling glistened with dampness and flickering torches fixed to the surrounding walls cast eerie shadows over the surface. The brandy must have been drugged; but why?

He heard a noise. Raising his head as far as his bonds would allow he saw a group of figures enter his prison. There were four, no, five of them, their slender bodies covered entirely in black. As they drew closer he saw that the clinging material was rubber, and that their shapely forms were clearly female. Their breasts, bottoms and crotches were explicitly defined. Even their heads were completely encased in the stretch material, with small holes cut for the eyes and mouths. They surrounded the stone altar where he lay and stood silently, regarding him through expressionless eyes.

'Who are you?' he croaked, his throat dry and parched. 'What do you want?'

They said nothing and remained motionless for what seemed like an eternity. At last, one of the females reached down and picked up a silver jug from beneath the altar, held it over his chest and tipped it forward. Slowly, cool soothing oil poured on to his torso, running in little rivulets down his sides and around his neck. She moved the jug to allow the liquid to flow over his arms and then down to his stomach, then along each of his outstretched legs and back up to his genitals. She held the container over his crotch until the last drops of oil had fallen on to his thickening cock, his arousal at that time more than unwelcome in view of his fearful circumstance.

Setting the jug down, the eerie figure leant over him and began to run her gloved hands over his chest, massaging the thick oil into his skin. The other four black-clad nymphets followed suit, rubbing his body all over but carefully avoiding his penis, which now lay fully erect against his stomach. The sweet scent of the rubber material filled his nostrils and the sight of the five perfectly-formed female bodies, their breasts jiggling rhythmically with their labours, made him forget his terror.

One of his delightful tormentors produced a string of pearl-like beads and soaked them in the oil on his stomach, rolling them back and forth over his flesh. Then she deftly pushed a finger inside his anus, turning it to relax the muscles of his tight sphincter before carefully pushing the beads, one by one, into it until just a short strand of thread remained. Alex wondered as to the purpose of this, pleasurable as it was.

Still they avoided stroking him between his legs. His cock ached for their touch and to feel the oil smoothed over it but no, they seemed to be deliberately avoiding such contact. He felt his body warming under their erotically stimulating caress. The back of his neck ached from holding his head in such an awkward position but he continued to watch them, their hands everywhere but where he wanted them. His cock throbbed and a small drop of white fluid seeped from the thick, purple-coloured end and slipped into his navel. He wanted to free his hands, grab his stalk and rub it furiously until he came all over these shadowy but intensely sexual strangers. But he was helpless, only able to relax his oil-soaked body on the bed of cold stone.

One of the women clambered on to the altar with her back to his face and lowered herself over his head while leaning forward and resting her hands on either side of his hips. Slowly she lowered her bottom to his face until his mouth pressed against the shape of her sex, enticingly displayed within the silken, powerfully-scented rubber. He breathed the aroma deeply, filling his lungs with its erotic substance, then pushed his tongue against the soft

130

material, tracing the shape of her cunt. The taste was as delicious as anything he'd ever savoured before.

At last, he felt someone gripping his cock and the velvety, fluttering touch of delicate fingers ran through the copious amounts of oil that had been poured over his stiff phallus. How many hands caressed him he could not guess as his face was all but smothered by the delightful, sumptuous bottom and warm pussy that he continued to lick. A tongue touched the tip of his cock, then he felt the full lips of an unseen mouth encircle his stalk and take half of his length within the wet, fluttering sheath. He began to move his hips up and down as much as his bonds would allow and two or maybe three hands rubbed his exposed stem as he fucked the face of his anonymous lover.

He groaned as he felt the swell of orgasm building up within his loins, chewing the rubber-covered sex-flesh in his mouth as the sperm surged along his penis and streamed into the welcoming mouth. He could sense her drawing his fluids from his body; draining him; swallowing all he could give.

Gradually he relaxed, his breathing difficult under the cushioning buttocks, and sweat pouring from his body. The girl clambered from his face, stood once more alongside her companions, and they watched him silently. Then they moved away quietly in an almost military fashion; their task complete.

Alex didn't know how long he had lain there in the dank, damp silence of the dungeon. Time had lost its meaning. Although his ethereal lovers had gone, their scent remained with him and their taste was still on his lips.

Alone with his thoughts his concerns returned, the gloomy atmosphere of his surroundings and the occasional scurrying of vermin in the darkness compounding his fears. His body remained heavily oiled and his skin glistened in the torchlight. The cold, unyielding stone against his back was becoming unbearably uncomfortable. He tugged at the shackles that gripped his wrists, the severe metal digging into his flesh. There was no give in the chains; no hope of escape.

He lay his head back, exhausted. In his naked vulnerability he once again became incongruously aroused and his cock began to stretch as the ache within his lower body returned. He thought again of the rubber-clad nymphets and their wondrous ministrations and his fear subsided as he pondered on what other delights might be in store for him.

Suddenly he was aware of a presence. He was no longer alone. He raised his head and peered into the gloom. Silhouetted against the torchlight was the unmistakable figure of Melissa, standing silently before him.

'Lady Harman . . .' he began. She glided slowly over to his side, the flickering light now revealing her fully to his excited gaze. Alex swallowed hard. If the spectacle of five erotically-garbed females had been thrilling, the vision that now presented itself to his hungry eyes was electrifying.

She stood tall and statuesque, her flame-red hair falling wildly over her bare shoulders. Her superb body was encased in a black leather basque drawn in tightly at the waist and her huge, melon-sized breasts swung free, each of her long nipples pierced with tiny gold rings joined by a thin sliver of gold chain. The basque ended just above her crotch and her pussy was completely shaven. The thick pouting lips were engorged with her obvious arousal. On her legs she wore high-heeled boots of the same leather as that of her basque, reaching to less than an inch below her brazenly displayed sex and tightly encasing her shapely legs. In her hand she held a wicked-looking lash, the strands of which she playfully drew across her breasts as she fixed his gaze with a hypnotic stare.

'Did my angels please you?' she asked huskily.

Alex nodded. 'Why am I chained like this?'

Melissa grinned, running the whip slowly over his torso. He shivered. 'To please me,' she said simply. She drew the flail down to his cock, circled the thickening stalk at the root with the fine strands of leather and pulled them tightly. His erection rose quickly and the veins became engorged with blood while the head turned painfully purple. She licked her lips lustfully.

'My, what a splendid specimen,' she breathed. 'See how big it grows.'

Alex looked down at how the whip acted as a tourniquet and made his cock at least an inch longer than any previously proud achievement. His delight was short-lived, however, because the pain was quickly becoming unbearable. He winced. Melissa relaxed her grip on the whip and allowed the strands to slip away. He looked down again. His cock remained hard and huge against his belly.

'Set me free,' he begged, 'and I'll give you the best fuck you've ever had.'

'Later,' said Melissa seductively, 'but first I must have my amusement.' She climbed gracefully on to the altar and stood over him, her feet placed on either side of his waist. She looked down on his face haughtily. Dropping the whip to the floor, she put her fingers to her hairless pussy and pulled the lips apart to afford him a perfect view of the pleasures to come. Her sex-flesh glistened with her arousal. The lips were far thicker than any he'd seen before; the hole juicy and inviting.

It was just a trickle at first, then a torrent, as her piss sprayed over his chest and face, soaking him. He closed his eyes to the stinging fluid, the stream seemingly endless as she moved herself along the stone until she was able to direct the remainder of her flow on to his stiff cock. Alex opened his eyes again and watched as the final droplets fell onto his genitals. He'd experienced such pleasures before of course; Sarah had been particularly adept at the pastime, but somehow, in this chained and defenceless predicament, it had been all the more erotic.

Melissa moved forward carefully on her precarious heels until she stood with her feet placed on either side of Alex's head. He gazed upwards at the delicious sight of her open pussy lips, his cock aching to sink within their plump succulence. She squatted over him, lowering her cunt to his mouth.

'Lick me,' she commanded. 'Swallow my juices. Make me come with your tongue.'

Alex gladly obeyed, his tongue lapping greedily around

133

the puffy lips before moving deep into her soaking hole. The tough leather of her thigh-boots rubbed against the cheeks of his face as she ground her sex against his suckling mouth. The taste and scent of her hairless pussy thrilled him. He longed to grab her bottom and fondle the magnificent globes of firm flesh as he devoured the creamy fluids of her arousal. He moved the tip of his tongue upwards and found the erect bud of her clitoris. He flicked over it like the wing of an insect, hearing her groan softly to herself. She moved her crotch against his mouth, pressing hard on to his lips.

Suddenly she yelled, her cry echoing around the damp, stone walls. She pressed her cunt hard against his teeth, making his jaw ache. Her orgasm was long and obviously powerful. Her taste seemed to change and become sweeter and her wetness soaked his face as she shuddered above him. Then she relaxed and he licked her again, carefully avoiding her clitoris while running his tongue around and around her honeyed flesh, savouring every drop. He sucked the thick lips of her pussy into his mouth and suckled until she clambered from him and stood shakily at his side.

Melissa breathed deeply, her eyes staring into the distance. Her mountainous breasts heaved and the thin gold chain between her stiffly erect nipples glistening in the torchlight.

'Free me now,' he pleaded. 'I need to fuck you.'

She shook her head, smiling. 'Oh no, not yet,' she teased, 'I have only just started.'

She reached down to the floor and retrieved the whip, holding it at the end from where the strands splayed out and putting the other end to her mouth. She licked the foot-long handle suggestively, as though it was a firm, black cock, then took a few inches of it into her mouth. She soaked it with her saliva, all the time keeping her eyes fixed on Alex's. She turned her back on him and bent forward almost double, displaying her exquisite bottom to his excited gaze. Such an arse! Such perfection! He yearned to sink his long, thick shaft between those luscious globes and impale the tiny, puckered orifice just inches away from his leering eyes.

Melissa put the whip-handle to her pussy and pushed it in, the full length sinking quickly inside her until just the strands of leather could be seen. Then she drew the monster out, then slid it back and out again; steadily fucking herself. Her free hand parted the flesh of her buttocks so that Alex could see every detail of her self-stimulation.

'Let me,' he begged. 'Let me fill you! That's a poor substitute for the real thing!'

She turned and climbed once more to kneel over him, the whip-handle still firmly held within the grip of her pussy. She moved her hips so that the leather strands stroked against his lower body, then leant forward, her breasts close to his face. 'Take the chain between your teeth,' she demanded. Alex did so, clenching his teeth against the thin sliver of gold. Melissa arched her back and pulled herself upwards, her nipples stretched forward by the grip of the chain on the piercing rings. She supported herself with one hand while the other pumped the handle in and out of herself. The nipples jutted ludicrously and her breasts became almost conical in shape. She must have been in pain but the expression on her face betrayed only ecstasy as she came for a second time, her cries even louder than before.

When he was sure that she was sated, Alex let the chain fall from the grip of his teeth and she fell forward on to his body, her breasts smothering his face. The whip clattered to the floor.

After a moment, Melissa climbed from his body and, retrieving the flail, stood once more at his side. 'And now,' she said in a mildly threatening tone, 'the ultimate pleasure!'

Before Alex could prepare himself she brought the whip down on him, the leather stinging the flesh of his thighs. Another stroke, then a third quickly followed, the look in Melissa's eyes becoming near-manic. She turned her attention to his stomach, then his chest, then back to his upper thighs and getting closer and closer to his genitals but never quite touching them. The leather strands were soft and the pain was slight but exquisite. Alex's cock swelled in response to their erotic kiss. Melissa paused and lowered the whip to her side, her breasts heaving with the effort of her labours.

'He seems to like that, doesn't he?' she said, gazing hungrily at his throbbing erection. Alex was visibly shaking with lust, desperately striving not to come before he could sink his hard shaft into her lovely body. Melissa seemed to sense his urgency. She clambered yet again on to the altar, squatted over him with her back to his face, and gripped his thick cock with one hand to guide it to her open pussy. He feasted his eyes on the sight of her perfect bottom as she lowered herself on to him. At last his engorged, throbbing cock slipped between the spongy folds of her soaking cunt, and the hot, undulating flesh enveloped him to the hilt.

She leant forward slightly, resting the palms of her hands on his thighs as she moved her backside steadily up and down, treating Alex to an unencumbered view of his swollen phallus slipping effortlessly in and out of her.

'Oh God, hold still, just for a moment,' he pleaded, his climax near. Melissa turned her head and grinned at him, holding his full length inside her wet sheath. His cock throbbed and a jet of pre-come shot up inside her. He breathed heavily, biting his lower lip. The urgency quickly passed.

Slowly, Melissa resumed her erotic dance, at first allowing little more than an inch of his hard cock to slip out of her cunt before sitting down again and absorbing everything he could offer. Then she raised herself until just the tip of his distended knob was held within her heavenly grip. He stared at the perfection of her bottom, his neck aching from the effort of holding his head up from the altar. The tiny, puckered orifice was invitingly visible and the sumptuous globes were framed by the black leather of her thigh-boots and basque.

This time he was going to come; there would be no stopping it. She seemed to sense it too and increased the power and rapidity of her movements, pumping her hips up and down heavily as she gripped his thick shaft with her inner muscles.

136

'Oh, God, yes!' he cried, arching his back to force his cock deep into her as she tensed her upper-thigh muscles to grip him at the root. He felt her fingertips exploring between his clenched buttocks, and remembered the beads. He came, the sperm gushing from his body to join with his contemptuous lover's copious juices, while at exactly the same time she pulled the thread hard. The long string of beads were hauled from his anus in one swift movement, the combination of sensations making him gasp for breath. Melissa continued to bounce herself up and down on his hips, then almost leapt from the altar and turned to face him, taking his throbbing cock into her mouth and sucking him voraciously.

Then something happened which he had never thought possible. The ache within his loins returned and his orgasm built up for a second time. Melissa carried on sucking and licking him, while she rubbed the thick stalk of his cock rapidly. He groaned and a second jet of sperm shot from him into her willing mouth.

'Oh my God,' he panted as he watched her swallow his juices avidly. 'I just don't believe it!'

Gradually the feelings of blissful release subsided and the tenderness of sated flesh returned. Melissa let his drooping phallus fall wetly from her mouth, running her tongue across her lips lest a trace of his juice be lost, then ran her hand over his cock and smoothed the dampness over his stomach.

He watched her tenderly, smiling proudly as he felt his stalk thicken yet again. The lascivious powers which had been bestowed on him by Demonia amazed him, and he delighted in the knowledge that he could fuck this beautiful creature as much as she wanted.

To his surprise, however, her expression changed into one of abject annoyance. She squeezed his stalk roughly but her action only served to stiffen his quickly rising erection. She slapped it angrily against his flesh and stood up, towering over him with her hands placed squarely on her hips. Even in her apparent displeasure she looked devastating. She oozed a powerful sexuality that he found irresistible.

137

'Is he prepared?' The thickly-male voice boomed out through the dank atmosphere. Alex turned his head in the direction of the sound, seeing a huge, dark figure in the shadows. Although the features were hidden from him, he sensed that he was in the presence of evil. Melissa rushed towards the figure, throwing herself at his feet.

'Oh, my lord Mansola,' she wailed, pitifully. 'He has come three times and yet still has the strength for more!'

The baron pushed her to one side harshly and stepped forward, the torchlight catching his malevolent expression. He glared at the prone figure of Alex then turned to Melissa as she struggled to her feet. 'Take him to your bedchamber,' he growled. 'Bring my angels to him and have them sate his lust and drain his spirit.' He turned to Alex again, his fang-like teeth bared sinisterly, 'And then bring him to me.'

The huge man swept quickly from the dungeon, his long black cloak billowing behind him and the iron door crashing against the wall as he flung it open. Melissa clapped her hands sharply. The five sylph-like girls reappeared in the room, drifting silently over to where Alex lay. Their heads were still completely covered by their masks but they now wore just a tiny pair of clinging, rubber shorts each. The material was split at the crotch, revealing their pink, down-covered pussies. Each was a clone of the other; white-skinned, delicate forms of pure femininity with their slim, boyish hips, pert, inviting bottoms and small, firm breasts.

Alex watched with rising ardour as they busied themselves unfastening the shackles around his wrists and ankles. His long cock was once more stiff and ready for action. He thought of the baron's words and dismissed them from his mind. Let them do whatever they could, he thought arrogantly. They would not defeat him.

They led him silently from the room, two of the nymphets supporting him as he walked because his legs were cramped from lying on the stone for so long. They guided him up a long, steep stairway to the main hall, then on up a grand staircase to the upper floor of the mansion and into a large sumptuously-furnished bedroom. The room reminded him of Demonia's bed-chamber – the room where he had plundered the welcoming depths of Sinitia's delightful, black bottom. It was similarly designed and the walls were festooned with mirrors while heavy drapes covered the large windows.

He was manoeuvred towards the large bed that was the centre-piece of the room and made to lie on his back, the warm softness of the mattress a welcome relief to his aching muscles. The girls stood around him motionless, as though awaiting instruction. Alex wondered if he should make the first move.

He was about to reach out to touch the nearest girl when Melissa entered the room and handed a black, rubber garment to her. The girl held it up as though seeking his approval. It was a pair of shorts, similar to those that they all wore, although the split at the crotch was much larger and its purpose was clear. He watched as they were slipped over his ankles, noticing a phallic-shaped protuberance, roughly six inches in length, sewn in the back of the shorts. Another of the girls poured some oil from a small decanter into the palm of her hand and smoothed it over the small, stiff rod, then the shorts were pulled up his legs and over his thighs. He felt the lump prod against his anus and stiffened his body, seeing the mouth of the girl closest to him broaden in a grin as she gently eased the phallus inside him. She pulled the shorts up tightly around his hips, drawing his thick, hardening cock and heavy sack through the split in the sensuous material.

Alex felt the unexpected intrusion to be extremely arousing and his penis rose quickly to full erection. He looked at the five girls with their tight, skimpy shorts, wondering if they too were subject to the same erotic invasion of their pert little bottoms. He was soon to find out.

One of the girls knelt on the bed and drew her leg across his body so that she faced him, her eyes shining mysteriously through the small holes in her black mask. Carefully, she took hold of his hard stalk and guided it into her wet pussy, pushing her hips down as he slid effortlessly into the warmth of her soaked sheath. He could feel the unmistakable pressure of a thick rod against his cock, making the grip of her cunt even tighter. She sat upright, undulating her hips back and forth and moving up and down, so that the sensuously soft rubber of her shorts rubbed against his throbbing stalk. With each forward movement of her hips the phallus inside her bottom pressed hard against his own. The knowledge of her intimate intrusion and the sight of his long cock slipping in and out of her pussy filled Alex with utter delight.

He was not to enjoy the spectacle for long. Another of the girls squatted over his face with her back to her colleague and lowered her cunt to his mouth. His tongue obediently slipped within the silken folds of her delicately-perfumed sex-flesh. The strong smell of rubber invaded his senses. His studies had told him of the powerful aphrodisiac properties of rubber, but it was his first experience of the hypnotic exhilaration that could be enjoyed from merely the touch and aroma of the material. It was a diversion that he promised himself he would savour again.

He sensed his ankles being raised by unseen hands and felt his feet being pressed against two hot, wet pussies and his toes quickly slipping between the open folds of sex-flesh. The fifth girl positioned herself between his splayed legs, deftly licking his testicles as the first nymphet continued to fuck herself on his raging stalk. He lapped hungrily at the little pussy in his mouth, his face becoming soaked with her juices.

He wanted to come but knew that it could be his last, and feared that his sated, weak body would be at the mercy of the evil Baron. He had to hold back, even though he didn't know why. But it was becoming more and more difficult; the incessant, rapid pumping of the young girl's crotch against his, the taste of sweet pussy and the overpowering scent of the rubber driving him to distraction.

Suddenly, as one, their movements stopped and the girls clambered from the bed, standing motionless around him. Despite their recent exertions they hardly seemed to breathe and Alex found their eerie silence unnerving. He sat up and looked across at Melissa, who stood in a corner of the room, toying with her whip. She nodded towards the girls who, in one practised movement slipped their shorts down and stood up again, now completely naked save for their bizarre head gear.

Melissa nodded again and one of the girls took Alex by the hand and made him stand at the side of the bed as her four companions moved on to the mattress and knelt side by side, their backs arched, their arms stretched out in front of themselves. The fifth girl joined the others, so that five, virgin-white bottoms were presented to Alex's eager gaze.

Melissa walked over, held out the whip and drew the strands of leather delicately over each pair of inviting buttocks in turn. Then she handed the flail to Alex. 'Beat them,' she whispered. 'They delight in the kiss of the lash.'

Alex had enjoyed the pleasure of spanking Sarah's wonderful bottom many times and she had thrilled to the stinging slaps of his hand, but this was different. He was torn between a powerful desire to do as Melissa commanded and concern for the willing victims who knelt obediently before him.

'Whip them!' ordered Melissa brusquely. 'Then you can take them all in the way you love the most!'

The thought of impaling five beautiful, pert bottoms, one after the other, was enough to cloud Alex's mind with uncontrollable lust. He raised the whip and brought the strands of soft leather down on them again and again, the force of his strokes increasing as he thrilled to their cries of delight. Over and over the lash thwacked against reddening flesh and his painfully stretched cock bobbed ludicrously in time with his exertions.

Then he was lost. If he was to become a victim to the nameless terrors that the baron had in store for him he would at least hold this final memory. He threw the whip to the floor and approached the first girl, holding his thick stalk as he directed it to her puckered orifice. He sank in easily, the young girl's bottom well prepared for his invasion. He drove his long cock deep inside her until his stomach touched the softness of her creamy flesh. He pumped in and out of her anus about six times then pulled it slowly from her and moved to the next girl, thrusting his stiffness deep into her arse as the muscles of her sphincter gripped him tightly.

Then the third, the fourth, the fifth. One by one he fucked each pretty little bottom in turn before moving back to the first and impaling her once more. His legs ached and his cock throbbed heavily. He knew that he could hold back no longer. Pulling himself from the heavenly grip of her tight anus he gripped his thick stalk and rubbed it rapidly until jets of thick white sperm streamed over the prone bodies. All five bottoms were coated with his creamy fluid. For a moment it seemed that his orgasm would never end, his loins torn with raging lust as he rubbed himself furiously until at last he collapsed to his knees, exhausted.

Helplessly, he watched the girls stand and troop out of the room, their come-streaked bottoms swaying seductively and their eyes once more expressionless. Melissa walked over to him and grinned, her features betraying an expression of joyful conquest. Alex tried to move but he couldn't. All he could do was wait for the baron.

He could hear sounds from outside the room. Heavy, resounding footsteps on the long staircase. He glanced in panic at the door, then turned to look at the heavily-draped window for some means of escape. A shaft of bright light shone from a small gap in the curtaining. With the renewed vigour of restored hope he dragged his aching body over the carpet towards the window and summoning up all his remaining strength, tugged at the heavy material. Suddenly, the hooks and rings gave way to the force of his efforts and the curtain collapsed about him, filling the room with the sharp light of the dawning sun. The door behind him opened then closed with a crash, a muffled curse coming from behind the heavy oak.

Mansola would not be calling on him that day.

Demonia and Sinitia sat gravely silent in their armchairs as Alex stood before them and recounted the story of his experiences with the mysterious Lady Harman and his

142

chance deliverance from the clutches of the malevolent baron. As he told his tale, he began to feel the terror that had somehow eluded him during the excitement of his panic and he began to visibly tremble, finally needing to sit on a small footstool. His hands were shaking, and his brow was covered with sweat.

'You have indeed had a miraculous escape,' said Demonia presently. 'Mansola is not one to let a prize elude him so easily.'

Alex looked up at her. 'What do you mean? Do you think he let me get away on purpose?'

Demonia shook her head, rising gracefully from her chair and walking over to him. 'No,' she said thoughtfully. 'He wouldn't do that. His powers have not yet fully returned, although he is still to be feared. He needs something, perhaps from me or possibly from this house. I wish I knew what it is that he seeks.' She rested her hand lightly on Alex's shoulder.

'From the house?' he asked, warming to her soothing, comforting touch. 'What sort of thing? A talisman, token, what?'

'That is the stuff of fiction,' said Demonia, walking back to her chair. 'It is something far more powerful, the essence of mortality itself. I believe he intends to destroy me.'

Alex gasped. 'Why should he want to do that? You are the same . . .' He stopped short, the words turning sour in his mouth.

'Not the same, Alex,' chided Demonia quietly. 'You are still not able to understand. The sisterhood merely seek hedonistic pleasures; he and his kind are the embodiment of evil.'

'But what would he gain from destroying you?'

Demonia sighed, glancing into Sinitia's startled eyes. 'I don't know. I'm just certain that the key to his power lies within this room.'

'Perhaps it is me,' ventured Alex. 'Maybe if I'd let him capture me to suck my blood he . . .'

'He has taken much sustenance from mortal blood already. No, it is not so simple. We must discover the secret before it is too late. In the meantime, we must arm ourselves.'

'How? With garlic and crosses?'

Sinitia laughed out loud. 'Useless, I'm afraid,' said Demonia. 'No, we need to draw more companions into the sisterhood. Only in numbers and strength of will can we have a hope of vanquishing the baron. You and Sarah already have the power and in less than a day Belinda and Karen, as well as Stuart and Andrew, will possess the knowledge also.'

'What would you have us do?' asked Alex, his heart captivated by the sight of the two beautiful vampires sitting in exquisite serenity before him.

Demonia smiled broadly. 'You must go out. You, Stuart and Andrew must share the taste of your seed with as many strong, young females as you can. The will is already within you, dear Alex. Your libido is strong, ferociously tearing at your loins through every waking moment. Such is the joy, or possibly the curse of the vampire. Sarah and the girls will be experiencing the same feelings of near insatiability. They must share their erotic joys with both men and women, to draw them into our fold. Through your efforts we may be saved.'

'If you think we can do it,' said Alex, the idea clearly appealing to him. Sinitia stood up and walked over to him slowly, the light from the blazing fire and the flickering torches catching the sensuous shape of her body through the translucent material of her flowing, white dress. He felt his cock begin to stiffen.

She stood at his side and pressed her palm over the bulge in his trousers. 'Oh, you can do it, Alex,' she breathed, slowly easing down his zip. He trembled, but this time it was through lust, not fear.

Alex glanced at Demonia as she watched them fondly from her armchair. Sinitia was now easing his rampant erection from the confines of his pants, and rubbed the full length gently for a moment before putting the thick end to her mouth. He wondered at the strength of his libido and his almost incessant need for release. There were dangers, certainly, in his new-found existence but for the moment at least it seemed worth it.

He shivered as he felt Sinitia envelop his rigid stalk with her thick, wet lips. Her tongue playfully circled his aching sex-flesh while her hand steadily pumped his exposed length. He looked down at the kneeling figure, meeting her eyes with his own. Her gaze held an expression of divine innocence coupled with an almost submissive worship as she suckled on his long rod. The contrast between his pink flesh and her flawless, ebony skin was arousing in the extreme.

'Feed her,' whispered Demonia. 'She needs the sustenance of your thick, succulent seed.'

The sheer eroticism of her words filled Alex's mind as he felt his cock being drawn down the throat of his young lover until her thick lips pressed against his bushy groin. He stiffened his buttocks and closed his eyes, the surge from within his loins tearing at his emotions. His penis throbbed heavily and his sperm gushed down Sinitia's throat as she sucked him all the harder, draining him once again. His legs began to tremble and he steadied himself by resting a hand on her bobbing head. He groaned happily.

Sinitia pulled her head back, taking his cock from the luscious, fleshy grip of her mouth and licked swiftly up and down the long stem to lap the remains of his release from his stiff phallus. He braced himself for what he knew was about to happen. His cock thickened once more, the entire length feeling as if it would burst, and a second stream of thick, white cream spurted from the end, soaking her lovely face.

He stiffened his backside again in the hope of achieving a third orgasm but his penis softened rapidly and hung loosely from his aching groin, the end resting on the cushion of Sinitia's pouting lips. He watched, panting as she drew her fingertips through the juices that covered her perfect features and put them to her mouth. She swallowed more, not wanting to lose a drop.

'You have learned well,' said Demonia, rising from her armchair and walking over to them. She gripped the tender

145

flesh of Alex's wilting manhood and held the end to Sinitia's lapping tongue.

'It gets better every time,' he mumbled, his heart pounding.

'And so it will and when you join us fully your desires and experiences will be such that you would never have imagined possible.'

'Will you join us?' asked Sinitia, rising to stand before him. Her eyes shone with desire and the dark skin of her face was still streaked with evidence of their recent pleasures. Alex smiled but said nothing. The uncertainties and the fear of the unknown still burned deep within his brain. The two divine beauties turned from him, accepting his indecision, and returned to their chairs. Then they watched silently as he clumsily pushed his wet penis back into his clothing.

'I had another of those dreams last night,' said Sarah as she lay in Alex's arms on his bed, the noisy cavorting of students at play sounding through the open window.

'Was the baron in the dream?' asked Alex, tenderly stroking the tousled, blonde tresses of her hair.

'Yes. It was weird, but incredibly erotic. It was as though I knew I was dreaming, and could wake up at any time, but I didn't want to.' She wrapped her arms around his naked body, gripping him tightly. 'I'm scared, Alex. He seems to be taking over my mind.'

Alex kissed her lightly on the forehead. 'Demonia feels we can beat him,' he said, enjoying the warmth of her soft body against his own. 'We just need to increase in numbers. Karen and Belinda are already out there, no doubt mercilessly hunting for some willing victims, and I'm sure that Andrew and Stuart will rise to the occasion.'

Sarah laughed gently. 'I'm sure you're right, darling,' she said, snuggling against him, 'and, of course we must do our bit.'

'You're not objecting, are you?'

She laughed again, gripping his penis tightly. 'What do *you* think?' she asked, bending down and kissing the tip of his thickening erection.

146

'Easy,' said Alex. 'I'm feeling a bit tender at the moment.'

'I'm not surprised, the number of comes you've had this morning. I don't think I'll want to eat for a week!'

'They said that it was all part of the gift of becoming one of them. The better it gets, the more you want.'

'I feel the same,' said Sarah, lying back on the pillow and staring at the ceiling. 'Perhaps that's why the dreams are so real.'

'What happened, in your dream last night?'

'Like I said, it was weird. I couldn't see. My head was completely covered by some sort of mask, with just a small hole where my mouth was, so that I could breathe.'

'Rubber?'

'Yes. How did you know?'

'Just a guess,' he lied. 'Go on.'

'That was another strange thing. I could actually sense the aroma of the rubber. It was incredibly strong. I didn't think you could smell in dreams.'

Alex said nothing but lay back, his cock thickening to full erection as he remembered the experiences of the previous night. Sarah noticed his arousal. 'Are you into rubber, then?'

'I never used to be. Lots of things have changed recently.'

Sarah circled her fingers around his stiff stalk and rubbed him slowly. 'Anyway, back to the dream. As I said, I couldn't see a thing. I sensed that I was being carried along. There were hands all over my body, touching and fondling me as well as supporting my weight. I felt my nipples being squeezed and fingers slipping inside my pussy and my bum, driving me crazy.

'Then I was lowered into something that felt thick, wet and slimy, a bit like mud but with a strong, erotic scent. The hands spread whatever it was all over my body, pushing me through the mush and rolling me in it. The feeling was exquisite.

'Then I felt the cock, *his cock* going into me. I knew it was the baron, from the sheer size of it. He pushed it right

147

up me until his groin pressed against mine. Somehow, it didn't seem strange that I was accommodating a prick that was well over a foot long; it was as though I was used to it, expected it. There was no pain, not even discomfort. He started to fuck me, really hard, pounding in and out of me, my body slithering through the goo and hands gripping my wrists and ankles so that all I could do was submit.

'Like I said, it was so incredibly *real*. I could feel every nerve-ending in my body tingling and every thrust as he hammered into me, my poor little cunt being stretched impossibly. I could sense that my climax was coming and I started to buck my hips, urging him to fuck even harder, to slam that monster pole into me.

'Then, suddenly it was all gone. The baron, the hands, the mask, everything. I was floating, drifting in a thick white mist, not touching anything with my feet. My pussy ached, more from the need to come than the pounding that it had just received.

'The mist seemed to clear and I saw you, and all the others – Demonia, Sinitia and the students – in the distance. You were laughing, rolling about in the ether, fucking each other like crazy. I attempted to move towards you but you carried on drifting away. Then I saw his face, the baron's, but it was huge, right behind you. I tried to call out, to warn you, but I couldn't make a sound. All I could do was watch helplessly as you drifted towards his grinning, open mouth. It was horrible.

'Then I was awake. I'd been spared the sight of you being devoured by the beast, thank God. I was sweating like a pig, and shaking. The strangest thing of all, and the most frightening, was that my pussy still ached as though I really had been fucked.'

Alex put his arms around his lover and kissed her gently on the mouth. 'Just a dream, Sarah, nothing more.'

'I don't mind the dreams normally. They are always very erotic, but this one, God, it was vile.' She shuddered. Alex hugged her close to his body, his hard erection pressing against the softness of her stomach.

'Fuck me, Alex,' she said tenderly. 'Fuck me like you used to, like you love me.'

'I *do* love you, Sarah. Don't worry, we'll be OK.' He slid across her, slipping his lower body between her legs. His cock quickly found its target and slid effortlessly into the wet, spongy sheath. The warmth of her sex-flesh gripped his rigid stalk. They gazed fondly into each other's eyes as he moved gently back and forth and fucked her slowly with a sensitivity he had somehow forgotten.

'Oh, yes, Alex,' she breathed, 'make love to me. It's so good, so perfect.'

Alex continued to slide his hard shaft slowly in and out of her, letting her feel the full length with each movement and drawing it out until just the tip touched the welcoming lips of her pussy. Then he eased it inside again, feeling her close over the thick ridge before slipping deep into her until he touched her cervix. He moved back and forth, up and down, with a steady rhythm of deeply sensuous delight. He thought of nothing but her pleasure and thrilled to her sighs of enjoyment as they fucked. Her hips moved in time with his and her vaginal muscles gripped him tightly. He kissed her mouth passionately and their tongues entwined and explored as his hands fondled her large breasts. She stroked his firm buttocks, her fingertips delving between the cheeks and teasingly stroking the tight sphincter of his anus.

Alex raised himself, supporting his weight on his hands and toes, and began plunging his hard length in and out of his lover's beautiful body with long, deliberate strokes, ensuring that every inch of his big cock filled her cunt with each forward thrust. Sarah pulled her legs back until her knees pressed against her breasts, allowing him even deeper penetration of her softly undulating sheath. Alex ached to come and fill her stunning body with his juices but instead he moved her leg in front of him and twisted his body so that he lay behind her with her leg resting across his waist.

The mirror on the dressing-table caught the reflection of the couple, both of them now able to enjoy the image of his huge stalk impaling her soft, widely-stretched cunt. As he pulled out of her, almost withdrawing completely, Alex noticed that her tight sex lips seemed to pout as they moved with him. They gripped him, as though unwilling to let him go. His cock throbbed as a jet of pre-come shot inside her, making his movements even more easy as he increased the rate of his thrusts. He moved his hand to her mound and his fingertips found the swollen bud of her clitoris and caressed it rhythmically. He bent his head and took a long, thick nipple into his mouth.

Sarah moaned and pushed her pussy against his fingers, her eyes closed in ecstasy. Alex wormed his free arm under her lithe body and his hand cupped her bottom and stroked the smooth globes delicately before snaking one, then two, fingers into the tight orifice of her anus.

This was too much for her. With a sudden shout she came, her entire body shuddering with the force of the orgasm. Alex pumped hard and fast into her, desperate to join her in her climax. He suddenly held himself still, Sarah still mewing with passionate joy as her orgasm slowly subsided. He felt his cock swell within her and the pressure of his seed within his body build up rapidly at the base of his stalk. For an instant, the pressure sudsided and he held himself stiff, controlling the moment for what seemed like an eternity. Then he was lost. With gut-wrenching force he came, his sperm surging up the long, thumping shaft in regular, solid spurts. He sucked hard on her nipple, his teeth raking the tender flesh, and his fingers pumped in and out of her bottom as his climax took control of his mind. Every nerve-ending in his body was set on fire by the power of his orgasm.

Gradually the feeling subsided. They lay quietly, still entwined, their breathing slowly returning to normal. He kissed Sarah's cheek lightly, easing his wilting manhood from her. Then he lay back, stroking her hair tenderly.

Whatever the baron had in store for them and whatever dangers lay ahead, he knew that as long as he had Sarah he would be content.

Six

'Haven't seen you here for quite a while.'

Sarah had hardly noticed the grinning face of the young man behind the health club reception desk as she fumbled in her kit-bag for her membership card. She looked up and smiled. 'I've been very busy,' she said lamely.

'Pity,' he replied, making a cursory examination of the card. 'We don't get many chicks as tasty as you coming through.'

She raised her eyebrows in mock sarcasm. 'I expect you say that to all the girls.' Normally, she might have taken offence at his impertinence but today she couldn't have cared less. She regarded him closely. He was tall and black with soft, Afro-American features. His hair was shoulder-length and in tight ringlets, and his grin was broad and dazzling. She remembered him from the gymnasium; his slim, muscular torso was often arrogantly displayed for all to see as he worked the machines and weights. His tight, pert buttocks and the promising bulge in the figure-moulding shorts he invariably wore were a tantalising diversion from her own efforts.

Demonia would welcome him into the fold, that was certain. Sarah smiled again, sweetly, making a mental note to speak to him after she had enjoyed her swim.

The changing-room was busy. An aerobics class had obviously just ended and the showers and cubicles were filled with overweight, middle-aged women chattering incessantly. Sarah stripped and slipped on her tiny costume, ensuring that the narrow sliver of stretch material fitted snugly between her buttocks as she pulled the straining garment over her voluptuous form. She stood for a moment, admiring herself in a mirror while smoothing the material over her curves. She noticed in the reflection two women sitting behind her; one nudging the other and pointing at her brazenly exposed buttocks, her expression more one of envy than disgust. She managed to suppress a proud, if conceited, smile and turned to walk towards the swimming pool.

The pool was empty when she entered the smooth, crystal-clear water, one of the benefits of being a member of a private health club rather than having to do battle with hordes of screaming children at the local public leisure centre. Sarah glided along with a gentle stroke, savouring the soothing warmth of the water as it lapped over her body. For once, thoughts of Alex and Demonia were dismissed from her mind. She imagined the handsome receptionist swimming naked alongside her, his hands occasionally straying to touch her. Her fantasy developed quickly and he was sitting waiting for her at the end of the pool, his big, black cock in his hand. He was ready for her.

'Hi.' The voice snapped her from her daydream, causing her to flounder in her stroke. She spluttered to a halt, standing up in the relatively shallow water. He was sitting on the edge of the pool; not the receptionist but Colin, her enigmatic young lover of a few days previously. He slipped into the pool and stood next to her, his slim, athletic body rekindling memories of their shared moments of erotic joy. She smiled, brushing her wet hair from her face.

'Sorry, did I startle you?'

'It's OK, I was miles away. I didn't know you were a member here.'

'I'm not. I saw you coming in and took a day membership. I thought I'd surprise you.'

'That's nice.'

'It's a great club; really flash. Maybe I'll join it.'

'It's very expensive,' she said, realising immediately how patronising her words must have sounded. Colin didn't seem to notice.

'Mind if I swim with you for a while?' he asked, moving off into a gentle breaststroke without waiting for her reply. She followed, quickly catching up with him and swimming

152

by his side. They moved steadily up and down the full length of the pool for some time, Colin having some difficulty in keeping up with Sarah's powerful stroke.

Eventually they paused and rested their arms on the side of the pool, their legs kicking lazily in the warm water.

'When can I meet the others?' asked Colin suddenly.

'Soon.' Sarah knew that her task was to attract more people into the fold but she couldn't fight the deep unease that she felt about this young student.

'I really am looking forward to it,' he said, with schoolboy eagerness. She said nothing and slipped back into the water to move away from him. He followed immediately, vainly trying to catch up with her.

They swam for some time, Colin grinning enthusiastically each time they passed in the narrow lane. Finally, she stopped and hauled herself out of the water. 'I'm going for a jacuzzi,' she said, making her way to the small pool at the far end of the plushly-tiled area. He followed, sliding into the frothing, white-foamed water next to her.

They sat in silence, Sarah leaning her head against the side. Her eyes closed in the relaxing caress of the churning warmth. Suddenly, she felt the brush of Colin's fingertips against her upper thigh. She opened her eyes. He was staring at her intently, his handsome features drawn into a broad grin.

'We could do all sorts of things in here, and no one would be any the wiser,' he said.

She pushed his hand away. 'You'll get me thrown out of the club,' she chided.

'Oh, come on,' he complained, 'there's nobody here. Anyway, even if there was, they wouldn't be able to see a thing.' He put his hand back, this time resting it between her thighs. She looked down and had to admit that he was right. The bubbling water concealed the lower halves of their bodies ideally. She began to warm to the idea and parted her thighs slightly, allowing his exploring fingertips to touch her between her legs. She closed her eyes again, the sensuous prodding against the thin, wet fabric of her costume arousing in the extreme.

She reached over and ran her hand up Colin's thigh, her fingers quickly finding his bulging swimming trunks. His cock was already fully erect within the restraining material. He shifted his position slightly and Sarah felt him pull the costume away from his crotch, enabling her fingers to encircle his thick, hard stalk.

The door to the changing-rooms opened suddenly. They removed their hands quickly, sitting benignly side by side, purposely avoiding each other's eyes. The newcomer was a woman of immense proportions, a gigantic testament to the ravages of good living; her multiple folds of fat encased in yards of paisley material. Sarah silently willed her to go to the swimming-pool though in her heart she knew that it was unlikely.

Sure enough, the woman lowered herself carefully into the quickly overflowing water of the jacuzzi, sitting directly opposite them. She nodded by way of a casual greeting. Sarah smiled.

Colin's fluttering fingertips returned, caressing Sarah deftly between the legs. She pushed his hand away but it quickly returned. She looked down. His movements would be invisible to their unwelcome companion. She moved her own hand back to Colin's crotch and felt his erection still naked beneath the water, his trunks now pulled well down his legs.

Casually they fondled each other, both staring directly in front of them. Colin wormed a finger underneath the elastic material of her costume and slipped it inside her highly-aroused pussy. Sarah swallowed hard.

'Lovely in here, isn't it?' said the woman.

'Marvellous,' said Colin. Sarah began to pump his hard cock steadily, slipping her body down so that the water covered her shoulders lest the woman notice the rhythmic movements of her upper arm. She felt a second, then a third finger slip inside her, and knew the wetness of her sex lips had nothing to do with the water. She began to move her hips involuntarily.

'Let's go and have a steam bath,' she said suddenly, releasing her grip of his hardness. Colin sat back, looking a

154

trifle disappointed. Sarah grinned mischievously. 'I'll see you in there in a minute or so,' she said, her eyes glinting.

She climbed out of the foaming water and opened the translucent glass door to the steam room, pausing briefly and looking back to see Colin clambering after her. The large woman's eyes were fixed on his ludicrous bulging swimming trunks.

To her delight, Sarah found the small room empty and thick billows of steam made visibility near impossible. She felt her way to the back, sat on the fixed bench and waited. The door opened almost immediately and Colin entered.

'Shut the door quick, before the steam goes,' she said, shifting along the bench to make room for him. He closed the glass partition and sat next to her, putting his fingers immediately between her open thighs and gently stroking her aching pussy. She reached across him and with one hand pulled his tight trunks forward while the other gripped his still raging stalk and manipulated it once more to full erection.

'Nobody ever comes in here in the afternoon,' she breathed, rubbing him steadily. 'We can get up to anything and if someone does arrive we'll be able to pull apart before they see us in this fog.'

'What d'you want to do?'

She let go of his cock and stood up, pulling the material of her costume to one side at the crotch. 'Thank God for lycra,' she said as she bared the juicy, open lips of her cunt to his excited gaze.

'Do you want me to fuck you?' Colin sounded nervous, even afraid.

'Come on, it'll be all right.' She turned her back to him and lowered herself slowly down on to his lap, thrilling as she felt his long stalk slipping into her hungry sheath. She sat down hard on him, holding his full length deep inside her, then began to move evenly up and down, absorbing and reabsorbing him into her tightness.

'I once saw a couple doing this in here,' she panted. 'The steam was so thick they didn't even know I was in with them! I've wanted to do it myself ever since.' She moved quicker, Colin returning her downward motions with thrusts of his own. The steam continued to billow thickly and sweat poured from her face, her bottom slapping wetly against his thighs.

The door opened suddenly. Sarah flung herself from her heavenly perch and tugged at her costume, but the material obstinately clung to her matted pubic hair leaving her engorged sex lips totally exposed. The steam seemed to clear dramatically, revealing the unmistakable dark form of the receptionist. She looked at Colin through wild, nervous eyes. He was vainly trying to stuff his hard cock into his ludicrously small trunks.

'Well, what's going on here then?' asked the big man, his voice booming against the tiles.

'Nothing,' said Sarah weakly, still attempting to cover herself.

'Don't worry, I won't say anything,' said the receptionist kindly. 'People are always at it in here. Please, carry on.'

'Are you going to watch?' asked Sarah, rather relishing the thought.

'Unless you'd like me to join in?' posed the newcomer. Sarah looked at Colin. He shrugged.

Oh, what the hell, thought Sarah, moving back to Colin and resuming her erotic position so that she straddled his lap with her back to him. She reached between her legs and grasped his cock, guiding it once more into her sopping wet pussy.

'My name's Jim,' said the big man, pulling his trunks to his knees and pushing a long, black prick towards her face. She opened her mouth willingly, the thick bulbous end slipping between her lips. She found the slightly salty taste highly arousing and circled her fingers around the gnarled, ebony stalk, pumping it slowly as she moved her body up and down on Colin's throbbing intrusion.

'Hey, baby,' said Jim, thickly, 'don't make me come. I gotta get inside you first.' With that he pulled from her and knelt between her legs on the tiled floor of the steam room, pointing his massive phallus at her already stretched pussy. She raised herself so that just the tip of Colin's cock remained inside her and watched hungrily through the misty haze as Jim pushed the end of his weapon to her sex lips. Slowly, he slid inside her and Sarah gradually lowered herself until she held both hard cocks within her, the sensation of total fullness thrilling her beyond measure.

The big man began to fuck her evenly, rubbing his length against Colin's, and Sarah manoeuvred her hips so that she sank down on Colin's lap at the same moment that Jim thrust forward. It was awkward and very uncomfortable, but the sensation of being impaled by two large cocks simultaneously was one that she wanted to savour forever.

She felt her legs begin to cramp; the position was simply too hard to hold for long. She raised her body, allowing Colin's thickness to fall from within her pussy, then reached between her legs again and carefully directed his hard erection to her anus as she leant back against him. She sat down again slowly and lifted her legs, Colin's stalk sliding effortlessly into the tight orifice as she rested her heels on the edge of the bench. Jim continued pumping steadily into her, plunging every thick inch of his superb length deep inside her aching pussy while she rotated her hips gently on the erotic pivot of Colin's stiffness held within the snug confines of her bottom.

'Hey, baby, you really are something,' grunted Jim as he realised what she'd done, his hips beginning to move rapidly and his cock swelling monstrously inside her. 'Not every chick likes to be ass-fucked.'

Sarah knew that the time had come to welcome Jim into the fold. 'Lick me,' she breathed. 'Lick my cunt. Make me come.'

The big man pulled from her, crouched down and put his mouth to her sex, the lips pulsating with the rhythm of Colin's thrusts from beneath her. She gasped as Jim's tongue lapped at her, her juices flowing into his eager mouth. He was hers. Sarah howled as the orgasm tore through her loins, contracting her buttocks and gripping Colin's erection deep inside her bottom. She felt him throbbing, and knew that he was filling her with his seed. She groaned as though in pain as Jim's tongue licked rapidly across the tender bud of her clitoris until she had to put her hand to his head to make him stop.

Jim stood up quickly, grasping his cock by the root and directing the weeping end to her mouth. Sarah parted her lips and took him inside greedily, sucking heavily on the hard monster while still feeling the gentle throbbing of Colin's stalk deep within her bum. Jim threw back his head as his sperm gushed into her mouth. Sarah sucked all the harder as he climaxed, swallowing hard.

The door opened again and the huge woman from the jacuzzi groped her way through the steam. She regarded the scene before her, her lips pursed. 'Selfish cow,' she grumbled, and stomped back out of the room, slamming the door behind her.

Sarah walked slowly into the health club's snack bar, her face flushed from her exertions and her hair still damp from the shower. Colin sat alone at a table, waiting for her. He stood up as she approached.

'Can I get you a coffee?' he ventured, pulling a chair back.

'Thanks, that would be nice,' she replied, dumping her kit-bag on the floor and sitting down. She watched him go to the counter. The sex had been great but now the old doubts were returning. She couldn't put her finger on why she felt so uneasy; perhaps the new, intuitive powers that she and Alex seemed to be developing had something to do with it. Whatever it was, she needed to discover why she was being nagged by such uncertainties.

Colin returned, carrying two steaming cups of coffee. He set them down on the table and sat close to her, looking intently into her eyes. Sarah felt uncomfortable.

'What d'you think of the club facilities then?' she asked, trying to make light of the situation.

'Very nice. Er, look,' said Colin, clearly ill at ease, 'I must know, I must know when I'm going to meet the other vampires.'

'Don't be so impatient; you'll meet them soon enough.' Sarah looked hard at him. Something was quite definitely wrong.

'When though? I . . .'

'What are you not telling me, Colin?' she asked suddenly. He drew back sharply.

'Nothing. I . . . what d'you mean?'

'There's something, Colin, and you'd better tell me if you ever want to meet the others.'

She watched in an accusing manner as he drew a deep breath. 'OK,' he said presently. 'The truth. These creatures are *evil*. I can save you from them.'

Sarah's eyes opened widely. 'What do you mean, evil? What are you saying?'

He seemed to relax and sat back in his chair. 'What I told you, about being a student of vampires. Well, that's only part of it. I'm a member of an organisation, a group dedicated to eliminating the scourge of vampirism from the face of the earth once and for all. I have to find the whereabouts of your leaders, put them to the stake and release you and all the other poor souls from their control.'

Sarah swallowed hard, finding it difficult to accept what she was hearing. 'But you had sex with me!' she said with a sudden realisation and so loudly that the waitress looked up from her labours in startled amazement. Colin just shrugged. Sarah leant forward, lowering her voice. 'You must have known that you would become one of us,' she hissed. 'If you tasted . . . if you drank from me.'

He nodded. 'It was a risk I had to take,' he said, his voice trembling. 'Which is why I must find them soon, before they take complete control of me. Already, I am experiencing strange dreams, and my sexual desires increase by the hour. Please, Sarah, before it is too late!'

'But you are so wrong, Colin,' she pleaded. 'They are not all evil. The female vampires and those who serve them seek only to share pleasure.'

He shook his head benignly. 'No, Sarah, it is you who is wrong. They are taking over your mind.'

She stood up angrily. Colin's expression was that of a convinced evangelist; she knew she was wasting her time. 'I will never tell you, Colin. I will never betray them. They are my friends and my lovers. Soon you will learn the truth and you will join us.'

He stood up, his face inches from hers. For the first time, Sarah knew why she had held such doubts about him. The tender expression in his handsome face was gone and he glared at her with a malevolence that she had only seen once before – in the eyes of the baron himself. 'I will kill you first,' he growled, and strode away from her, disappearing into a crowd of babbling students who were forcing their way through the main entrance.

She watched him go, realising that pursuit was pointless. She clasped her cup and sipped the steaming drink, her mind racing. How could she have been so stupid? She'd let them down: Demonia, Sinitia, the others. She knew she would have to warn them, and take the consequences of her naïvety.

There was an aura of excited expectancy in the sitting-room of the house on Gallows Hill Road as Alex and the four students awaited the arrival of Demonia and Sinitia. The evening sun still bore down on the heavy drapes covering the windows and shafts of bright light caught the slowly-drifting particles of dust in the air. The time was not yet ready for their lovely hostesses to arise.

The message had been clear. Alex had been given strict instructions to draw the group together so that Demonia could explain their position and plan their mutual fight against the evil of Baron Mansola. He and Sarah had already told the students as much as they knew but they were all very aware that they all had much to learn, not least about their own futures.

Sarah was unusually quiet, sitting alone in a corner of the room. Alex smiled at her but she glanced away quickly, clearly troubled by something.

'What does the baron look like?' asked Belinda.

'A huge man,' answered Alex soberly. 'Well over six feet tall and powerfully built. Not a man to be trifled with, that's for sure.'

'And incredibly handsome,' followed Sarah, 'but with the most piercing, evil eyes.'

160

'I wouldn't say he was particularly handsome,' grumbled Alex, feeling a little hurt despite being pleased that she had joined in the conversation, 'and, besides, you've only seen him in dreams. I came face to face with the monster.'

Sarah smiled at him. 'And speaking of monsters,' she continued, her expression one of amusement at Alex's jealousy, 'he's got the biggest prick I've ever seen ... dream or no dream.'

'Even bigger than Andrew's?' laughed Karen, gently patting the young man's bulging jeans. Sarah nodded.

'Much bigger. Longer, and very thick.'

'The creature sounds deformed,' growled Alex, tiring of the discussion.

'Show Sarah and Alex your party-piece,' said Belinda suddenly. 'Go on Andrew. You know, what you showed me and Karen last night!'

Andrew blushed. 'Oh, no, they won't want ...'

'Yes, go on!' said Karen excitedly. 'You won't believe what he can do!'

'Well Andrew,' said Sarah impatiently, 'let's see your little trick.'

'I'll have to strip first,' said Andrew, standing up and beginning to pull his T-shirt over his head.

'I'll help you!' said Karen, gleefully tugging at the zip of his jeans.

'Oh, must we?' asked Alex, hardly relishing the impending sight of Andrew's huge cock springing up before him. 'Demonia and Sinitia will be here soon. It's hardly seemly; we are guests, after all.'

'Oh, don't be such a misery, Alex,' chided Sarah. 'They won't mind. In fact, I think that they'd be more likely to be surprised if they found us waiting in here still fully dressed.'

Alex shrugged his shoulders and watched as Karen and Belinda pulled down Andrew's briefs. His long, thick manhood drooped between his muscular legs. The two girls caught hold of the swelling stalk and rubbed it slowly, grinning happily as the monster rose quickly to full erection. Belinda opened her mouth and took the plum-sized

161

end between her pouting lips while Karen continued to pump the thickly-veined stalk with her small hand.

Alex looked across at Sarah and saw her staring intently at the engorged phallus, licking her lips hungrily. He felt a twinge of possessiveness that was ridiculous in view of their circumstances. He dismissed such thoughts from his mind. At least she seemed to have cheered up.

'Where's the trick in that?' he asked mockingly.

Belinda drew back her head, letting the glistening cock fall from her mouth. 'Watch,' she ordered, 'you ain't seen nothing yet!'

With that, Andrew lay on his back on the carpet then, with the grace and adeptness of the gymnast that he was, he raised his legs in the air and brought them over his head. He supported his lower back with his hands. Gradually, he eased his legs back still further so that his gnarled, raging erection pointed straight at his face. The purple-coloured knob was still wet with Belinda's saliva. Slowly and deliberately he brought it towards him until he was able to open his lips and take the bulbous head within his mouth.

Karen and Belinda cheered and clapped their hands in mock applause as Andrew made a point of drawing his cheeks in and out, as if to prove he was genuinely sucking his own cock. Alex grimaced, more in envy than distaste.

'A clever demonstration.' The voice was Demonia's. She and Sinitia had, as always, silently entered the room like ghosts. Andrew quickly unfolded himself and grabbed his jeans, sheepishly trying to cover his stiffness. Demonia walked over to him and grabbed the garment away, gripping his hard cock with her other hand and smiling lustfully. 'Don't hide such a beautiful thing,' she said softly.

Andrew stood motionless as Demonia squeezed his throbbing flesh, her fingers barely able to encircle its massive girth. She stared into his eyes as her lips parted suggestively, the hint of a smile playing across her mouth. Andrew began to sweat and his entire body trembled. Alex watched the scene intently. Demonia clearly had the young man completely under her control. This was another facet of the beautiful vampire's increasingly dominant powers, and he found it highly stimulating. Like Mansola, she clearly grew stronger with every conquest that she made.

Andrew suddenly closed his eyes and uttered a dry, guttural groan from the back of his throat. Demonia continued to grip his cock and despite her not having moved her hand in any form of erotic caress the sperm jetted from the engorged knob, sending streaks of white fluid up her bare arm. She grinned, holding him firmly until he was done, then she let him fall from her clasp.

'Wow,' breathed Belinda. The others said nothing but watched as Demonia drew her forearm across her mouth, voraciously licking the thick cream from her skin. Alex felt his erection rising. The sight of their stunning hostess relishing the fruits of Andrew's copious ejaculation was one of supreme eroticism. She ran her tongue slowly over her lips, savouring the last drops of her sustenance. She drew the back of her hand across her mouth and regarded the assembled group with detached haughtiness before walking casually across the room and sitting in her customary armchair. Sinitia joined her at her feet, curling her legs under her lithe body and resting her arms on Demonia's lap. The ache between Alex's legs grew as he looked at the innocent expression on the younger girl's face. Her brown eyes seemed larger and wider than ever; her lips fuller and even more succulent, ready to suckle on his hardening cock. She smiled coyly when she caught his gaze, looking down momentarily at the plush carpet.

'The time has come for me to be more open with you all,' began Demonia, her tone one of utmost gravity despite her recent display. Alex looked up at her. The beautiful features held the mark of seriousness. Her eyes were sharp and clear.

'Mansola is near. Thanks to Alex and his episode with the delightful Lady Melissa Harman,' she continued, her accent on the word *delightful* indicating her disdain, 'thanks to that we know where his lair is. Also, he has visited me here, and made it clear that he means us harm and I in turn have told him that we will not be subjugated by his evil will.

'As I have explained before, we need to draw many more into the fold if we are going to vanquish this foul entity forever. You have all now tasted the orgasmic juices of a true vampire – either Sinitia or myself or indeed both of us. For the duration of a full cycle of the moon your bodies will adjust and you will learn more of the new powers that have been bestowed upon you until at the end of that time you may make the decision as to whether to join us in an eternity of lustful pursuits or return to your former, mortal selves.

'On the last day you will be brought before us and asked to either drink the juices of our lust from our bodies and in so doing become at last one of us. Alternatively, you may leave us forever. The choice will be entirely yours and should you choose mortality we will remain forever grateful for the help you have given us.

'In the meantime, we must hunt. We must search for young, strong-minded men and women who can be willingly drawn into our circle and thereby swell our numbers and increase the power of our spirit. You can be sure that the baron is doing the same thing in his own demonic way, so there is no time to lose. Sarah, Karen and Belinda, you have been asked to go out into the world and take as many men as you can, preferably those of a promiscuous lifestyle, so that they too can act as messengers in our cause. Andrew, take that fine weapon of yours and continue to impress as many young females as are willing. But Stuart and Alex, you must remain here as our guardians and of course our sources of pleasurable diversion. It is no longer safe for us to venture into the night.'

With these last words, Demonia looked pointedly across at Sarah, who looked away quickly.

'How long do you think we've got?' asked Belinda, somewhat nervously.

'Three days, no more. Return on the fourth night and regale us with tales of your conquests. As I suggested, it is too dangerous for Sinitia or I to venture from these walls now. We are relying on you.'

'No problem,' said Andrew, casually pulling up his

jeans, having fully recovered from the mind-blowing orgasm he'd just experienced.

'There is one more thing,' continued Demonia, her tone deepening. 'Sarah has told me of her meeting with another who will do us harm; a member of an organisation that sees us as much of a threat as the baron himself. This group of people are manic in their hatred of vampires and they will try to find and destroy us all. We must all be vigilant, and not trust anyone.'

Alex looked across at Sarah. 'Colin?' he asked simply. She nodded.

'I was so stupid,' she said quietly. 'I *knew* there was something wrong, and yet I . . .'

'It was a mistake that any of us could make,' said Demonia, her voice lighter if not entirely convincing. 'Just remember, we must all be on our guard. Now, go, enjoy yourselves. I look forward to hearing the tales of your exploits! Meanwhile, Alex and Stuart, wait in the great bedchamber. Sinitia and I have need for you. Great need.'

Alex lay naked on the huge bed, casually stroking his stiffening erection. Stuart sat nearby on a small chair, absently flicking through the pages of an ancient book. Outside, the rain began to spatter on the window and the occasional flash of lightning promised a storm.

'Do you think you will join them?' asked Stuart, resting the book on a table.

Alex lay back against the pillows and stretched his arms above his head, his cock resting heavily on his stomach. 'I don't know,' he said, after a moment. 'It's a big step.'

'I can't see the problem,' said Stuart, getting up and walking to the window to pull back the drapes. 'An eternity of endless screwing; what's wrong with that?' The bedroom door opened slowly and candles flickered as a sudden draught blew across the room from the partly-open window. Alex shivered. Demonia and Sinitia entered, both completely naked. The contrast between the flawless colouring of their skin was enhanced in the shimmering light. Demonia was carrying what seemed to be a whip. It was

165

similar in appearance, in Alex's eyes, to that so expertly used by Lady Melissa. He felt his erection stiffen rapidly.

The two women glided over to the bed, their smiles broad and their eyes glistening with lust. Stuart joined them and slipped his arm around Sinitia's tiny waist. The young girl immediately allowed her fingers to encircle his hard cock. Demonia sat on the edge of the bed. Alex could see now that she held not a whip but a massive, black phallus; a fearsome dildo with straps and buckles attached to the perfectly-formed root.

Demonia playfully put the end of the implement to her lips and with her eyes fixed on Alex she took two or three inches into her mouth, bending the thick stalk as she did so. The unmistakable scent of rubber invaded Alex's nostrils, rekindling recent, highly erotic memories.

'Sinitia found this toy in a little shop not far from here,' said Demonia as she took it from her mouth, the end wet with her saliva. 'It's amazing the things you can buy. These are enlightened times.'

Alex grinned, wondering what other treasures Sinitia might have been tempted to purchase. 'We thought you might like to watch us give you a little demonstration, to prepare and arouse you.' She gripped Alex's stiff shaft firmly. 'Although perhaps it is unnecessary.'

'No, please,' said Stuart, releasing himself from Sinitia's grip, 'give us a show!'

Demonia let go of Alex and handed the dildo to the young black girl. Sinitia quickly donned the strange apparel, drawing the straps around her waist and between her legs tightly until the monster jutted from her crotch, looking for all the world like the real thing. The sight made Alex's mouth become immediately dry. The pert buttocks were raised to even greater perfection by the action of the straps, and the ludicrously large phallus swung in front of her menacingly.

Stuart sat down again on his chair, his gleeful expression resembling that of a member of the audience at the first night of a new West End play. Demonia placed a pillow on the floor then lay on the carpet, her legs splayed apart

166

with the cushion under her bottom. Her pussy was already wet and aroused; the pink slit open and eager. Sinitia knelt between her lover's legs and carefully directed the monster phallus towards its target. The thick, rubber end parted the pouting sex lips and the long shaft slid in effortlessly.

From his vantage point, Alex could see the padded root pressing against Sinitia's sex, no doubt allowing her to stimulate herself against it as she stabbed the fearsome weapon back and forth, steadily fucking the unusually submissive form of Demonia. The two girls pressed their mouths together and the pumping of their hips came ever faster. The sight of Sinitia's delightful little bottom stiffening and relaxing in time with her rhythmic thrusting drove Alex to distraction.

It was Stuart who moved first and crawled over to the rutting couple. He then knelt across Demonia's face. She immediately took his testicles within her mouth and began to suckle him while Sinitia took his cock between her succulent, full lips. Alex was quick to join the happy threesome and crouched behind the two girls, holding Demonia's legs in the air by the ankles and kissing and licking Sinitia's exquisite bottom. The mixture of her heavenly scent and that of the rubber phallus filled his senses. The young girl slowed her movements as he lapped wetly between her buttocks then pushed the tip of his tongue inside the tight little orifice, curling it and moving it in and out until he sensed the muscles of her sphincter begin to relax.

Without moving his face from his delicious cushion, Alex brought Demonia's ankles together and gripped them both with one hand, then moved the fingers of the other to caress the dampness between Sinitia's gently undulating buttocks. He heard her groan with pleasure as he pushed two fingers deep into her bottom, then withdrew them slowly before easing four inside her. He twisted his hand, finding little resistance.

He removed his hand and inched along on his knees until his stiff cock pointed directly at the tiny hole. Pushing forward, the end of his supremely hard cock entered her easily, the puckered orifice closing tightly over his thick ridge. Sinitia began to move her hips backwards and forwards once more, steadily slipping the huge dildo in and out of Demonia's cunt. Each time she withdrew the monster she absorbed more of Alex's steel-like length inside her tight arse until every inch was within her.

Alex merely had to hold still; Sinitia's movements were enough and the incessant rhythm of her coupling with Demonia and the tightness of her anal muscles gripping his engorged shaft were leading him ever nearer to the ultimate joy of release.

But he didn't want to come. He knew that the night would be long and he wanted to savour every delight that their combined knowledge and imaginations could manifest.

He pulled himself reluctantly from his enchanting position, a thin sliver of pre-come momentarily joining the end of his penis with her sweet little hole. There was a sudden flash of lightning – a searing brightness that tore through the gaps in the curtains – followed almost immediately by a deafening clap of thunder. The lightning repeated, filling the room with a blinding, white light. The power of the storm erupted, serving to heighten Alex's arousal with its majestic electricity. The thunder crashed again with an ear-splitting crack so loud that it seemed to him that its force would split open the ceiling above them. The chandeliers rattled with the sudden vibration in the air.

The four lovers made their next movements smoothly, as though rehearsed. Stuart lay on his back, holding his hard cock erect. Demonia untwined herself from beneath Sinitia. The huge, black phallus slipped out of the silky confines of her pussy and she knelt across him, taking his stalk between her fingers and guiding it between her soaked sex lips. She leant forward and arched her back, moving her bottom in an erotic, circular motion as Stuart thrust upwards. The sight of her perfect, white globes was too much for Alex to resist. He put his face to her soft buttocks licking wetly across the hole and probing inside her with his fingertips. As he did so, he felt Sinitia push two or maybe three fingers inside his own bottom, turning them and readying him in the same way that he was preparing Demonia.

After a few moments of this exquisite torment he pulled himself erect on his knees and aimed his thick tool at Demonia's flawless bottom, holding her still as he pushed slowly inside her to the hilt. He could feel Stuart's cock rubbing against his through the thin membrane that separated them. He held himself rigid as he throbbed within the tight confines of her fleshy bum before matching the student's movements with his own.

Alex leant forward, still pumping heavily into the delightful orifice and kissing and gently biting the alabaster-white skin of Demonia's shoulder. He felt a pressure against his anus, then a sudden, wonderful fullness as Sinitia pushed the dildo carefully inside him, a sensation he could never have imagined in his most wild fantasies. He glanced at a nearby wall-mirror, the image filling his mind with its sheer eroticism. The beautiful Demonia, her sublimely magnificent body sandwiched between Stuart and himself, and Sinitia, fucking him in the way that he had fucked her so many times before.

He lost all self-control in that instant and the sperm surged up his long penis, his stalk throbbing mercilessly as he pumped his seed deep into Demonia's bottom. Sinitia forced in as much of the monster phallus as she could. Stuart groaned, his own cock throbbing within the purse of Demonia's pussy, and the lovely vampire squealed as she joined the two men in blissful release. Only Sinitia didn't share in the orgasmic joy. She slowly withdrew the huge intrusion from Alex and sat back, grinning as her colleagues collapsed in an exhausted heap.

'Now you know how it feels,' she said sultrily. 'Is it not the most wonderful experience?'

Alex said nothing but lay back on the floor, his eyes staring at the reflection of the four, sweating bodies in the mirrored ceiling. He pondered over what other exquisite delights awaited him.

* * *

169

Sarah stood at the crumbling gate of the ancient manor house, her heart pounding. It was nothing like Alex had described it. There were no lights in the tall windows, no sounds emanating from within the grim, stone walls. The house was dead; as dead as its nameless, unearthly occupants.

She began to regret her decision to go there to face up to the baron once and for all. The idea had seemed so acceptable and so realistic in the reassuring surroundings of her bedroom but now, as she walked slowly along the gravel driveway towards the looming edifice, she wasn't so sure. But she had to go ahead and offer herself to Mansola. That way she would gain his confidence, learn of his plans and hopefully his weaknesses.

The air had grown suddenly cold, a thin mist drifting through the eerie shapes of the twisted, gnarled trees. Their skeletal branches swayed nakedly in the slight breeze. The waning moon offered her little comfort as her feet crunched against the path, the steps to the main entrance closing fast. Sarah swallowed hard and took a deep breath. She had to go through with it. She had to at least try to save the others.

She paused as she reached the steps. One of the two massive, oak doors was slightly ajar, as though beckoning to her. She walked slowly towards it, her shadow appearing against the old wood, elongated like the image of a monstrous creature. She pushed the heavy door firmly. It creaked, the noise echoing about her as she entered the hallway.

The place stank of dampness and decay. There was no furniture, save for a few broken remnants and the floors were littered with rotting carpets and dead leaves that had drifted into the house over the years through the open door and broken window panes. She began to wonder if this was the same house that Alex had talked about, but remembered the incredible transformation that had happened in Demonia's home and realised that the baron would have the same powers. Perhaps he preferred it this way; it seemed fitting.

She moved to the foot of the long, curved staircase and looked up. A huge window at the top of the flight illuminated her way, almost inviting her to ascend. There was a sudden, loud crash behind her. Sarah swung round, her heart in her mouth. The old door had swung closed, probably caught by a freak gust of wind. The hallway was silent once more.

She turned again to look up the long flight of stairs and gave a start. Standing at the top of the stairs was the form of a woman – tall, statuesque and silhouetted against the large window. Her white shroud billowed gently, and the superb shape of her body was highlighted by the silvery sheen of light that shone through the diaphanous material. This must be Melissa, she thought. The Lady Harman. Sarah began to climb, step by crumbling step, clutching the flaking bannister rail for comfort as well as support. Her feet felt like lead. As she neared the figure she saw the beautiful face. It was haughty but kind.

Melissa held her arms outstretched. 'Come sister,' she said, her voice gentle in tone. 'Welcome to my home.' Sarah ascended the last few steps and stood in front of her, unsure what to say. Melissa rested her arms on the trembling girl's shoulders. She had half-expected her touch to be icy but her hands felt warm through the thin fabric of her shirt. She breathed deeply again, the delicate perfume worn by the woman reassuring in its pleasantness.

'I have come to offer myself to him,' Sarah said presently, her voice small and quivering. 'To join with you.'

Melissa smiled and kissed her lightly on the cheek. 'The baron will be pleased,' she whispered, 'but first, come with me and I will prepare you.'

The tall figure turned, the moonlight once again catching the divine shape of her voluptuous body through the thin, gossamer-like material of her garment. Sarah felt a strange mixture of trepidation and lust as she followed her down the long corridor. Lady Harman was certainly as beautiful as Alex had said; small wonder he had almost fallen victim to the evil baron.

Melissa ushered her into a large bedroom where the

opulence of the furnishings and drapery were at odds with the decay of the remainder of the house. It was as Alex had described – almost an exact copy of Demonia's luxurious chamber, right up to the giant bed that stood in the centre of the room.

Two young men stood, one on either side of the bed, like silent sentinels guarding their queen. Their bodies were criss-crossed by strands of leather which did nothing to hide their superb, muscular physiques and their genitals were concealed by black pouches. The bulges were promisingly large.

Melissa walked over to the bed and drew the white shroud over her head, dropping it lightly to the floor and turning to face Sarah. Sarah gasped in awesome envy at the perfection of her body: the huge, firm breasts with their pierced nipples, the tapering waist and broad hips, the long, lithe legs and the smooth, hairless mound of her pussy. She licked her lips, the sight of Melissa's puffy, engorged sex lips filling her mind with desire.

'You're beautiful,' she breathed, feeling a sudden dampness between her thighs.

'So are you, Sarah. Come, strip and lie with me.' Melissa lay on the bed, her legs wide open and inviting. She ran the fingers of one hand along her wet, pouting slit. Sarah pulled her shirt quickly over her head, struggled out of her jeans and sandals and clambered next to the reclining body, forgetting all fear and feeling only a strong desire to possess this stunning creature. Melissa moved her hand from her pussy and put it between Sarah's legs.

'My, you're soaked already,' she said happily, her fingers delving into the soft lips. Sarah said nothing and closed her eyes and moved her hips in response to the expert caress of Melissa's fingertips. She felt all four fingers slide inside her and the thumb playfully rub against the hard bud of her clitoris. Then the whole hand moved within her pussy, turning and twisting ever deeper into her hot sheath. The fingers were curled into a fist within her.

'Ah, so accommodating,' breathed Melissa. 'The master will be delighted.'

Sarah looked down, watching in fascination as Melissa moved her slim forearm in and out of her, the outer lips of her pussy stretched widely to accept the unusual intrusion. She glanced up at one of the men, his face remained impassive, and his eyes looked forward. She breathed slowly as Melissa eased her hand from within her, her arm coated with a sheen of juice.

'The master has a splendid, thick weapon,' she said, lying on her back, 'but you will have no problem with him, I'm sure.'

'When will he come to us?' asked Sarah, sitting up and gently stroking Melissa's flat stomach.

'Later. When I call him. Come, rest your lovely head between my thighs and put your lips to me, and I, in turn, will taste the delights of your sweet juices.'

Sarah moved her body across her new lover, kneeling with her pussy over Melissa's face. Her own mouth quickly pressed against the soft flesh of the beautiful woman's sex. She licked the hairless mound, drawing the fleshy lips between her teeth and nibbling them playfully. Melissa's scent was intoxicating; her taste succulent. She felt the hard touch of the nipple-rings against her stomach as the huge mounds pushed against her. She gasped, feeling Melissa's tongue fluttering over her clitoris and her fingers once more delving inside her.

There was a movement on the bed. Sarah lifted her head to see one of the guards knelt between Melissa's legs, pushing his thick cock towards her face. She stretched her tongue out and licked the end, tasting the salty pre-come, then parted her lips and took it inside her mouth, suckling avidly while continuing to caress Melissa's wet cunt with her fingertips. Then she took hold of his stalk and guided it to the pouted opening, licking around it as it slid into the accommodating succulence. The guard soon began to move in and out, drawing Melissa's tightly-gripping outer lips forward with each withdrawal. Sarah licked the distended flesh greedily.

She felt the unmistakable pressure against her pussy as the other guard began to enter her from behind while

Melissa continued to flick her tongue rapidly over her swollen bud. She returned the compliment, licking swiftly as Melissa's hips rose and fell in time with the long, deep thrusts of her lover. Each time he withdrew, Sarah licked up and down his shaft, relishing the taste of Melissa's juices then returning her tongue to her clitoris as he slowly plunged down.

She felt the man who was fucking her, whose face she couldn't even remember seeing, withdraw his thick cock from inside her and immediately press it against her anus. He eased it into her expertly as Melissa allowed her mouth to completely engulf her aching pussy, her long tongue circling around the inside of her sex lips. She took hold of the stalk in front of her face and pulled it from Melissa's pussy, guiding it to enter the other, tiny hole. She watched excitedly as it slipped into the tight confines of her beautiful bottom.

The guard made a few cautious movements, then groaned loudly and pulled his cock from Melissa, his seed spurting rapidly over the flesh of her pussy. Sarah licked the cream voraciously, swallowing all he could offer as she felt the inevitable climb to orgasm begin to take hold of her senses. The other guard was pounding into her rapidly and Melissa was still sucking her engorged sex lips, her tongue slipping in and out of her like a small, wet cock. Sarah groaned and stiffened her thighs as her climax hit her, burying her face within the soaked warmth of Melissa's crotch. The guard suddenly pulled his thick cock from her bottom and his hot sperm splashed on to her sweat-covered back. She fell forward, slipping from the soft cushion of Melissa's body to lie on her stomach on the cool, silk sheets beside her.

As she drifted off into inevitable sleep, Sarah sensed the gentle touch of Melissa's tongue on her skin, drawing a snail-like trail between her bottom and her shoulders, and knew that she too had been sated.

The first sensation that Sarah felt as she slowly eased back into consciousness was the tingling of her skin, as though

174

her body had been freshly bathed. The second was the gentle, delicate touch of something between her legs. It was too soft to be a finger or even a tongue. She opened her eyes drowsily, slowly focusing on the image of Melissa kneeling between her widely-splayed legs, lovingly stroking her with a long, white feather. The strands were soaked and matted with her juices.

She tried to move but found that she couldn't. Her wrists and ankles were secured to the huge bed by soft, silken ropes. Two or three pillows had been placed under her bottom, raising her sex in a blatant display of submissive availability. She felt totally vulnerable, and highly aroused.

Melissa looked up and moved the feather up and down her open slit more purposefully. 'I think that you are ready now,' she purred, putting the wet strands to her mouth and tasting Sarah's wetness. 'The master will come to you soon.'

Sarah felt suddenly afraid. She had never in her short life felt so sexually excited and so hungry for orgasmic release. She longed to feel the huge phallus that she had seen in her dreams enter her small body and fill and stretch her, and yet she knew that she had put herself in great peril. She tugged at the ropes that secured her wrists.

'Why am I bound?' she asked.

'The baron demands it,' answered Melissa simply. Sarah watched helplessly as the beautiful woman slipped from the bed and walked to the door, savouring the perfection of her naked body despite her trepidation. Melissa paused at the door and looked back at her with an expression of triumph in her suddenly cold eyes. 'Yes,' she said quietly, 'the master will be pleased.'

Sarah was alone. Her terror only served to heighten her desire. She strained again at her bonds; they were securely tied. She thought of Alex and of Demonia and Sinitia. She had caused them to take shelter in their house through her own stupidity. She owed them this sacrifice.

The door opened slowly. She raised her head as high as she could and saw the tall, broad form of the baron enter

175

the room. He stood at the doorway, his body shrouded entirely in black and his handsome features passive. His eyes, however, were filled with lust. She shivered, feeling a trickle of her juices slip between her buttocks to dampen the pillow below her bottom. He moved silently forward until he stood at her side, his expression severe and dominant. She trembled as he reached over and cupped her large breast. Her long nipple hardened against the leathery palm. She made an effort to smile seductively but his countenance remained impassive as he squeezed her flesh.

'So, you have come to me at last, Sarah.' She heard the words but his lips didn't move. She made no reply, her eyes saying everything. The baron drew back from her and unfastened his cloak, casting it quickly from his shoulders and revealing his naked body to her lustful gaze. His cock thrust monstrously from a thick bush of hair, the heavily-veined stalk as thick as her forearm. He gripped the shaft and held it against himself. The huge, bulbous head pressed between his sharply-defined pectoral muscles. Too big, she thought, but so magnificent.

Mansola moved forward and held the massive phallus to her face. She licked the end cautiously then opened her mouth wide, eager to close her lips around the peach-sized end. With a suddenness that startled her he ejaculated, and streams of hot, thick cream soaked her face and hair. She licked his juices from her lips, savouring the strong, exotic taste. Her loins throbbed with her arousal.

The baron made not a sound. He drew back from her and gripped his huge erection, a trickle of white fluid slipping down the long stem. She stared in fascination at his immense hardness and knew that he had barely started. He would not disappoint her.

He moved on to the bed, kneeling between her wide open legs, staring at the soaked lips of her pussy. For an instant he smiled – a leering, malevolent grin – then aimed the head of his huge cock towards her. A sensation like a charge of electricity ran through her body as she felt the spongy tip touch her aching sex lips. She raised her head as high as she could and watched as the monster slid within her, the feeling of total fullness causing her to gasp with delight. Melissa had prepared her well. She accommodated inch after inch of the throbbing rod, its thickness stretching her beyond belief until at last she felt his balls pressed against the soft globes of her buttocks. She wanted to raise her legs and curl them around his powerful body so that she could absorb even more of him into her, but the unyielding bonds prevented it.

The baron began to fuck her steadily, drawing the full length of his cock from her until her tight pussy lips gripped him around his thick ridge then plunging back, slowly but deliberately, into the hot sheath of her cunt. She groaned with the sheer pleasure of the magnificent intrusion. She looked into his face; his eyes held hers in a hypnotic stare. There was no passion or desire in his expression. He was using her, yet in her situation of hopeless vulnerability she gave herself completely, surrendering her soul to his incessant thrusts. Her orgasm built up within her ravaged loins rapidly.

She cried out as she came, bucking her hips against his, and for a moment feeling as though she was taking control as the sensations of shattering release tore through her emotions. Then she relaxed and he continued to move in and out of her, as though unaware of her joy.

He fucked her for what seemed like hours, unrelentingly pumping his phenomenally large weapon in and out of her. Her orgasms came thick and fast. She felt wild and insatiable; a willing victim to whatever he chose to do with her. With each climax she cried out and mouthed obscenities. Every nerve-ending was concentrated on the soaked, hot area between her legs.

Suddenly, he began to move rapidly. Plunging his big cock savagely into her, he hammered hard against her aching loins. The great bed creaked and shook and sweat poured from their bodies. Sarah gasped for air as he thrust brutally into her. She felt his cock swell inside her, stretching her to the limit. She looked again at his face; the handsome features strained, his teeth bared, his eyes ablaze. He roared; a long, low cry from the depths of his massive body

177

and she felt him throbbing inside her. His movements became easier as he filled her tight sheath with his cream. With a sudden, sharp cry she came with him. The sensations exploded within her mind as she arched her back and raised her bottom from the pillows beneath her, meeting his heavy thrusts with frantic lunges of her hips.

He held still deep inside her for a moment, hardly seeming to breathe. Sarah panted heavily, her heart pounding. Suddenly he began to pump into her again, his cock as hard as ever. Then, with another guttural roar, he pulled from her, pushed himself over her body and forced the huge end of his fearsome weapon to her mouth. She parted her lips and took him in, jets of hot sperm shooting immediately to the back of her throat. She swallowed greedily and sucked hard on his thick stem until he had no more to give.

Mansola moved from her quickly, taking up his cloak and drawing it over his shoulders. 'Welcome, Sarah,' he said. 'You are soon to be one of us.'

Demonia sat up quickly, staring wildly into the distance. 'He has Sarah!' she exclaimed, her expression one of abject horror. 'The baron has her!'

'What do you mean?' asked Alex, wearily trying to raise himself to a sitting position on the floor. 'How do you know?'

'I *know*. Sarah is lost to us, unless we can save her before she enters the pit.'

'The pit? What's that?'

'The final initiation. Thanks to the intervention of your ancestor I was spared its terrors. Once the baron has taken her there she will become as he is. She will crave not only for sex but for blood! Come, there is no time to lose!'

Seven

'You must go to the house of Mansola today, Alex. Both you and Stuart, as soon as the sun rises.'

Demonia's tone allowed for no dissension and no discussion whatsover. Despite his misgivings, as well as his fear of returning to the house from which he had had such a lucky escape, Alex knew that she was right. He glanced across at Stuart; the young man showed no sign of concern. The typically youthful arrogance of the perception of immortality was a blessing at times like this.

'What would you have us do?' he asked, dreading her reply.

'Hopefully, like Sinitia and I, the baron sleeps during the hours of daylight. You must search the house and find Sarah, but be assured, he will have hidden her well. She must be rescued from his clutches before it is too late.'

'What if we find the baron himself?' asked Stuart, clearly excited by the prospect. 'What if he's there, lying helpless in his coffin? Couldn't we stake him, and finish him off for good?'

Demonia smiled benignly. 'Don't even think of such a thing,' she warned. 'Mansola is not so easily destroyed. Should he catch you, the consequences would be too awful to contemplate.'

'Have we any protection?' ventured Alex. 'Perhaps if we carry crosses, or holy water?'

'Such items offer some measure of defence, were you to encounter him or any of his brood. A vampire cannot approach anyone bearing a crucifix and should it be blessed the mere touch of it against his skin would burn his flesh.'

'What d'you mean, blessed?' asked Stuart.

179

'Just what I say. A simple piece of metal in the shape of a cross would be useless. The crucifix or holy water would need to have been consecrated by one versed in the mysteries of exorcism.'

'But we haven't time . . .'

Demonia shook her head sadly. 'No, and unless you hurry, Sarah's soul is doomed to everlasting damnation.'

'How will we ever defeat this creature?' asked Alex despairingly.

'When we discover the secret; when we learn what it is in this house that he needs so much. I'm convinced that the key to his weakness lies within these walls. But first, we must think of Sarah. If we fail her, we will never forgive ourselves.'

'We will not fail her,' said Alex, manfully trying to conceal his uncertainties. He stood up and walked to the window, carefully holding back the drapes. 'It will be dawn soon. We'd better get dressed.'

'And Sinitia and I must leave you,' said Demonia softly. She joined him at the window as he let the curtain fall back into place, hiding the brightening sky from her eyes. She looked so beautiful and, for a brief moment, so very vulnerable. She touched him lightly on the shoulder; a tender, affectionate brush of her fingertips. 'Take care, Alex, please take care.'

He felt deeply moved by her concern as he watched her quickly pull the sensuous silk of her dress over her sumptuous curves, the material doing little to conceal her abject sexuality. He felt the familiar stirring within his loins as he watched the lovely Sinitia slip her diaphanous robe over her slender shoulders. Demonia took her hand and led her from the room to find solace in their unearthly resting places. Above all, this was what bothered him most about joining them; the need to find sanctuary in a death-like sleep during the daylight hours.

The old manor bore little resemblance to how it had appeared on his fateful visit with the evil Lady Harman. Now, the greying walls stood coldly in the warmth of the day, defiant against the soothing rays of the sun. The black windows stared at Alex and Stuart as they walked along the crunching, gravel path, the thick convolvulus creeping through shattered panes of glass to invade the ghostly interior like serpents. The surrounding trees and bushes stood in uniform death, their grey-black branches choked by the same, all-pervasive growth.

Alex glanced at Stuart, the student's ashen face mirroring his own terrors. Deep inside him his good sense was gnawing at his emotions and ordering him to turn back, but he knew that he must go on. He had to enter this vile mausoleum and find Sarah. He patted his pocket, assuring himself that he still had the small torch he had had the presence of mind to retrieve from the car's glove compartment.

'Christ, what a dump,' said Stuart, staring up at the towering walls.

'If you were a vampire, wouldn't you choose a place like this?' said Alex in a poor attempt at humour. Stuart merely shrugged and walked up to the entrance, pushing open the creaking door.

Alex took a deep breath as though it was to be the last gulp of fresh air that would ever enter his lungs and followed the young man into the dingy hallway. The putrid aroma of damp and decay filled his nostrils.

'God, there's something dead in here,' said Stuart, holding his hand over his mouth.

'I think we can be certain about that,' replied Alex gravely. 'Let's just hope it stays that way.' Stuart laughed nervously, moving slowly towards the huge staircase. 'I think we should start with the cellar,' continued Alex, noticing a small door at the back of the hall. 'It's probably through there.' He walked quickly to the door, his desperation to flee their oppressive surroundings almost as powerful as his desire to rescue his lover.

The door opened with the now expected groan of aged wood straining against rusting hinges. Foul-smelling air wafted from the darkness within, causing Alex to gag. He turned his head away, taking a long breath of the relatively fresher atmosphere of the hall like a diver about to plunge into deep water. Stuart followed his example. They moved slowly into the dark corridor, their way illuminated by Alex's torch. Their cautious steps echoed against the damp, stone walls. The air became slightly more breathable as they reached the top of a narrow flight of steps that descended into eerie blackness. Something howled far below them, an animal-like cry of anguish.

Alex swallowed hard and led the way slowly, the torch-light barely cutting through the darkness. Gruesome shadows played against the harsh walls like scurrying creatures watching their every move. He could feel his heart pounding in his tight chest, and could see his breath billowing in the ice-cold beam of light. The steps seemed to be endless, cutting ever deeper into the very bowels of the earth.

He was scared, of that there was no doubt, but there was another sensation, an incongruous urge within his body that seemed to be strangely quelling his fears: an immense desire for sex. Somehow, the unearthly atmosphere of their surroundings seemed to be playing tricks with his senses. His loins were beginning to ache and his erection was steadily rising.

'I don't know about you, Doctor,' whispered Stuart from behind him, 'but I feel incredibly horny!'

Alex grunted a reply, not wishing to admit to his own, bizarre arousal. His feet slipped slightly on the damp steps and he steadied himself by putting his hand against the wall, finding the rock cold and slimy with lichen. He pulled his fingers away in disgust. On and on they trudged, ever downwards, as though they were heading to the gates of hell itself.

At last the stairway ended and the firm, flat stone of the floor offered some comfort after their long descent. They stood still for a moment and peered into the blackness, the shaft of torchlight cutting a swathe through the gloom. The beam caught the glint of a barred, metal door, then another, set within the forbidding stone wall. Alex walked over to the first and shone his torch through the grill. Inside, he saw a small, empty cell. A pitiful cot and an up-ended water jug were the only furniture.

'She's not here,' he whispered. 'Let's try the other.' He peered through the tiny aperture into the second room, at first seeing nothing. His loins ached, his cock maddeningly erect. The vampires were close, of that he was certain.

'Anything?' asked Stuart. Alex shook his head. Suddenly, he sensed a movement within the grim cell and the torchlight briefly captured the whiteness of flesh. He shone the beam directly, his eyes widening at the image the light revealed. It was a girl, barely eighteen or nineteen years of age. Her slender, naked frame was ghostly white, and her large, startled eyes shone like those of a cornered animal. Her hair fell in tangled, silver-blonde tresses over her slim shoulders, and cascaded over her small, pert breasts to her narrow waist. He felt his cock swell in the tight confines of his trousers. The ache was becoming unbearable.

He shone the torch downwards, his mouth becoming dry as he gazed at her downy-covered sex. The lips were unusually prominent, as though in a state of considerable arousal. He heard a shuffling sound from the darkness beside her and shone the beam across the cell. Another naked young girl, a perfect twin of the first, sat hunched in a corner. Her frightened eyes glistened in the torchlight.

'What is it?' said Stuart, pressing his face close to Alex's and peering through the small, barred grill. He took a deep breath as Alex shone the beam over the two delicate figures. 'God, they're beautiful!' he exclaimed. Alex had to agree. The virginal loveliness of the two hapless girls and the innocent, fearful expressions on their young faces captivated him. With immediate resolve he knew that they had to free them from their grim prison.

He looked quickly around the passageway for something to break the ancient padlock on the door and swiftly found a large stone which lay, possibly too conveniently, at his feet. He took up the rock and smashed it against the lock, the crash of the straining metal resounding in his ears. A second blow and the job was done. The padlock fell shattered to the ground with a noisy clatter. The two men held still, scarcely breathing, their ears tuned to any sound that might have emanated from the blackness around them. There was none.

Slowly, Alex pushed open the heavy, iron door, the hinges squealing in defiance. He shone his torch again and saw the two girls shrink back against the far wall, their eyes wide in apparent terror.

'It's all right,' he whispered, as kindly as he could, 'we won't harm you.' He turned the beam of his torch as wide as possible in order to illuminate the whole cell and set it down on an unsteady, wooden stool. Then he held his hands forward in a gesture of friendliness. The first girl walked cautiously towards him.

'Can you help us?' she whimpered, the gentle sound of her voice lilting in the air. He nodded. 'Oh, thank God,' she cried, falling into his outstretched arms and pressing her slim nakedness against his body. He was conscious of the hard bulge in his trousers pressing against her soft stomach and felt more than a little embarrassed. Stuart walked over to the other girl and took her hand, raising her slowly to her feet. She immediately flung her arms around him, kissing his face and neck in a demonstration of pitiful relief.

The beautiful girl in Alex's arms took hold of his hand, putting it immediately between her legs. She was soaked, the lips of her pussy engorged with lust. She looked up into his face, her eyes filled with pleading. 'Sex,' she breathed. 'Please, give us sex.'

Alex tried to pull his hand from her grip but she held it firmly against her softness. 'No,' he struggled, 'we must take you out of here.'

'No, no,' continued the girl, rubbing her thighs against him as his fingers slipped inside her welcoming sheath, 'we must have sex! Please, it has been so long. We must have it! Please, fuck us now, then we can escape!'

Without waiting for his reply she fell to her knees, grasped wildly at the zip of his pants and yanked them open, wrenching them to his feet in one swift, determined movement. His cock sprang up, fully erect. There was no way that he was going to be able to resist the advances of this seemingly innocent waif. The aura of the eerie surroundings had worked its magic.

He glanced across at Stuart. He was naked, save for his small T-shirt, and his cock was firmly implanted within the suckling mouth of the beautiful twin. The sight thrilled him and his shaft throbbed as a jet of pre-come gushed down the throat of the girl at his feet. His entire length was now held within her voraciously sucking lips. He glanced at the door nervously. This was madness! They had to free these two nubile nymphets and continue their search; there was no time . . . no time.

He looked down again. His entire length was held inside the gently undulating mouth of the beautiful, blonde vision at his feet. Her lips clasped tightly around the root and her tongue fluttered across the hard stem. The heavy, swallowing movements of her throat threatened to draw his seed from within his tortured body.

He felt his orgasm rising within his loins and pulled himself from her, anxious that he should impale her delicate body. He closed his eyes until the urgency had passed. His stalk throbbed, a long sliver of his cream slipping from the swollen end to trickle suggestively between her small, firm breasts. The young girl slipped her fingertips into the cream then put them to her mouth, staring at him seductively through wide, shining eyes. He turned his gaze away as his cock throbbed again. His desire to bathe her lovely face in his juices was achingly intense.

She clasped hold of his arm, pulled herself to her feet and walked over to a small bench by the wall. Turning her back to him, she rested her hands on the wooden surface so that her bottom was presented to his excited gaze in the most appealing manner. Alex struggled to pull his pants over his shoes and cast them to one side. Sarah would have to wait.

Stuart was lying on his back on the stone floor, its coldness apparently not concerning him as his twin lowered her delightful body on to his. His cock slipped between the folds of her pussy to plunder the hot depths of her sheath.

The young man groaned as he entered her, his hands caressing her lithe form as she began to ride him wildly, taking complete control.

Alex looked back at the soft, white buttocks so brazenly offered to him and moved over to stand behind her, his cock jutting hugely before him. Gripping it by the root, he pressed the thick, bulbous end to her soaked pussy lips, his length slipping easily into her. She groaned with pleasure. 'Yes, oh, how I need it!' she moaned. 'Fuck me, fuck me as hard as you can!'

He moved cautiously in and out, desperately trying not to come and anxious that he should sate this beautiful nymphet. His cock throbbed again and he held himself still, gritting his teeth. She began to move her bottom back and forth, rapidly increasing her pace in her need to fuck herself on his long, hard rod. He gripped her buttocks tightly, vainly attempting to slow her movements, but she was in control as she rammed her white-skinned backside forcefully against his crotch. He looked away and saw Stuart and the other twin humping crazily. The groans of the two young girls echoed around the walls of the cell.

Alex tore his gaze from the sight of the others and looked down at the perfection of the creamy-white bottom pumping backwards and forwards. He watched his long shaft appearing and disappearing within the tightly-gripping folds of sex-flesh, and the tiny, puckered orifice of her anus seemed to beckon to him. He groaned, the surge within him taking complete control of all of his emotions at last.

'Aargh!' He cried out through clenched teeth, his fingernails digging into the soft flesh of his nubile lover. His moans of orgasm were matched by her own as she came suddenly. The sounds of Stuart and the other twin engaged in their own noisy release filled his ears as he pumped heavily in and out of the heavenly sheath, and the silky lips of her pussy appeared to suckle his thick stalk as he filled her with his jetting cream. His cock throbbed continually and the searing, surging ache within his loins tore at his every nerve-ending, his vision clouded with the intensity of the moment.

His movements slowed and the feelings subsided. Then, to his delight, he felt the now familiar second surge of orgasm building up within his loins. His thick cock was swelling to massive proportions inside her. He thrust wildly in and out of her, pumping his stalk as hard as he could and thrilling as she cried out once more. Suddenly, she pulled herself from him and fell to her knees, grasping his cock and stuffing it quickly into her mouth. He groaned loudly as jet after jet of thick, creamy fluid flooded to the back of her throat as she pumped his throbbing erection with both of her small hands.

Eventually, the tenderness that inevitably follows a perfect orgasm took hold of him and he fell back, exhausted. Stuart dragged himself stiffly from the floor and sat next to him on the bench, the two men breathing rapidly as the beautiful twins stood before them smiling in apparent triumph.

'Now for the ultimate release!' said one of the girls, her eyes shining with lust. Alex groaned inwardly, glancing at Stuart. They had no more to give. He looked back at the girls and for a moment his heart stopped. Their innocent, albeit lustful, expressions had disappeared. They grinned malevolently, their full lips drawn back and their gleaming white teeth bared. Alex jumped to his feet in horror and Stuart made a dive for the door. The heavy iron crashed closed as though sealing their fate. Alex shrank back, pressing his body against the cold, stone wall as his twin approached him, her eyes filled with evil. Her mouth was open and saliva dripped from the sharp fangs.

'Stop!' The voice was strong, roaring from outside the cell. The girls swung round fearfully as the door was flung open, revealing the unmistakable figure of the baron himself. The huge man stood impassively as the twins scurried out like frightened rats into the darkness of the passageway. Alex swallowed hard, angry that they had so easily been duped and terrified for his life.

Mansola turned his evil face towards them, his teeth bared in a leering grin. 'So,' he boomed, 'you come in search of your unfortunate colleague. She is lost to you, as

187

you will witness tonight when she faces the rigours of the pit of Mansola!'

With that, he swept from the cell, the door crashing shut behind him. The clatter of a new padlock being fitted to its clasp resounded around the room, confirming the hopelessness of their situation.

'I thought vampires only came out at night.' Stuart's voice echoed in the two prisoners' dark solitude. Alex flicked the torch into life. The battery was fading; the light dim.

'Obviously they are safe down here,' he replied. 'Those old horror films have a lot to answer for.'

'What d'you think he meant by "the pit"?'

Alex shrugged. 'God alone knows,' he said, quietly. They sat in morose silence for some minutes. Suddenly, the now familiar clatter of the padlock reverberated around the cell. Alex stood up, his heart pounding. The door swung open and two hooded men entered swiftly, roughly grabbing Stuart and deftly fixing manacles and chains to his wrists. Alex glanced at the door but they were too quick for him and the brief possibility of escape was snatched from him before he could collect his thoughts. His wrists were quickly shackled and the two struggling captives were dragged into the passageway like slaves bound for transportation.

The long corridor was illuminated by flaming torches and the grim rock glistened with dampness. The hooded men tugged at the chains, forcing them to walk quickly. Their legs were still weak from their earlier excesses with the vampire twins.

Presently, they came to another iron door, larger than the others and set in the very core of the rock. Slowly, one of their captors dragged the heavy barrier ajar and they were ushered through.

Once inside, they found themselves in a huge, cavernous space illuminated by thousands of black candles. The sheer walls rose far above them into the blackness. Ahead of them, at the foot of a short but steep flight of steps, the floor opened suddenly into a chasm, well over fifty feet in depth. Its floor was covered by sharply-spiked stalagmites, offering a lethal bed to any hapless individual who should fall into the gruesome pit. At the centre of the chasm was a tall pinnacle of rock, the surface of which was flat and approximately ten feet in diameter. On this had been placed a large, circular table of heavy oak to which were attached numerous straps and shackles. A long, raised bridge, held by an intricate system of chains and pulleys, was held suspended near to where they stood, clearly the only access to the central column of rock.

Alex and Stuart were pushed unceremoniously down the steps and made to sit at the edge of the pit, their manacles swiftly chained and secured to iron clasps set in the stone. Alex tugged vainly at the unyielding irons. The rough metal of the manacles around his wrists dug painfully into his flesh. All they could do was wait.

After what seemed an eternity the door swung open again and more robed men entered. There were twelve in all, and their faces were completely hidden by their hoods. They marched in procession around the perimeter of the pit and circled it twice before standing silently at the edge, their heads bowed as if in prayer.

'I don't like the look of this,' whispered Stuart. A hefty kick in his back from one of the guards precluded any further comment.

The door opened for a third time and the baron entered. The hooded men immediately fell to their knees in cowering deference. He stood for a moment, his long black cloak billowing gently in the slight breeze that appeared to emanate from the pit itself. He surveyed the scene before him. Apparently satisfied, he turned and held out his hand. Alex gasped as Sarah entered – naked and as beautiful as ever. Her face was heavily made up and her long, blonde hair was tied up above her head, accenting her regal features. A thick, metal clasp encircled her neck, to which was attached a long chain which the baron grasped. He pulled her behind him like a pet animal as he walked towards the bridge.

Alex tried again to force his wrists free of the severe grip

189

of his bonds, but knew that it was useless. Whatever nameless fate awaited his lover, he could do nothing but sit and
watch. He caught her gaze as she stood by the baron but
her eyes were empty, as though hypnotised. He cursed his
earlier stupidity, his heart aching.

Mansola clapped his hands sharply and one of the
hooded men leapt forward immediately and began to
wrench at the heavy chains that secured the bridge. The
massive frame slowly lowered into position. Once the span
was secured he bowed low and scuttled back to kneel with
his colleagues at the edge of the pit. The baron pulled the
long chain that was fixed to Sarah's neck and tugged it
roughly, leading her as she seemed to drift in a dream-like
state across the narrow bridge to the centre. Once there, he
stooped and took her in his massive arms. He then lifted
her bodily on to the table, laying her across it on her back.
He pulled her arm above her head and secured it to one of
the straps. Then, heaving the frame of the huge table, he
moved the entire surface around on its pivot. He fixed her
other wrist to a second strap then rotated the table again,
securing both of her ankles so that her legs were spread
wide apart. Her sex was displayed for all to see in the most
blatant manner.

Turning the table again, he checked all the bonds and
having satisfied himself that she was securely tied walked
back over the bridge to stand at the side of the pit. He then
raised his arms high above his head.

'The pit of Mansola!' he bellowed. 'The final initiation
of a mortal into the arms of the vampires!' He directed his
gaze towards Alex and Stuart. 'Watch, and understand,' he
growled, his leering expression filling Alex with disgust.
'Your beloved Sarah will be willingly impaled by the twelve
leaders of the brood, they who kneel before me now. She
is fully aware of what is to happen to her and delights in
the thought. Is that not so, my dear?'

'Yes.' The word came weakly from Sarah's mouth, her
eyes now wide with lust.

The baron grinned. 'Already, she has become insatiable
like your consorts, Demonia and Sinitia. Her needs will

hardly be met, even by the twelve. When they have finished I will take her and with the thirteenth intrusion of her lovely body her soul will be mine and the ceremony will be complete.'

'You evil monster!' yelled Alex, his body shaking with anger. Mansola merely laughed.

'Your turn will come, my friend,' he said, 'and you will find the male initiation far less pleasant.'

'Isn't there something we can do?' hissed Stuart.

'What, for Christ's sake?' shouted Alex, glaring at the student angrily.

'I don't know! We can't just let it happen!'

Alex didn't reply, turning to look again at the lovely image of his lover lying spread-eagled across the table, her expression clearly indicating her eagerness for the initiation to begin. Her hips moved up and down rhythmically, as though she were already engaged in an act of copulation. Her large breasts heaved, her nipples sharply erect.

The baron nodded to the kneeling group and the first man stood, walking slowly to the bridge. He drew his long robe back over his shoulders, revealing his naked body, and his long cock jutted forward as he approached the supine form on the table. Sarah's breathing became heavier and the thrusting movements of her hips more pronounced as the man joined her on the table and knelt between her wide open legs.

There was no kiss or caress and no words as he pushed his thick stalk towards her, the glinting wetness of her sex lips in the flickering candlelight a testament to her extreme arousal. She groaned with pleasure as he entered her in one slow push, until his long cock filled her to the hilt. Alex felt his own erection rising as he watched her enjoying the steady, pounding thrusts. Her hips rose from the table to meet the incessant driving movements of her unknown lover. There was no finesse, no technique; just a hard, solid fuck. From his vantage point Alex could see every detail of the long, gnarled shaft sliding in and out of Sarah's soaked pussy. Her moans of ecstasy filled his ears.

He heard the familiar sound of her cries of orgasm and

191

the man threw back his head as he joined her in blissful release. His hood fell from his head to reveal his handsome, young features. Alex's cock throbbed, a thin trail of semen slipping down the long shaft. He desperately wanted to grab his stalk and rub it hard to join his lover in her delight but his bonds denied him such a pleasure. Instead, he could merely watch as the man withdrew his drooping phallus from Sarah's wet pussy and walked silently back over the bridge, his place quickly taken by a second, hooded figure.

Once again, the actions were the same, as though rehearsed. The cloak was thrown back, the thick stalk driven quickly into Sarah's open sex lips, and her groans of delight were constant as he fucked her mercilessly until he filled her with his seed.

So the procession continued, until all twelve of the hooded figures had sated themselves within her ever more demanding body. Not a word was spoken throughout, the only sounds being Sarah's cries of pleasure each time she came and the occasional groans from her nameless lovers.

When the last one had filled her and withdrawn his flaccid cock from her ravaged pussy there was a long silence and a quiet expectancy. Sarah lay still, panting heavily. Semen seeped from her open sex lips – a sight so erotic that Alex felt he would explode. He looked across at Stuart. The young man's cock lay limply on his thigh, his stomach wet with evidence of his release. Alex felt a twinge of envy but his stalk remained stiff and erect. His desire to orgasm tore at his loins.

'And now, the thirteenth.' The baron spoke in a grave, ceremonious tone as he withdrew his robe to reveal his massive, naked body and his huge cock. He walked slowly across the bridge, his phallus swinging menacingly, until he stood at the table. He gazed down at her submissive form, her hips once more moving up and down in brazen invitation. He knelt and pressed his mouth to her pussy and drank from her sweet chalice. Sarah groaned and thrust her mound against him, his tongue darting in and out of her rapidly. Then he drew back, gripping his thick stalk like a weapon.

'Are you ready, Sarah?' he boomed. 'Ready to join the brood?'

'Yes, oh yes,' she whimpered. 'Take me. Sink your massive shaft within my body!'

The baron knelt on the table and aimed the huge head of his immense phallus at her cunt. Alex looked away.

'Stop!' The word was screamed from behind him. He swung his head round and saw a young man standing at the door with a large crucifix clasped in his raised hands. 'Stop this carnage and be damned, foul entity!'

The baron jumped from the table and turned in the direction of the newcomer, his cock still fearsomely erect and his face twisted in vehement anger. 'What is this?' he roared. 'You dare to defile the inner sanctum? You will die for this!'

'Not I,' continued the young man, walking slowly forward with the cross held high before him. Alex could see that he was trembling and clearly terrified.

'Colin, please, no!' shouted Sarah from the table, recognising the intruder immediately. 'I want him; I *need* him!'

'I know you, Mansola,' said Colin, ignoring her pleas. 'This cross has been blessed by the Lord High Exorcist himself! You cannot resist!'

Mansola lunged forward and ran across the bridge towards the quaking figure. Colin stood his ground and the baron stopped just feet away from him. There was a long pause as their eyes met. Neither gave way until suddenly, the baron turned. Flinging his cloak around his nakedness, he stormed out of the room, contemptuously shoving the slight figure of the young man to one side. The other figures followed immediately, Colin proffering the crucifix towards them as they scurried past.

Then there was silence, save for the sound of Sarah weeping quietly. Colin set down the cross and unfastened the shackles that held Alex and Stuart.

'How did you know?' asked Alex as he rubbed his aching wrists.

'I knew you would come here eventually,' said the young man. 'It was just a matter of time. I knew of your relationship

193

with Sarah, and that you were probably involved with the vampires. I simply had to follow you, until you led me to their lair.'

He walked over the bridge and gazed down at the sobbing figure lying on the table. 'I was nearly too late,' he said, beginning to untie her bonds.

'I wanted to be with them,' she wailed. 'Why did you stop them?'

'I have learned much since I last saw you,' he said quietly. 'I believe you spoke the truth about Demonia and the others. But the power of Mansola is great; he has bewitched you. Come, let us leave this place. Let me return you to your sisters.'

Sarah climbed stiffly from the table, clutching his arm for support. 'You will not harm them?' she asked, her expression fearful. Colin shook his head.

'No, I was wrong. But I believe I can help them in their quest to rid the world of this evil.' He led her carefully over the bridge and Alex immediately took her into his arms, hugging her sweat-soaked body and feeling her wetness against his groin.

'I need sex so badly, Alex,' she whimpered, her body trembling. 'Even after all that, I need it so much.'

Alex kissed her lightly on the cheek, the desire to impale her there and then with his rigid stalk tearing at his emotions.

'Not here,' he whispered. 'Let's get back to Gallows Hill.'

The power of the blessed crucifix was indeed very strong. The passageways remained silent and empty as Alex and Stuart quickly retrieved their clothing. Sarah covered her nakedness with a discarded robe, then they hurried up the long flight of steps, through the hallway and out into the open. They all filled their lungs with the welcome scent of fresh air and the afternoon sun bathed them with its agreeable warmth.

'Don't drive too fast,' said Colin as he clambered on to his ancient motor scooter. 'I don't want to lose you.'

Alex helped Sarah into the back of his car, sliding in beside her. Stuart positioned himself at the wheel and started the powerful engine. 'D'you think we can trust him?' he asked, as he moved the vehicle into the narrow, winding lane that led away from the grim mansion.

'I don't see that we have much choice,' replied Alex, slipping his arm around Sarah's shoulders. She smiled at him sweetly, her face flushed from her recent experiences. He looked out of the rear window to see Colin struggling along behind them, clouds of acrid smoke billowing from the exhaust of his bike. No, he thought, no choice at all.

He felt Sarah's hand slip to his groin, her fingers delicately stroking the bulge in his trousers. His cock began to stiffen immediately. 'Fuck me, Alex,' she breathed, squeezing his thickening length. 'Please.'

He didn't need to be asked a second time. Quickly unzipping himself, he dragged his pants down to his knees as Sarah lay back on the wide seat, opening the front of her robe to reveal her sumptuous, naked body. He swallowed hard; she looked even more beautiful than ever. Her large breasts were rising and falling heavily and her pussy was wet with her juices and those of her many lovers. The sight filled him with an intense, erotic desire.

Alex moved forward and pressed the thick, swollen end of his rigid stalk against her soft sex lips, his stiffness sinking quickly between them until their groins met. Her incredible wetness served only to heighten his arousal as he pumped steadily, kissing her mouth passionately and pinching her nipples between his fingers. He knew that he wouldn't be able to last long – the memories of the sights that he had just witnessed made it impossible for him to hold back. With a groan he came, his seed jetting deep inside his lover. Her quiet sighs indicated that she had shared his joy.

'You are one of us, Sarah,' said Demonia, with more than a hint of pleasure in her voice. 'Now that you have lain with the baron, your fate is sealed. Are you unhappy?'

Sarah shook her head, snuggling close to Alex on the sofa. 'No,' she said, 'I had already decided to join you.'

'Beware that you do not allow him to touch you again,' continued Demonia, 'or you will yearn for blood, as well as sex.'

'I understand.'

Demonia smiled warmly, then turned to regard Colin, who was sitting rather nervously on a chair at her side. 'And you, Colin, how is it that you have changed your mind, when you told Sarah that you intended to stake us all?'

'It was the book. The notes written by Doctor Tankard's ancestor, the old professor. I searched through Sarah's desk, mainly to try and find out where this place of yours was, and I came across them. I've studied other pieces of the professor's works before as part of my research, so I knew he was telling the truth.'

'You realise that, in making love to Sarah you are destined to become one of us yourself, should you so choose?'

Colin nodded. 'I do, and I intend to join you.'

Demonia looked at him in surprise. 'You seem very certain,' she said, imperiously.

'I have always felt that it was my destiny,' he replied simply.

The door to the sitting-room opened and Karen entered, closely followed by Belinda and Andrew. 'Hi everybody,' said Karen with customary cheerfulness. 'Ooh, who's this?' She walked over to Colin, resting her hand on his shoulder.

'This is Colin, a new member of our group,' said Alex.

Karen looked shocked. 'Colin? But I thought . . .'

'He has seen the error of his ways,' said Demonia. 'Come, tell us what you've been doing these past days. The party is becoming too sombre.'

Karen sat down, her grin broad. 'I've had a fantastic time,' she said, with marked enthusiasm. 'I think I've done more screwing since I last saw you than in the rest of my life!'

'Tell us about it,' said Demonia, clearly warming to the idea.

Karen giggled girlishly. 'Do you want all the gory details?'

196

'Everything,' said Demonia, sitting back in her armchair. 'And then perhaps Belinda and Andrew can cheer us with their tales.'

'OK then. As Doctor Tankard and the others already know, I'm the cox for the university's rowing eight.' She stopped, noticing Demonia and Sinitia's puzzled expressions. 'It's a team sport, you know, rowing a boat up and down the river.'

'Go on,' said Demonia. 'Please excuse our ignorance of such matters.'

'Well,' continued Karen, gleefully getting into her stride, 'I think they picked me because I'm so small as well as being very fit. I joined because the team are eight of the most gorgeous, hunky men on the campus. One of them, Ron his name is, is a divine piece of male flesh, and I've wanted to get into his pants for ages. He's got a hell of a reputation with the girls, and I thought he'd be ideal for our little group.

'I decided to make a play for him after training. Things didn't work out quite like I intended, though. The session had been particularly good and the lads decided that they would celebrate by going to a nearby pub for a quick pint. I knew that once they'd started drinking they wouldn't stop, and then Ron would be no use to me or anybody else. I could never understand that with blokes; after a few drinks I'm game for anything, but guys seem to lose interest or, at least, the ability to perform. I didn't want a quick, drunken screw in the car park; that's not for me. It was now or never.

'The opportunity came all of a sudden. Ron suddenly announced that he wanted to have a quick shower before joining them for a drink, and went off to the changing-rooms. The others set off for the pub while I pretended to be adjusting various pieces of equipment. Once they were out of sight I followed Ron to the changing-rooms.

'I could hear the water spraying from outside. I waited a moment, to be certain that he was in the shower, then slipped quietly into the hut. I could hear Ron singing tunelessly from the showers, and could make out the shape

197

of his lovely, muscular body through the steamed-up glass. I pulled my clothing off quickly, chucked it on to a bench and opened the door to the shower.

'The steam billowed out. There were about six shower-heads in a row. Ron was standing at the furthest end with his back to me, soaping his legs, and the sight of him rubbing the soap over his lovely, tanned thighs made my pussy twitch. He's got the most delectable arse – tight, firm buttocks with a line of thick, black hair running along the cleft between them. Lovely.'

Karen paused and licked her lips, her eyes glazing with the memory. 'Go on,' said Demonia impatiently, her hand snaking under the folds of her dress to fondle herself. 'What happened next?'

Karen blinked. 'Oh, sorry,' she chuckled, 'I was just thinking about his lovely bum. If there's one thing about a bloke that will make me drool, it's a nice, tight little bottom. Anyway, I turned the tap of the shower at the other end of the line and stood under the stream, taking up a small piece of wet soap and beginning to nonchalantly smear it over my breasts. Ron turned suddenly, realising at last that he was not alone. "Karen," he stuttered, "I . . . er . . .." I grinned at him and carried on soaping myself, as if it were the most natural thing in the world to do. I looked pointedly at his body, examining his superb, muscular shape and the thick, matted hair that covered his broad chest before running in a thin line over his stomach to his crotch. I glanced down, seeing his prick hanging heavily between his legs, covered in soap. I looked up at his face, grinning again, then let my eyes travel slowly down once more until my gaze became fixed on the bush of hair between his legs, his cock visibly stiffening. "You don't mind, do you?" I said. "Only I wanted to shower before I went to the pub."

'He shook his head, nervously starting to wash himself again. I looked away and rubbed the soap over my stomach, smoothing the thick cream over my flesh sensuously before slipping the slimy bar down to my crotch and working it slowly around my hairless sex-flesh. I didn't need the water from the shower; my pussy was already soaked, and the soap was bubbling between my legs.

'I turned and glanced again at Ron, seeing him look quickly away as though afraid that I might catch him watching me. I wanted to rush over to him and grab him, forcing him to fuck me there and then, but I was enjoying the game. I turned my back to him and pretended to drop the soap. Spreading my legs but keeping them held stiff and straight I bent over at the waist to retrieve it, giving him a perfect view of my naked bum. I knew that he'd be looking at me, seeing the soapy, open lips of my shaven pussy and wanting to ram his thick cock up me. I let the soap slip out of my hands a couple of times, ensuring that he had a good look, then stood up again, turning slowly.

'This time he didn't look away. His cock was sticking out like a flagpole, a monster with a thick, heavily ridged head. His eyes darted about nervously. "Wash my back, Ron," I said, seductively. He moved over to me and took the cake of soap from me. I tried not to look at his cock, jutting out in front of him, my eyes firmly fixed on his while I fought the temptation to reach out and grab the object of my desire. I turned my back to him, looking over my shoulder as he cautiously began to soap me, running his strong hands over my flesh, the leathery touch of his palms sending shivers down my spine.

'He concentrated on my shoulders at first, then ran his hands down, massaging my back smoothly. "Don't forget my bottom," I said. He didn't need asking twice. He cupped my buttocks immediately, rubbing the soap over them thickly. He put down the bar and smoothed the cream over my bottom slowly, moving closer so that the tip of his prick touched my back. I rotated my hips slightly, letting him know the effect that he was having on me.

'That was the only signal he needed. He slipped the fingers of one hand between my buttocks, running the tips up and down along the cleft. I shivered and groaned, arching my back slightly and pushing my bum out, almost coming when I felt a fingertip touch the little hole. He slid his other hand around my body to my stomach, then down, agonisingly slowly, to my crotch. The shower sprayed warmly over our bodies, streams of soapy water running erotically over my breasts, down, over my stomach to his hand as he gently wormed his fingers inside the soaked lips of my cunt. I reached behind me and gripped his thick shaft as he slipped a finger inside my bottom, the sensation making me shudder with delight.

'I leant my head back and our mouths met. I kissed him awkwardly as he slipped his fingers in and out of my two holes, my hand slithering over the soapy wetness of his cock. He managed to work four fingers inside my pussy now, and at least two in my bottom. I needed him badly. I turned my body to face his and kissed his chest, then slid my tongue down his body as his fingers slipped from me. I crouched in front of him, took hold of his thick stalk with both hands and pumped it rapidly. I opened my mouth and took him inside, feeling the shaft throb between my lips and tasting his delicious saltiness. I looked up at him, his cock still held deep in my mouth, and began to bob my head back and forward. I was rubbing his thick stem between the palms of my hands, and running my tongue round and round his huge knob. He rested his hands on my head and moved his hips, fucking my face, his breathing heavy.

'I managed to only get about half of his length inside my mouth, my hand quickly rubbing the other four or five inches and the fingers of my other hand gently caressing him between his buttocks. I began to worry that he would come before he tasted me, and before I'd had the fucking I so desperately needed, so I pulled from him and stood up, my face barely level with his muscular chest. I licked and sucked his nipples in turn, my hands gripping his cock tightly.

'Ron slipped his hands around my waist and lifted me bodily from the floor. I wrapped my arms around his shoulders and my legs about his waist, kissing his mouth passionately as I sensed him positioning his lovely dick to enter me. He lowered me slowly, his thick shaft slipping effortlessly into my soaking wet pussy, filling me completely. He gripped my bottom and we humped against each other, our bodies soaked by the constant stream of warm water from the shower. Then he started to lift me up and force me down rapidly, hammering my small body on to his huge shaft like I was a rag doll.

'We heard noises, but we didn't care. I guessed that someone had come in to shower; boy, were they in for a surprise! Ron pushed me against the wall, pressing my back against the cool tiles and thrust wildly in and out of me, my heels digging into his backside, my fingernails clawing at the back of his neck.

'The door to the shower opened and two naked figures entered – two more of the crew. There were more noises from the changing-room. The whole damn bunch of them were there! Either they'd changed their minds about the pub or more likely I'd been set up. Needless to say, I didn't mind.

'Both of them quickly sported marvellous erections, and I knew that Ron wasn't going to be the only new member of our little group. One of them, Pete I think his name is, came to the side of us and turned my face towards his, kissing me on the mouth, his hand cupping my breast. Ron carried on as though nothing untoward had happened, pumping heavily into me as the other guy, Joe, slipped his hand under my bum. I came with an explosion of sensations as I felt him slide a finger into my soapy little hole. Ron's superb length swelled inside me as he fucked me violently until he groaned loudly as he filled my pussy with his creamy seed.

'I remember sobbing as I bit into his shoulder; feeling the incessant throbbing of his cock deep within me, Joe pushing his finger rapidly in and out of my tight little arse, Pete now sucking and nibbling my nipple. Gradually, I was allowed to put my feet on the floor and Ron's cock slipped from inside me and hung heavily between his legs. I knelt down and took it in my mouth, tenderly licking and sucking the wilting stem.

'Somebody turned off the shower, and Joe and Pete lifted me by my arms, carrying me triumphantly out of the

201

shower into the changing-room. As I had suspected, the other five members of the team were there, all naked. A cheer went up as Joe and Pete carried me in like some sort of willing sacrifice. I don't think I've ever felt so horny in my life, knowing what was likely to happen to me.

'The men moved over to us, their hands roaming over my wet nakedness, fondling every part of my body. Fingers were slipped into my pussy and my bottom, hands groped my breasts as I was held there, powerless to resist their every demand. I reached out with both hands, clutching an erect cock in each, rubbing them vigorously.

'At last I was set down on my feet. I stood still for a moment, taking in the scene before me. Eight, gorgeously athletic young men, all fully naked and all but one hard and ready. Only Ron was drooping slightly, although even his cock was already beginning to show signs of recovery.

'Joe lay on a bench on his back, holding his cock erect; his intentions clear. I walked over to him and spread my legs across him, lowering my little body until I felt his stalk slide into me. I sat down on him, taking every inch while leaning forward, holding on to his shoulders with my hands. I felt an unmistakable pressure against my anus and relaxed myself. A lovely, thick shaft slipped into my bottom easily, the constant probing of God knows how many fingers before making me more than ready.

'Almost immediately, Pete positioned himself in front of me, his lovely cock jutting out towards my face. I opened my mouth and let him push it between my lips, sucking on him greedily as he moved back and forth, slipping his long, hard flesh in and out. Another guy moved to stand next to him, shuffling Pete to one side so that I could take both pricks in my mouth while my nether regions were pummelled mercilessly.

'I heard the chap behind me groan and felt his cock throbbing in my bottom, filling me with his seed. The next moment Pete cried out, his sperm gushing to the back of my throat. I swallowed hard, my actions stimulating the other guy to instant orgasm, and their combined ejaculations filled my mouth with delicious cream.

'I felt the softening erection being pulled from my bum,

only to be replaced by a longer, thicker shaft plunging deep into me. He hardly moved at all before withdrawing again and jets of hot, thick fluids streaked across my back. Again, another thick stalk plundered my tight little orifice, Ron now standing before me and offering his huge tool to my mouth, the thick stem as hard as ever. I sucked him in greedily, my mouth stretched by his massive girth. I was in heaven.

'All the time, Joe pumped up into me, his staying power amazing. I began to wonder if he'd ever come. I got my answer when he suddenly arched his back, thrusting his cock into me as far as it would go, the shaft throbbing heavily. I came with him, an earth-shattering climax that made me cry out loudly, my shout muffled by the huge dick in my mouth. The guy behind me started to hammer his wonderfully hard stalk into my bum until he groaned and came, his fingernails gripping my buttocks painfully, his crotch grinding against them as he tried to force more and more of his length into me.

'Ron was not to be outdone. With a quiet moan he began to throb between my lips, his luscious juices jetting into my throat. I held his seed within my mouth when he pulled from me, then pushed it out with my tongue, soaking my chin, offering him a sight that I knew would fill his dreams for years to come.

'I sat quietly on the bench, the men sitting or lying around me, exhausted. It had been fun, but they had still not tasted me, and I knew that was essential if they were to become members of our group. After a few moments I suggested that they lick me, each in turn, so that I could judge who was the best oral lover. They readily agreed, despite their tiredness, and one by one they took their positions at my feet, their tongues lapping at my poor, ravaged pussy, little knowing that their fates were sealed.'

'Oh, oh!' All eyes of the occupants of the sitting-room turned in the direction of the sounds, seeing Sarah, her face flushed with arousal and embarrassment. 'I'm sorry,' she said breathlessly, 'I've just come. That was quite a story!'

'I'm nearly there myself,' said Andrew, patting the huge erection displayed through the tight material of his jeans.

'Oh, don't waste that,' cooed Demonia. 'Come and sit by me and let me pleasure you while we listen to Belinda's story.'

Andrew rose willingly, carrying his chair and placing it next to hers. Demonia immediately unzipped him as he sat down, taking hold of his monstrous stalk and gently rubbing the long, thick shaft.

'Oh no!' moaned Andrew, his sperm suddenly jetting up into the air and spraying over his jeans.

'What a pity,' said Demonia, smoothing the cream over the end of his throbbing cock. 'Still, I'm sure that once Belinda's tale has been told it will rise again.'

Belinda stood up, her skin-tight jeans and flimsy sweater doing little to hide the perfection of her voluptuous, young body. Her breasts bounced hugely as she took her seat in the centre of the group, her nipples visibly erect through the thin cotton. Alex felt his mouth go dry. His cock stood firmly erect within his trousers as a result of Karen's story; he wasn't sure how much of Belinda's account he would be able to hear before nature would take its course.

'My story's a little more straightforward,' began Belinda, 'but no less exciting, as I think you'll agree. I'd seen an advertisement for a singles group, you know, where people who are unmarried or divorced get together, and I'd heard that these things usually ended up in orgies, so I decided to give it a try.

'When I telephoned the bloke who was running things – a chap called Jeff – he told me that they were having a party that night, so it looked as though my luck was in. Then he asked me my age. When I told him, he seemed shocked, saying that most of the members of the group were much older, and did I mind? I said not, although I began to worry just how old they might be, as Demonia had made it clear that we need strong, able people to join us.

'Nevertheless, I agreed to go along. To be honest, I found the idea of joining in with a bunch of bonking strangers quite a turn-on! When I arrived at the house, however, I began to wonder what I'd let myself in for. Everyone was fully dressed – and very smartly – and sitting around the lounge of this big house holding glasses of wine and making small-talk. It was more like a vicarage tea party than what I'd hoped for.

'Because of Jeff's reaction when I told him my age I'd gone there dressed rather like a precocious teenager with a tight, knitted sweater over my braless breasts, the roughness of the material causing my nipples to jut out, a very short, pleated mini-kilt and knee-length, white socks. I hadn't bothered to put any knickers on, believing that they'd soon be wrenched off anyway.

'There were a few perceptible looks of admiration from the men as I sat down in an armchair, carefully crossing my legs so as not to reveal too much, at least not yet. Jeff handed me a glass of wine. "This is our newest member, Belinda," he said, beaming with pride as though he had created me himself.

'One of the women looked at me quizzically. "You're very young," she said petulantly. "Are you sure you've come to the right place?" I told her I was, although I was beginning to have my doubts.

'Jeff sat on the arm of my chair, resting his hand nervously on my shoulder. When I didn't shrug him off he became bolder, slipping his arm around me and stroking the side of my breast as he chatted aimlessly with the others. I looked around the room. There were a couple of people in their fifties but generally the age range wasn't too bad: thirty to fortyish, I suppose. There were about twenty in all, none of them what I'd call bad-looking, so I decided to stay and see if things progressed.

'I uncrossed my legs, ensuring a chap sitting opposite me got a good view of my naked pussy, then crossed them again. I saw him lick his lips and I smiled at him. He looked away in embarrassment. I shrugged and sipped my wine, the acrid taste of cheap plonk making me wince.

'Still the incessant chatter went on; I found myself looking at the clock, willing the hands to move quickly around the dial, to bring an end to this torture. Jeff's hand remained against the side of my breast, unmoving. I was beginning to feel desperately randy, but nobody seemed to be taking much interest.

'Jeff leant over me to whisper in my ear. "There's a rule in this club," he said. "New members have to go to bed with the host." I glared at him, annoyed at the crassness of his approach. He looked mortified. He was quite good-looking, actually, a sort of city-gent type. I let my expression soften. "I'm sorry," he said. "Bad joke."

'I smiled as sweetly as I could. "I didn't think it was a joke," I lied. "I was just wondering what the others would say if we disappeared to a bedroom." He laughed nervously, leaning further forward and pushing his hand around me to cup my breast. I lay my head back and closed my eyes, my lips parted in invitation. He kissed me, his tongue delving into my mouth, playing against my own. I uncrossed my legs again, letting them fall slightly apart, knowing that twenty pairs of eyes would be able to see my hairy little pussy.

'"Look at that!" It was the woman who had chided me for being so young who spoke. "They'll be doing it on the carpet in a minute."

'I looked at my host and grinned. "I don't mind if you don't," I teased. His eyes widened. Obviously nothing like this had happened before at these so-called parties.

'Another woman spoke up. "She's got no knickers on! Look, you can see everything!" I was past caring. They could throw me out if they wanted to. I reached up and slipped my arm around Jeff's neck, pulling his face to mine and kissing him passionately. He moved his free hand to my other breast, cupping them both and kneading them with his fingers.

'"Go on," said a male voice, "fuck her, Jeff. She looks like she needs it!" Still Jeff refused to move from his perch on the arm of the chair. I'd had enough of the formalities. I pushed him off and stood up, surveying the faces of the group before me. A couple of the women frowned, but the men all gazed at me excitedly, willing me to go further. I wasn't about to disappoint them.

'I reached and caught hold of the hem of my jumper,

quickly pulling it over my head, letting my big breasts spring free to gasps of admiration from the throats of most of the crowd. I caught hold of the clasp on my mini-kilt and held still for a moment, looking at their faces, making them wait. They wanted to see more, that was obvious.

'Slowly and teasingly I unzipped the skirt and let it fall down my legs to the floor, stepping out of it and standing wearing nothing but my white socks and little black shoes. "Jeff told me that new club members have to do this," I lied. "I expect that you've all done it, so I suppose that I must."

'"You don't have to if you don't want to, my dear," said a female voice. I looked in the direction of the sound through the sea of admiring faces.

'"But I want to," I said, reaching out and taking Jeff by the hand. He stood awkwardly, looking about him in almost shamed embarrassment. I knelt at his feet, unzipping his trousers slowly. He stood there lamely, not knowing what to do or say. I tugged down the front of his underpants and drew out his small, but very erect cock, putting it straight to my mouth. He came the moment that I started to suck him, his legs trembling with the effort. I swallowed hard, the warm taste of his seed awakening every nerve in my body.

'Jeff staggered back to his seat, leaving me alone in the middle of the carpet. I looked nervously around me, wiping my mouth on the back of my hand, wondering if I'd gone too far. The atmosphere was electric. "God, Jeff," shouted the chap who was sitting directly opposite me, "she needs more than that!" He stood up, wrenching his trousers and pants down to his knees, his cock springing up before him. I lay back gratefully, opening my legs wide. He was much older than Jeff, a real company director if ever I saw one. He was very distinguished but at that moment looked slightly ridiculous as he knelt between my splayed legs, his big cock jutting forward.

'He pushed himself on to me, his body heavy as his stalk slid into my aching little pussy. I looked to one side, seeing the woman who had disapproved of me so much swiftly unbuttoning her blouse and pulling it from her shoulders, revealing the biggest pair of tits I'd ever seen. Almost immediately, a guy sitting next to her grabbed one of the huge mounds and put it to his mouth, sucking her long nipple like a baby. Another man did the same to her other breast, both of them pushing their hands up her skirt, shifting the material up to reveal her stockings and suspenders.

'The guy who was fucking me pulled out suddenly and turned his body, crouching over me on his hands and knees, his long cock hanging inches from my mouth, his face quickly burying itself between my legs. I groaned as his mouth touched my pussy, his tongue rapidly licking around the sodden lips before concentrating on my throbbing clit. I took hold of his thick stem and drew it into my mouth, swallowing the full length down my throat, arching my neck so that I could continue to breathe. I swallowed continuously, knowing that the movements of my throat muscles would be giving him the most wonderful of sensations, my tongue lapping back and forth across his hard stalk. I raised my hips, pressing my mound to his mouth and came, a gut-wrenching orgasm that tore at my upper thighs, shockwaves of pleasure shooting down my legs. The heavy throbbing of his cock within the sheath of my throat told me that he had shared my delight.

'Presently, my lover struggled wearily from me to sit on the floor with his back resting on the sofa. I looked around me. The big-breasted woman was on her knees on the floor, some guy pumping into her from behind, another bloke feeding her mouth with his cock. Everywhere, people were getting into it, sucking, licking and fucking. The party was getting started at last.

'I noticed a handsome, but rather shy-looking young man sitting awkwardly on a chair in the corner of the room. I picked myself up from the floor and walked over to him, stepping over numerous, writhing bodies on the way. "Hello," I said, "are you not enjoying yourself?"

' "Er, yes," he said, nervously looking over my shoulder. I turned my head.

' "That's my son," said the big-breasted woman, taking

the cock from her mouth for a moment. "He's not used to seeing his mother behaving like this. Go on, Clive, you know you fancy her."

'I turned back to look at Clive and smiled again, taking his hand in mine. "Do you fancy me, Clive?" I asked. The young man nodded. "Well then," I said, pulling him to his feet, "do you want to do it here, or would you rather go somewhere else?"

'He looked across at his mother, who had happily returned to her pleasurable tasks. "Can we go somewhere?" he asked quietly. "It's a bit difficult."

'I led him through the myriad of copulating bodies and out into the hallway. Once the door was shut I wrapped my arms around him, pressing my naked body to him and kissed him fully on the mouth. He barely responded, his arms hanging limply at his sides. "What's the matter, Clive, don't you like me?"

'He looked anxious. "Yes, I *do* like you," he said. "It's just . . ."

' "Is this your first time?" He nodded, hanging his head shamefully. "Don't worry," I said, "I'll be very gentle with you." He didn't seem to get the joke. I took his hand and pulled him behind me up the stairs, thrilling to the idea of making love with a virgin for the first time in my life.

'We entered one of the bedrooms, finding the big bed covered with coats. I heaved the various garments in a big pile on to the floor then lay on the bed, my legs wide open, my finger slipping along the length of my open pussy lips. Clive just stood there like an idiot. "Undress, Clive," I breathed. "I want you to fuck me."

'He began by nervously unbuttoning his shirt until at long last he stood naked at the foot of the bed. His cock stood fearsomely erect, the near-purple head pressed against his stomach. I patted the mattress, indicating that he should join me. He walked slowly around the bed, his cock barely moving, so full was his erection. I worried that he would come before he could get it up me, and I certainly needed to feel that wonderful stalk inside my body.

'He lay at my side, resting his hand cautiously on my

stomach. I took hold of it and put his fingers to my breast. "Feel me, Clive. Squeeze the nipple." He did as ordered, bending his head towards me. We kissed, a deeper, more passionate sharing of tongues than before and I sensed him relaxing. "I'm going to teach you how to please a woman," I whispered, holding my breast towards his face. "Suck it. Suck the nipple gently." He moved his mouth to my erect little bud, taking it between his lips and suckling the hard flesh. As he did so I took hold of his hand and put it to my wet pussy, moving it for him to show how I liked it. He soon got the idea, his fingers delving between the soft lips while his thumb rubbed against my erect clit.

'"That's it, Clive. Now, put your mouth to me, kiss me, down there." He paused for a moment, as if to be sure I meant what I said. I nodded my head in the direction of my aching crotch and smiled in encouragement. He inched his body downwards, until he lay with his head between my legs. "Lick it, darling," I said. "Especially at the top." He pushed his tongue forward, the tip touching the lips of my throbbing pussy, tasting the flavour of a woman for the first time in his life. He licked around the hole, rubbing his tongue flatly over the lips then slid it upwards along the slit until it reached the stiff bud, fluttering over it like an expert. I groaned, clutching his head and raising my legs into the air as I pressed his face hard against me. He lapped hungrily, clearly enjoying the new experience.

'I came with a shudder, crying out loudly. He sat up quickly and asked me if I was all right. I laughed, and he looked disappointed. I reached up and stroked the back of his head tenderly. "Clive, you have made me come with your tongue. It was wonderful." His face beamed with pride.

'"Now, Clive, I want you to fuck me." I accentuated the word "fuck", my eyes wide with lust. He knelt between my legs, his big cock inches from my cunt. I reached over and gripped it, my fingers circling the hard shaft, and guided him into me. He slid in easily, his groin pressing against mine. Suddenly he began to pump in and out at a ferocious rate. I pressed my hand hard against his bottom. "Steady,

210

steady, you'll come too quick. Take it nice and slow," I whispered.

'He began to move like an expert, resting his weight on his elbows, my breasts crushed hard against his slim chest. "That's it, Clive," I breathed. "Fuck me, fuck me." My words were ill-advised because the young man's movements became once again rapid and his face betrayed the fact that he was lost. With a groan he came, his cock throbbing inside me, his cream filling my soaked sheath.

'He fell from me almost as soon as he was finished, lying on his back and gazing at the ceiling. I knew what he must be thinking – feelings of pride and achievement as well as the pleasure of satisfaction. I'd felt similar things when I lost my virginity, quite some years before. I leant over and kissed him lightly on the forehead, then climbed from the bed and left him to his thoughts.

'Downstairs, the orgy was in full swing, the sounds and aromas of sex filling the room. Barely had I entered than I was virtually flung on to the sofa, someone's busy tongue lapping at my pussy, the juices of mine and Clive's ecstasy soaking my new lover's face.

'The evening wore into the night, and then to the morning. By the end of the party there wasn't a man who hadn't clambered over me, erection after erection slipping inside me, tongues licking my juices, cocks filling my mouth. A couple of the older women disappeared upstairs to see if Clive was OK; they didn't return until morning. I had taught him well.'

Demonia smiled. 'You've both done well,' she said. 'We will soon have enough members of our group to defeat the baron with the combined power of our will.' She looked at Andrew, noticing that his stupendous cock was once more erect, just as she had predicted. She reached to unfasten her gown as he quickly divested himself of the remainder of his clothing. Alex stood up and walked over to Sinitia, taking her small hand in his and leading her to the sofa. Within moments, Andrew had sunk his monstrous stalk deep inside Demonia's pussy and Alex was happily thrusting into the perfection of Sinitia's bottom.

Sarah, Karen and Belinda grabbed hold of Stuart, stripping him naked within a few seconds.

It would be another long, hot night.

Eight

'Tonight is the last in the lunar cycle.'

The atmosphere in the large sitting-room of the house on Gallows Hill Road was sombre as Demonia spoke, her expression one of extreme solemnity. Alex shifted uncomfortably on his seat. Sarah sat at his feet, clutching his hand tightly. The students sat like anxious schoolchildren on the long sofa, hanging on the beautiful vampire's every word.

'The time is significant in two distinct ways,' continued Demonia, rising from her armchair and standing in the centre of the room as if to stress the importance of her words.

'Two ways?' queried Alex. 'What do you mean?'

Demonia regarded him closely, her face for once unsmiling, and her body shrouded in a long black gown that seemed in keeping with her mood. 'As you know,' she said, slowly, 'all who have had sexual contact with any of the brood during the lunar month must make an important and difficult choice this night. They may join us forever, or return to their former, mortal state.

'Should they choose to become as us, they merely need to taste the fluids of our release, those of either Sinitia or I, and they will be at once transformed into the beings that you call vampires, lusting forever for the joyous sustenance of the creams of orgasm and, what is more important, blessed with eternal youth. Only Sarah is denied a choice; thanks to her experience with the twelve leaders of Mansola's evil brood her fate is sealed. She will live with us here, for ever.'

Demonia looked questioningly into Sarah's eyes, the beautiful blonde's face turning to hers in smiling acquiescence.

213

Demonia returned her smile and continued to address the group.

'The second matter is more immediate. At twelve midnight exactly the baron must come to this house to retrieve that which he seeks. Without it, his powers will fade until he becomes nothing but dust and earth. We must prepare.'

'What are we to do?' asked Colin, sitting with his arm wrapped protectively around Karen's slender shoulders. 'We don't even know what it is he wants.'

'I will call the others, those who have shared the pleasures of Eros with you all. Already, their awareness will be growing, their libidinous cravings for lascivious delights tearing at their imaginations. Through the power of my mind I will summon them and together we will learn the secret and defeat the monster.'

Demonia closed her eyes, her forehead becoming furrowed and her hands clenched tightly. The chandelier above the group began to tremble and the glass tinkled musically, ambiguously bringing a welcome lilt to the brooding silence. Droplets of sweat appeared on her face, the sheen of her alabaster-white skin enhanced by the flickering candlelight. Her body shook visibly, her fingernails dug into the flesh of her hands, and her teeth were gritted as though she were in great pain.

Suddenly she opened her eyes, breathing heavily. 'It is done,' she said triumphantly. 'They will be with us within the hour.'

Alex shook his head, marvelling at the demonstration of yet another of their hostess's ethereal strengths. There was so much to know; so much to understand.

'Now we must wait,' continued Demonia breathlessly, the immense strain of her endeavours clearly having taken its toll, 'and, sadly we may not make love until after midnight, when you have each made your choice.'

Her words burned into Alex's mind like a red-hot knife plunging into his heart. The thought of never again possessing her superb body, nor tasting the nectar of her juices, tore at his brain. He looked at Sinitia, seated on the far side of the room. No more would he be able to look

214

down at her perfect, pert bottom while his long shaft plunged between the ebony globes. Never again would he feel the tightness of her anus gripping his thick stalk. Unless ... unless he joined them, to reside for ever in the world of the undead.

Sinitia caught his gaze and smiled coquettishly. His choice would be difficult in the extreme.

'While we wait for our brothers and sisters to join us,' said Demonia, her tone becoming lighter, 'perhaps Andrew will tell us his story. Come, Andrew, delight us with tales of how many young maidens have become impaled on your wonderful cock.'

Andrew coughed nervously, sitting forward on the sofa. Belinda slipped her hand over the bulge in his jeans, squeezing the hardening flesh. 'Yes, go on, Andrew,' she breathed. 'Don't spare us any details.'

'OK then,' said the young man. 'It'll help pass the time. As I think Belinda knows, I've been supplementing my student's grant by earning a few quid doing a striptease act in pubs and clubs.' Demonia looked shocked.

'You mean, you bare your body before strangers, for money?'

'It's a laugh really, although the money's good. I was having a pee in a club a few months ago and this guy next to me kept peering over, looking at my dick. I was about to thump him when he suggested that with a cock the size of mine I ought to use it to earn some cash. At first I thought he was coming on to me, but it turned out that he was an entertainments agent, and he told me he could get me loads of work if I was willing to do it. I've always been proud of what I've got, so I thought what the hell.

'The first time was really nerve-racking, as you can imagine, but after that it became easier and I began to really enjoy myself. One thing I soon discovered, a sort of perk to the job, was that it was virtually impossible not to get laid after a show. It's incredible the effect it has on otherwise normal, ordinary women. They behave like animals!

'I was offered a booking a few days ago, so I thought it would be an ideal opportunity to find one or two new

215

recruits for our little group. It was a hen party – some poor girl getting married the following day – and they'd hired a private room at the back of a pub. I'd been asked to dress as a policeman. You know the sort of thing – pretend to arrest the bride-to-be, flash my tackle, give her a few kisses and quick grope then be on my way.

'I turned up in a cab at the appointed time. Apart from my constable's uniform I was only wearing a black leather posing pouch and a cock-ring.'

'What's a cock-ring?' asked Karen, giggling girlishly.

'All male strippers wear them round their balls and the root of their cocks. It controls the flow of blood, so that the longer you wear it the harder you become. It's very difficult to get anything like an erection when you're performing in public, so the ring is very necessary.'

'I can't imagine you having trouble getting a hard-on,' laughed Belinda.

'It happens,' continued Andrew. 'The only real problem comes if you leave the ring on too long. It can get quite painful. Anyway, I turned up at this pub and went in. The landlord was expecting me and directed me to the back room where the party was going on. The noise from the other side of the door was incredible – music blaring out from a disco mixed with the shrieking sounds of women having a good time. The landlord opened the door and led me in, signalling to the DJ to turn the volume down. The music went quiet and everyone looked at me. Most of them were in on the joke, of course, but I had to play the part straight.

'I took the microphone and stood in front of the small stage, trying to look as officious as possible. "Is there a Miss Reynolds here?" I asked, my voice booming out of the speakers. A lovely young girl – she can't have been more than about eighteen – was pushed forward. She was really gorgeous, a sort of half-caste I suppose, with the biggest, deepest brown eyes and waist-length black hair. She was a bit worse for wear, obviously well supplied with drinks throughout the evening, and from the look on her face she thought that I was the real thing, despite the fact that I was using the mike.

216

'I caught her arm and made her stand next to me, facing the audience of leering females. "Are you Miss Jennifer Alison Reynolds?" I asked. She nodded nervously. "Well, Miss Reynolds, I'm afraid that I have something to show you, something that you are required to take a hold of immediately." A couple of the girls laughed, but the poor bride-to-be looked terrified.

'I took off my helmet, then put it down on the stage with the mike. I stood up and quickly unbuttoned my tunic, throwing it to the floor. Needless to say, I wore nothing underneath. Jennifer clasped her hands to her mouth in mock horror as she realised what was going on. I wrenched my blue trousers off, pulling the boots from my feet at the same time.

'I took up the mike again, slipping my arm around her shoulders. My cock was already half-erect, the bulge in my leather pouch jutting out ridiculously, and at least twenty pairs of female eyes were fixed on it as I spoke again. "I have an item concealed about my person; a fearsome weapon which your friends here feel you ought to examine." Jennifer giggled and the other women cheered and shouted ribald comments. "Please remove the covering, Miss Reynolds," I ordered.

'The young girl stood in front of me and I pressed my hands on her shoulders, making her kneel at my feet so that the audience could get a good view of the proceedings. She hooked her thumbs in the string of the pouch at my sides and slowly pulled it down, staring intently at my gradually exposed crotch. My cock was hardening rapidly, so much so that when it sprung free of the leather it stood up stiffly, slapping her under the chin. The audience were applauding wildly.

'Jennifer gazed at my erection for a few moments, running her tongue suggestively across her upper lip. "Get hold of it, then!" somebody shouted. She reached out and circled my thick shaft with her slim little fingers. My cock throbbed and a big glob of white cream slipped from the end and ran down the stalk and over her hand. She pulled it away, letting my cock swing free, to further applause. I

217

thought I'd gone too far this time, but felt relieved when she put her fingers to her mouth and licked my sperm from them. From the look on her face she was clearly enjoying the experience.

'Somebody shouted "Give it a suck" and I began to get worried. After all, there *are* limits to what you can get up to at these performances, and I'd already gone past them. I didn't have a chance to argue, however, as Jennifer immediately grabbed hold of my cock again and pulled it towards her delicious little mouth, quickly taking the end inside. I throbbed again, knowing that she was tasting more of my juices inside her gently suckling mouth and prayed that I wouldn't come, knowing that that was *definitely* out of bounds.

'Someone else shouted from the back of the hall. "Why don't you sit on it, Jenny? You'll never see one as big as that again!" I looked across at the landlord, who was standing by the closed door, purposely stopping anybody from entering. He nodded, with a broad grin on his face. I didn't think for a minute that she'd do it, but I wanted to be sure that I wouldn't get into any trouble.

'Jennifer took her lovely mouth from me and stood up, looking me full in the face with the most erotic of expressions. The cock-ring was certainly doing its work. My erection was huge – at least two inches longer than normal and achingly thick. Another of the girls caught hold of it and gently rubbed it up and down, whispering "Me next" in my ear. I nodded. Well, who wouldn't?

'Jennifer pulled her little dress over her head, shaking her hair so that it fell over her lithe, slim body. Her skin was the colour of coffee. She was naked, except for a pair of white hold-up stockings and tiny, matching panties. Her knickers were quickly removed by two or three pairs of willing hands and she stood, waiting. Her body was a delight; slim, with small rounded breasts and the darkest, most prominent nipples I had ever seen, a narrow waist with a smoothly-curved stomach and a deliciously inviting bush of dark curls between her legs.

'Two of the women pushed me down to sit on the edge

of the stage. I must have looked preposterous, sitting there with this massive hard-on sticking up like a flagpole. Jennifer turned her back to me and raised her leg, resting one foot on the stage with the other on the floor, then began to lower herself down. I felt a sudden pang of conscience; after all, she was supposed to be getting married the following day, but as her wonderful little bottom came close to my raging stalk I thought what the hell and gripped myself by the root, directing the end to its ultimate target.

'I almost came as her hot, silky lips engulfed me, my huge prick sinking deep inside her as she sat down on my lap. There was a loud cheer, and then *she* began to fuck *me*. This girl really knew what she was doing, moving up and down at just the right pace, circling her hips occasionally so that my cock stretched every part of her soaking wet sheath. Her future husband has a lot of fun in store, that's for sure!

'There was a flash from a camera, followed by two or three more. I couldn't help wondering where the photos would end up, and whether I'd have some giant bloke knocking on my door, demanding revenge for me having fucked his fiancée! Jennifer wasn't in the least bit concerned; she just carried on humping herself on me, the other women pushing each other to try to get a better view of the proceedings, some even standing on tables. I'd had quick screws in the dressing-room or in parked cars after a show, but never anything like this. This was unbelievable!

'I was managing to control myself by now, to hold back the desire to come, although it wasn't easy. She was bouncing up and down on me as though her life depended on it, moaning loudly and tossing her head drunkenly from side to side.

'A pretty little blonde girl, about the same age as Jennifer, knelt in front of us. I assumed she was simply trying to get a close look at my big cock sliding in and out of her friend's accommodating little pussy, but I was wrong. I shuddered as I felt her start to lick my balls, her tongue trailing around them and tracing their shape before she took one, then the other, into her hot mouth. More cheers, more photographs.

'Jennifer suddenly leant forward and began to pump rapidly up and down on my thick stalk, knocking the blonde girl out of the way as she came with a sharp cry. I arched my back, resting my hands on the stage so that as much of my stalk as possible was absorbed inside her gorgeous, thrusting body. She seemed to like it, suddenly shouting, "Christ, what a big dick!" as she rammed her small frame down on me for the last time. It occurred to me that it was the first time she'd spoken, and here I was, with my cock held firmly up her sweet little pussy.

'After a moment, Jennifer raised herself from me, allowing my cock to plop back against my stomach. I looked down. It was enormous! Purple, and beginning to hurt a little. I knew that I'd have to come soon or I would be in trouble. "Look at that," someone called out. "He hasn't come! Let's see who can make him shoot!" The owner of the voice, a lumpish woman in her thirties, pushed me on to my back, my head nearly making painful contact with the amplification equipment. Before I could say or do anything she was astride me, her knickers wrenched to one side and my cock slipping effortlessly into her big, wet pussy. She pounded up and down on my poor, wrecked body for ages until she was dragged from me. I panted a quick thank you to my rescuer – a tall, Japanese-looking girl who was wearing nothing but a tiny T-shirt. My gratitude was short-lived, however, for this beautiful creature clambered over me almost immediately, forcing my engorged cock into her velvety sheath, and groaning as the huge end touched her cervix. "Bloody hell, I thought my husband was big," she moaned, then began to grind her crotch against mine, keeping my full length impaled deep inside her.

'Once again, my lover was dragged from me, only to be replaced by another, sex-hungry girl, then another, and another. It crossed my mind that I was going to have to fuck them all, but my cock ached terribly. Suddenly, with a shout of joyous relief I came, ramming my cock hard into the tightness that enfolded it, my sperm jetting deep into the gripping, wet sheath. The women cheered; the game had been won. My stalk throbbed and throbbed, my cream filling the tight pussy that seemed to be suckling on the stiff shaft and drawing everything from me. My orgasm lasted for a full minute, my groans drowned by the cheers and clapping of my audience.

'At last, it was over and I lay exhausted on the stage, trying to recover. The women quickly lost interest in me, barely seeming to notice as I retrieved my clothing and dressed myself. I felt rather cheeky taking my fee from the landlord as I left, but he was well pleased, and obviously intent on remaining at the party in the hope of enjoying a similar experience.

'As I went out of the door I glanced back and my eyes met those of the bride-to-be. She was fully dressed, looking as innocent as before. She smiled fleetingly, then looked away, turning to join her friends at the bar.'

The door to the sitting-room opened as Andrew completed his story, the large figure of the doorman appearing at it. Without a word, he ushered two men into the room, their faces showing signs of total bemusement. Karen recognised them immediately as members of her rowing team.

'Welcome, friends,' said Demonia, rising to greet the newcomers. The door opened again and three young girls entered, then more, until after less than half an hour the room was filled with people. Demonia and Sinitia busied themselves with short introductions, hugging their guests like old friends.

The clock chimed, signalling a sudden silence among the gathering. 'Eleven o'clock,' said Demonia gravely. 'He will he here soon. We must prepare.'

The group sat quietly in a large circle, the shimmering light of the long black candles bathing their flesh and casting erotic shadows around the hot sitting-room. All were now naked. Some were idly fondling each other's bodies and some were sitting motionless, as though awaiting a terrible uncertainty.

Alex pondered over the situation. Demonia's suggested

method of defeating the baron was so bizarre that it might work, yet even she had seemed more than a little uncertain. If only they knew the secret and what it was that would draw the monster to this house.

The old clock ticked loudly, as though intent on drawing the very life-force from their bodies with its incessant reminder of their vulnerability.

Five minutes before midnight. Alex glanced again at Sinitia, now sitting naked at Demonia's feet with her legs widely splayed, the thick curls of her delicious pussy brazenly displayed. His crotch ached and his cock rose steadily to full erection, his senses aroused by the sight of her blatant sexuality. She caught his gaze and looked quickly away, hurriedly bringing her thighs together so as to avoid offering him further temptation.

She needn't have troubled herself; he had made his decision. Even if it meant that he would never again taste the sweet nectar of her sex-juices or the tightness of her anal muscles gripping his thick shaft as he thrust his cock between her sumptuous, dusky buttocks he knew that he must remain mortal. There were too many dangers and too many unanswered questions.

He looked over at Sarah, who was nonchalantly sucking the stiff erection of one of the boat crew. The young man in question was staring into the distance, his eyes barely focused. Even she would be denied to him. This troubled him more than anything else in this wretched situation. Over the short time that he had known her he had grown to love her; her intelligence, her sense of humour, her seemingly insatiable libido. The foul entity that they called Mansola had taken her from him, and he hated him for it.

Sinitia stood up and walked to the door, Alex watching the gentle sway of her lithe body as she silently left the room. His urge to follow her and drag her into the bedroom to impale her to the hilt tore at his very soul. He turned away, catching the sight of Karen opposite him. Her tiny, delicate body oozed sexuality and arousal. She smiled broadly and shuffled across the carpet to sit at his side. She gripped his hard stalk immediately, her fingers

222

barely encircling the thick shaft. He looked down and watched as she soothingly rubbed his cock up and down. His manhood appeared huge within her small grasp.

The clock struck suddenly and Alex's heart leapt. Everybody sat upright, their eyes turned to Demonia, waiting for instruction.

'He is here!' she exclaimed. 'I sense it. He is within these walls!' The members of the group looked around the room, peering into the dark recesses as if expecting to find the monster crouching behind some item of furniture, ready to leap out.

'Sinitia!' cried Sarah suddenly. 'Where is she?'

Demonia leapt to her feet, her expression one of abject terror. She looked around in panic. 'She went out into the hall a few moments ago,' said Alex, his phallus rapidly becoming flaccid despite Karen's expert manipulation.

Demonia rushed to the door. 'We must find her! Alex, Colin, you come with me. The rest of you, stay here. Do not move from this room!'

Alex and Colin followed her out of the door, heading for the long staircase to the upper floor. They took the steps three at a time, the sight of Demonia's long legs striding purposefully up the flight for once not having an effect on Alex's libido. He and Colin caught up with her as she crashed the bedroom door open, rushing with her into the room that had been witness to so many past delights. They stood stock-still.

Sinitia lay on the bed with her legs held high and her fingers gripping her ankles, pulling them back towards her lovely face. The baron knelt before her in awesome nakedness, his hugely powerful body glistening with sweat and his sharply-defined muscles tensed. His massive phallus jutted out from his groin, the end purple with the rage of his lust. He was thrusting menacingly towards the wet, pouting lips of the young girl's open sex.

He turned his head and glared at the intruders, his lips curled in a malevolent sneer and his teeth bared savagely. 'You will not deny me this time!' he roared. 'I will take my prize, the virgin you took from me, sapping my powers over the centuries. I will have her; the first time for our mutual pleasure and the second to welcome her into my brood, to finally fill my body with the strengths for which I crave!'

Alex tried to move but he couldn't. It was though he was held by some invisible force. Demonia and Colin seemed similarly afflicted and the three of them stood helplessly by the door.

'It is Sinitia, she's the one!' said Colin, giving voice to their thoughts. 'She holds the key!'

The baron turned his head away from them contemptuously, gazing down at the lovely black girl lying acquiescently before him.

'No!' screamed Demonia, her entire body shaking with anger and frustration.

Sinitia lowered her legs, keeping them bent and widely spread, her heels resting on the bed. 'Please, Demonia,' she pleaded, her eyes filling with tears, 'let him take me, just once. I need to feel that wonderful rod sinking deep inside me, filling me, stretching me completely! I will not let him touch me a second time.'

The baron laughed, moving his body closer so that his huge cock was only inches away from his succulent target. 'See,' he hissed, 'she demands to be fucked! Leave us, and let her enjoy the ultimate pleasure of total intrusion!'

Alex felt his body relax; he could move again. Demonia moved forward, only to be halted in her steps by the power of Mansola's stare. She turned to Alex, a tear tracing its way down her ashen cheek.

'Go to the others, Alex,' she breathed. 'You know what is to be done.' He stepped forward, unwilling to desert her in this lethal predicament. He heard Sinitia groan loudly and looked back at the supine figure, her legs once more raised high. The monstrously thick shaft of the baron's cock was beginning to slip within the tight confines of her soaked pussy. 'Go!' Demonia ordered, her eyes blazing. 'Quickly, before it is too late!'

Alex and Colin made for the door, both turning their heads in response to Sinitia's ecstatic sighs, to see the baron pressing his groin hard against hers, the entire length of his enormous cock held deep inside her willing body. Demonia looked at them, her pleading eyes filled with tears. They turned and left the room, hurrying down the stairs to join the others.

'It has begun!' yelled Alex as they burst into the room. 'It is time! We must fuck like we've never fucked before! The house must be filled with the sounds of lust and the cries of orgasm! The combined essence of our mutual arousal has got to be strong enough to drain the baron's powers; to draw him to us.'

The entire group sat motionless, their expressions bemused.

'Now!' roared Alex, grabbing Karen by the arm and dragging her to him. Still nobody moved. Cocks hung flaccidly between male legs and pussies were hidden protectively between tightly closed thighs. Alex looked in panic at his own, heavily drooping member. 'Suck me,' he demanded, pushing Karen by the shoulders to kneel at his feet. 'For God's sake, make me hard!'

Karen opened her small mouth and took his cock between her lips. Her tongue immediately snaked around the bulbous head, and Alex stiffened the muscles of his backside in an effort to force an erection. If anything, he wilted slightly, then to his utmost relief he felt himself thicken and grow inside her steadily sucking mouth. Harder and harder it stretched until she was forced to move her head back due to his size. The thick shaft filled her mouth and the throbbing head pressed against the back of her throat.

He began to move his hips back and forth, fucking her beautiful, elfin face. Her hands gripped his big stem as though afraid to let go. Alex looked about him, happily seeing others in the group joining him in his bliss. Cocks were rising stiffly under the erotic caresses of fingers and tongues. Soon, the carpet was covered by seething, writhing bodies and groans of ecstasy filled the room. Only Sarah sat alone, unhappily unable to join in the bacchanalia, her fingers delving desperately into her sex as she watched the scene before her.

225

A sudden, female cry echoed around the room. Alex looked in the direction of the sound, discovering that it came from the lips of a huge-breasted woman whom he rightly assumed was the same person who had so recently disapproved of Belinda's open display of sexuality at the singles' party. Now she writhed in blissful orgasm on the prone form of Colin, his cock buried deep inside her pussy, while another young man plunged his not inconsiderable stalk into her bottom. Another cry followed from elsewhere in the room, then another. It was working. Alex sensed an incongruous warmth fill his body as Karen continued sucking on his engorged prick. He pulled himself from her and turned her to kneel on her hands and knees, her bottom in the air. He crouched behind her and ran his tongue over the pert, pink globes, licking between them until he found the smoothness of her hairless pussy. The lips were open and ready.

He lapped hungrily between the succulent folds of flesh, occasionally drawing his tongue upwards to lick her tiny, puckered orifice before returning to suckle her delightful cunt. Her body shuddered against his face.

He pulled himself up, gazing down at the inviting perfection of Karen's body and gripped his stalk by the root, aiming it at the open sex lips that appeared to be demanding his intrusion. He pushed himself forward, thrilling as his cock slid effortlessly inside the hot sheath, and eased it inch by inch into her until she held his entire erection deep within her trembling body.

Andrew joined them, kneeling in front of her, his massive rod close to her face. She opened her mouth and took him inside, swallowing as much of his immensely thick stalk as she could. Alex continued to pump heavily in and out of her pussy. He felt the wetness of a tongue running along the cleft of his backside. Turning his head, he saw the figure of the beautiful Japanese girl whom Andrew had introduced into the fold paying oral homage to his bottom. He slowed the movements of his thrusting into the other girl's delectable body in order to savour the sensuous caress of the tongue over his anus, and reached under

Karen's body to fondle her stretched pussy. His fingertips found the erect bud of her clitoris and rubbed it rapidly.

Somebody else groaned in orgasm and Karen followed suit. Andrew threw his head back and gritted his teeth as he filled Karen's mouth with his seed, the rapid movements of her cheeks making it clear to Alex that she was draining him and swallowing all that he could give. He pumped into her for all he was worth, ramming his long cock in and out of her ravaged sheath until her whimpers of joyous satisfaction eased.

Certain that she was sated, he pulled his engorged shaft from her silky wetness and turned to the oriental girl, easing her to lie on her back. She rested her head comfortably on the stomach of the prone form of Belinda, who was herself being happily serviced by Stuart, his hips moving at an alarming rate as he fucked the voluptuous blonde mercilessly.

Alex moved his body over the olive-skinned girl as she caught hold of his raging erection and guided him inside her. The honeyed warmth of her tightness quickly enveloped his throbbing stalk and he started to thrust into her immediately. His knees rubbed painfully on the carpet while the girl's legs wrapped themselves around his waist, her heels digging into his back. He leant forward and kissed her hard on the mouth, savouring the succulence of her thick, full lips. Their tongues met and slid sensuously against each other. He sensed the now-familiar delight of another tongue tracing a wet trail along the cleft between his buttocks until the tip searched out his tight hole and probed inside him, forcing its slippery length in and out. He bit his lip, feeling the inevitable surge building up within his loins but determined to hold back. He doggedly refused to allow himself the release for which he ached until he was certain that the baron's powers had been drained. He circled his hips, reluctantly forcing his anal intruder to move away, and held his cock motionless inside the Japanese girl's pulsating sheath. A jet of pre-come shot inside her, easing the urgency of his need for orgasm.

Arching his back, he supported his upper body with his

hands, thrilling to the sight of Belinda's mountainous breasts bouncing in steady rhythm as Stuart pounded into her lovely body. He leant his head forward and took one of her nipples into his mouth, nipping the long, erect bud between his teeth as he resumed his fucking movements. The girl beneath him moaned softly as she pushed her hips upwards to meet his steady thrusts.

Stuart suddenly groaned and pulled himself from inside Belinda, a jet of sperm spraying across the oriental girl's face before he pushed his throbbing cock into her mouth, her pouted lips encircling his stalk at the root. Alex managed to reach under Stuart's body until his fingers found Belinda's pussy and he rapidly rubbed them over her clitoris, feeling the movements of her crotch against his hand as she responded to his erotic caress. The Japanese girl began to moan loudly, her cries muffled by Stuart's slowly wilting manhood which she still held deep inside her mouth. Her crotch ground hard against Alex, her vaginal muscles gripping his engorged cock tightly as though sucking him within her hot sheath. Alex pounded harder and harder into the writhing body, fucking her as heavily as he could, his fingertips still rapidly rubbing Belinda's throbbing bud until, with a shout that accentuated the strength of his release, he felt his cream surge along the length of his cock and jet deep inside his lover's body.

The girl held her body stiff, Stuart's drooping phallus slipping from her mouth, then she groaned, bucking her hips wildly against Alex. Her cries of orgasm were echoed by Belinda who shuddered into release under the expert touch of Alex's fingers. Alex felt the surge of a second orgasm building within his loins and pulled himself from the trembling girl below him, moving quickly to push his massively erect cock towards Belinda's mouth. She took him between her suckling lips willingly, drawing in her cheeks and sucking hard, swallowing his entire length down her throat. He came again, the searing pleasure of yet another orgasm tearing at every nerve-ending in his body.

'Alex!' The voice was screaming, near-hysterical and hardly recognisable as Demonia's as she ran into the room, her lovely face stained with tears. 'He is winning, Alex,' she sobbed, gripping his arms tightly. 'He has sated himself within the body of my sweet sister, and now he intends to take her to the pit, to initiate her into his evil brood by impaling for a second time! We must stop him, Alex. We must not let him take her from this house!'

'How? What more can we do?' Alex looked around in panic. The other group members gradually unravelled themselves from their various positions of sexual delight to stand sheepishly in a circle around them. Demonia's eyes suddenly widened.

'That's it!' she exclaimed. 'Quick, everyone into the hall. the baron will have to pass through it to escape. When he reaches the foot of the staircase we must encircle him, our arms entwined, our wills directed at just one thing . . . his destruction!'

'Are you sure that this will be enough?' said Alex as fifty or so naked people pushed their way from the room. 'After all, you thought that the aura of our sexual excesses would be sufficient.'

'Yes, yes,' replied Demonia, excitedly. 'Don't you see? He *needs* to possess her to regain his full strength. Because Sinitia was denied to him all those years ago he became weak. She is his link with the past. The power of our wills *must* defeat him.'

Alex remained unconvinced but quickly joined the anxious murmuring group waiting in the great hall. Almost as he entered, the sounds of muted conversation ceased and all eyes turned to look up the long stairway. Mansola stood at the top. Sinitia's unconscious, naked body was draped over his arms like a small doll. He grinned at the assembled crowd, a sneering leer of triumph, and walked slowly down the steps. His flowing cloak parted at the front to reveal his manhood hanging heavily between his muscular legs and the sheen of Sinitia's release was clearly visible on the gnarled flesh. He glared at Alex, then at Demonia.

'I have her now,' he growled as he reached the foot of the stairs, 'and there is nothing that you can do to stop me from fulfilling my final destiny. Make way, lest great harm should befall you all!'

Alex stood his ground nervously, determined to conceal his terror. He felt Demonia's arm slip around his, gripping him tightly. He followed suit, circling his other arm around that of Colin, who stood at his side. He stared directly into the baron's cold, evil eyes as the other members of the group clasped each other in the same way, gradually forming a circle around the huge man and his delicate captive. Suddenly sensing the danger, Mansola let Sinitia slip to the floor and stood in front of Demonia, his features twisted in a fearsome rage. Sinitia stirred, her eyes opening lazily. Alex wanted to help her and take her to safety but he knew that he must not break the ring.

'You dare to defy me again?' he roared, the words spitting venomously into Demonia's face. She held his stare, her expression one of utter contempt.

'You are defeated, baron,' she retorted, her voice filled with confidence. 'Even you cannot break the will of this circle.'

Mansola turned around angrily, glaring at the trembling, naked figures that surrounded him. Suddenly, he rushed to the side towards two young girls, forcing them to step back in terror.

'Hold on!' yelled Demonia. 'Don't let go of each other! He cannot touch you.' Mansola swung around again, his body becoming strangely hunched and the skin of his face taking on a grey pallor.

'You have taught them well, Lady Demonia,' he hissed, stooping ever lower as he seemed to force the words from the back of his throat. 'Their will is strong, their bodies sated. You may have won this time but, be assured, I will return!'

There was a sudden, ear-splitting crack and all eyes turned to the sound as a huge mirror on a nearby wall shattered into a thousand pieces. Alex turned quickly and looked back into the centre of the circle. Sinitia was struggling to her feet, her expression one of exhilaration and her eyes wide and sparkling. Her pussy lips were still widely splayed as testament to her recent experiences. Be-

230

side her lay the cloak of Mansola, crumpled on the floor, a thin veil of green mist surrounding it momentarily until it faded into the flickering light of the candles.

Alex looked at Demonia. She was smiling, her large breasts heaving as she gulped in the air. He waited, anxiously.

'She is safe, Alex,' breathed Demonia, stepping forward and allowing her arm to circle Sinitia's slim waist. 'The baron is defeated. His evil form faded into nothing as I watched. He has gone; returned to Hades where he and his kind belong.'

'Are you sure?' asked Alex. 'He said he would return.' Demonia shook her head.

'I am sure,' she said, reaching out and taking hold of his hand, 'and it's all thanks to you, all of you. Your orgiastic indulgences would have weakened him; the circle was all that was required. I can never repay you for your kindness.'

Alex looked round at the group of naked people, their faces filled with a combination of bemusement and relief, and smiled wryly. 'It was our pleasure,' he said with a grin. 'Entirely our pleasure.'

Alex stood in the garden of the house on Gallows Hill Road, looking up at the old building in the dim light of the early dawn. Most of the others had gone; only Colin and Sarah remaining, lying together in the main bedroom. Colin had decided to join the others; making love to Sarah being the final step towards his acceptance. Alex felt a pang of envy, knowing that in his decision to remain mortal he had lost his love forever.

There was a sudden cracking sound and the great oak door at the entrance to the house swung open. Nobody stepped out from the darkness within. Another crack, louder than the first, resounded in Alex's ears, followed by the grating sound of stone against stone. He stepped back just in time as a large piece of masonry crashed to the ground at his side. He looked up in blind panic. The entire building seemed to be shaking against its foundations as though attempting to wrench itself from the very earth that supported it.

More stonework hurtled to the garden, smashing into thousands of pieces like delicate plasterwork. The house was decaying before his eyes!

His first impulse was to flee the shadow of the crumbling edifice, then he remembered Sarah and Colin. They would surely be crushed under the heavy walls. Without further thought for his own safety, he dashed into the house, adeptly dodging flying shards of glass that flew like daggers from the shattering windows. The noise was deafening.

He bounded up the stairs in four, massive strides, running down the hallway and forcing open the door to the bedroom which had become wedged within the grip of its warping frame. Sarah and Colin lay naked on the bed, clutching each other tightly, their faces drawn in sheer terror. Alex dashed to the bed and lifted Sarah into his arms. 'You've got to get out of here,' he yelled over the cacophony. 'The place is collapsing all around us!'

He rushed back to the door, heavy chunks of plaster falling around them and missing them by inches. Colin dashed down the stairs to the exit and Alex struggled to carry Sarah, her body stiff with fright. A huge beam suddenly screamed in surrender and thundered down in front of them, followed by tons of masonry. Their way was now blocked. Alex looked around him in confusion, desperately seeking an exit. A small, smashed window seemed to offer the means of escape. Quickly, he staggered to the aperture, carefully helping Sarah to clamber through. Sharp slivers of glass threatened to cut into her naked flesh. Once he was sure that she was safe on the outside he followed, falling heavily to the ground and clutching her arm. He then dragged her away from the shuddering walls.

They stood together in the garden, watching helplessly as the house crumbled into a pile of unrecognisable rubble. Sarah suddenly gasped. 'What about Demonia, and Sinitia?' she cried. 'They'll be killed!'

They should be safe down in the cellar where they rest,' said Alex, trying not to betray the hopelessness that he felt in the tone of his voice. He sat down on the grass. It was longer, much longer, and ugly weeds were forcing themselves through the once pristine lawns. The house was returning to death.

Sarah fell to her knees, sobbing loudly. Suddenly, a figure could be seen, dragging itself up the steep, stone steps to the crypt. Alex stood up and rushed towards it. The doorman ... Igor, as they'd affectionately known him! They'd forgotten all about him. At least he was safe.

But Igor was not alone. Carefully and dutifully he held out his arm, allowing it to be gripped by the alabaster-white hand that Alex knew to be Demonia's. Slowly, they struggled up the rubble-strewn steps into the half-light. Alex stood motionless, his heart thumping, then to his joy he saw the slim, dark figure of Sinitia. Her flawless, black skin was caked in dust.

Sarah leapt to her feet. 'Demonia! Sinitia! You're safe! You're ...' She stopped abruptly, Alex catching her thoughts like a savage blow to his breast. The sun had risen above the gnarled shapes of the trees and long, searingly bright shafts of light burnt across the scene of desolation. 'Go back!' yelled Sarah. 'Go back! The sun!'

Demonia stopped in her tracks, looking up at the rapidly brightening sky. At first her face betrayed her terror but then she slowly outstretched her arms as if in acceptance of the certainty of destruction. Sinitia joined her, gripping her shoulder tightly, and the two women breathed the cool, morning air deeply. They looked at each other and smiled.

Alex looked quickly at Sarah. 'Are you all right?' he asked, anxiously aware that she too should fear the bright sunlight. She ran her hands over her body, as if testing that all was as it should be.

'Yes,' she nodded, 'I feel OK. I don't understand.'

Alex rushed forward to the motionless forms of the doomed vampires, half-expecting them to crumble before his eyes. They turned to look at him, their smiles broad and their eyes bright with joy.

'It is over,' said Demonia, walking over to him quickly, Sinitia clutching her arm tightly. 'With the power of the evil one gone forever, so it is that our own powers have wilted. Because of that the house has returned to dust.'

'But the sun,' said Sarah fearfully as she walked over to join them, her eyes filling with tears. 'Won't you . . . won't we die?'

Demonia shook her head, taking hold of Sarah's hand. 'No, sweet child,' she breathed, 'the baron's hold is gone. We are free, we are mortal.'

'Mortal?' Alex looked concerned. 'You're not going to age suddenly, are you, or disintegrate into dust like the house?'

Demonia smiled benignly and shook her head. 'You must stop reading those silly books,' she said. 'Sinitia and I will live and breathe in the warmth of the sunshine, just like you. We will grow old, we will die, but in good time. Now we can exist as mortals, free of the curse of Mansola!'

'Does this mean that I'm not going to become immortal?' It was Colin who spoke, his face betraying a look of abject disappointment. Demonia shook her head.

'I'm afraid not, Colin, but you will have learned much. I'm sure that you will continue with your studies and, who knows, you may discover others like us.'

Alex looked at Sinitia, the perfection of her body still enticing despite its covering of white dust. Demonia also looked as ravishing as ever and of course Sarah . . . none were denied to him now. He felt the all-too-familiar stirring within his loins.

'We must see if we can retrieve some clothing from this mess,' he said, 'and then we will return to my quarters at the university. We have much to discuss, much to decide.'

Sinitia and Demonia looked down simultaneously, grinning as their eyes caught the sight of his rapidly-thickening erection. 'Yes,' said Demonia mockingly, 'much to discuss.'

The hotel was Sarah's idea. Alex had readily agreed, finding the idea of spending a couple of nights in pampered luxury with three devastatingly gorgeous and highly lascivious young women exciting in the extreme.

The food in the hotel restaurant lived up to the promise provided by their opulent surroundings. Sarah and Alex ate voraciously while Demonia and Sinitia merely picked

234

at their meals, unused to obtaining sustenance in this way. The waiters fussed about them, news of the lucky man sharing the grand suite with three beautiful women no doubt the talk of the staffroom and kitchens.

Alex regarded the two ex-vampires with barely-concealed curiosity. They seemed somewhat out of place in these normal surroundings. He considered how they would adjust to life in the twentieth century. In fact, he wondered how they would adjust to life itself. What would happen as time took its inevitable toll on their flawless beauty? Would they regret losing their chance of immortality?

They appeared content, although their expressions were distant, as though their thoughts were elsewhere. They maintained the air of regal detachment and sensuous aloofness that he found intensely erotic, and their responses were limited to nods and smiles as Sarah chattered enthusiastically like an excited schoolgirl.

'It's going to be *so* good,' she said, slipping her cutlery on to the empty plate before her. 'You can help me so much with my studies. I might even win a prize for my work!'

'Our guests must first find their place in our world,' said Alex calmly, 'and we must do everything we can to help them.'

'Of course,' continued Sarah, wiping her mouth on the linen napkin, 'but there is so much I want to learn. I can't wait to begin!'

Alex looked at Demonia, watching as she delicately chewed a morsel of food, her meal hardly touched. 'I expect you find it strange,' he said. 'Eating, I mean.'

Demonia nodded, resting her knife and fork on the plate. 'I hunger,' she breathed, 'but it is difficult. It has been so long.'

'I hunger too,' said Sinitia, her voice warm with emotion, 'but not for food.' She licked her lips deliberately, her mouth turning into a grin as she caught Alex's eye.

'It's odd that you should say that,' said Sarah, leaning back in her chair. 'The need for sex and especially the incredible desire to taste a man's cream, it's the same as before. I would have thought that it would disappear or at least return to how it was before, once the power of Mansola had gone.'

'You were never exactly undemanding before all this happened,' joked Alex. Sarah laughed girlishly.

'I sense that those yearnings will remain with us,' said Demonia, 'but what of it?'

'What of it, indeed,' said Alex, resisting the temptation to consume more of his delicious meal, knowing that his energies were likely to be called on very shortly.

The plates were cleared quickly, and small cups of strong coffee were served. Alec sipped the hot beverage slowly and looked fondly at his three companions, his loins beginning to ache with anticipation of the joys to come.

It would have been difficult to imagine three more different girls; Demonia, tall and haughty, the elegance of her features bordering on the aristocratic, her long black gown cut narrowly at the front to her waist, her mountainous breasts forcing the shining, satin material apart to reveal the alluring whiteness of her deep cleavage; Sinitia, dressed in a diaphanous, white dress of translucent silk, her breasts smaller but apple-firm, the long, black nipples clearly visible through the sheer fabric.

And, of course, Sarah; her superb, voluptuous body clothed in a simple, short halter-necked dress, the childlike innocence of her expression belying her high intelligence and robust libido. He felt his cock thickening within the tight confines of his clothing as he looked from one to the other. His need to possess them began to take control of his senses.

'Shall we go up to the room?' he said, his throat dry with lust. Sarah gulped down the remains of her coffee and stood up immediately.

'Yes, come on,' she said, a little too loudly for Alex's comfort. 'Let's go and have some fun!'

The other two women rose gracefully from the table, pausing for a moment while Alex signed the cheque. He followed them slowly from the restaurant, looking at each of them in turn. His erection throbbed, the bulge in his trousers clearly visible to the envious group of waiters they passed at the exit. 'Goodnight, sir,' said one, with unconcealed sarcasm. 'I hope you find your room comfortable.'

Alex offered him a cursory glance, then entered the lift.

The room was large and airy, the early evening sun streaming through the huge windows. Alex automatically moved to draw the curtains together, then stopped himself. Tonight there would be no need to shield his companions from its searing glare. Tonight their bodies could bathe in the warmth of its rays without fear.

Two large beds dominated the room, which they quickly pulled together. The sheets were thrown hurriedly to the floor as though they were clearing an arena for combat.

Alex stood awkwardly for a moment, then began to undress, his fingers trembling with the excitement of anticipation as he fumbled with his buttons.

Sarah was the first to be naked, her little dress cast to the floor as she leapt on to the mattresses. 'Come on, Alex,' she breathed, 'hurry up. I need a fuck.' Alex wrenched off his shoes and socks together then pulled down his trousers, his big cock springing up before him as he knelt on the bed before his lover, gazing in joyous desire at the perfection of her sumptuous body. Sarah reached out and grasped his thick stalk, pulling it towards her. Her legs were spread wide in blatant invitation.

He had little choice. He fell across her naked body, his cock sinking effortlessly into her soaked sheath, their pubic mounds crushed together as her vaginal muscles gripped his hard, throbbing flesh. He sensed an immediate surge from within his loins and his balls were drawn up into his tight sack as the sperm gushed along his pulsing stem to fill the welcoming warmth of Sarah's pussy. He groaned. 'Please God, not so soon,' he moaned between gritted teeth. He pumped his hips heavily up and down, driving the prone form of the lovely blonde into the softness of the bed, her large breasts bouncing rhythmically in time with his uncontrollable thrusts. She squealed, her orgasm surprising him with its suddenness. She ground her crotch against his as he gradually felt the intensity of his feelings subside.

He lay back, gasping for breath. Sarah leaned forward and caught hold of his cock, still firmly erect. 'Here's something else that we got out of our recent experiences,' she said, casually rubbing his hardness with her circling fingers. 'It makes a nice change, not to have a man come and then roll over to go to sleep.'

'I've never done that!' he protested, relaxing his body as her tender caress caused his cock to stiffen fully. Sarah laughed, letting his hard stalk fall heavily on to his stomach, the thick shaft wet with her juices. Alex looked up at the other two women, standing silently at the foot of the beds. Sinitia was naked and Demonia wore nothing but a pair of blood-red stockings and matching suspender-belt. For an agonising moment he felt that he was about to come again but he turned his gaze from the alluring vision until the urgency passed, a small stream of sperm slipping from his swollen knob to settle in a pool in his navel. Sinitia clambered on to the bed beside him and bent over him, pushing her tongue into the cream, glancing up at him through wide, dark eyes. Her hand cupped his balls. He watched her lick the wetness sensuously, raising her head back after a moment so that he could see the whiteness of his sperm glistening on the tip of her tongue as she drew it into her mouth.

Demonia knelt at his other side and leaned over him, her breasts hanging heavily close to his face. He opened his mouth willingly, taking a long, thick nipple between his lips and sucking the hard bud gently, occasionally nipping the engorged flesh with his teeth. He ran his hand down her long back to her bottom, his fingers tracing the line between her buttocks. His other hand quickly found the pert, firm globes of Sinitia's divine backside. Sinitia took his thick, swollen cock into her mouth and sucked him between her pouted, wet lips, her hand still cupping his tight sack, while a finger trailed mischievously to probe against his anus.

Sarah knelt between his legs, Alex quickly sensing her

238

tongue drawing wetly over his balls. Sinitia now concentrated on rubbing his thick shaft as she suckled the engorged end inside her delicious mouth. Alex moved his hand and wormed a finger into the tight orifice of her anus, following suit with the other hand and sliding two fingers deep into Demonia's bottom. Sinitia moved herself so that her bottom was pushed high into the air to give him easier access to her anus. His stalk was held upright within her thickly pouting lips, the position allowing him to see Sarah's head bobbing up and down as she lapped at his scrotum.

Demonia moved her body round to squat over his head. He gazed up at the white perfection of her buttocks and the open, reddening lips of her pussy as she gently lowered her body until his face was smothered by her creamy flesh. His tongue darted in and out of the wet slit.

He heard her groan as he lapped against her and drank the copious fluids of her intense arousal, his nose pressed hard between her buttocks. He could barely breathe, but couldn't have cared less. If he was to die, what better way than this; smothered by the creamy flesh of a perfect bottom, his cock steadily being sucked and his balls licked simultaneously by two beautiful women?

He concentrated the fluttering of the tip of his tongue against the hard bud of Demonia's clitoris, feeling her body shudder almost immediately. Her familiar, animal-like cry filled his ears as she came. She pressed her bottom down on to his face, her pussy crushing hard against his mouth. For an instant, he felt that he really might be suffocated by this heavenly pillow until at last she moved from him, leaving him gasping for air.

He had little time to recover. Demonia moved around him, squatting over his hips and gazing into his eyes with a lustful stare. Slowly, she lowered her body once more and Sarah and Sinitia clutched the long, thick stem of his cock and guided it to her wet opening, easing it within the silky folds of her cunt which seemed to grip and draw him within the tightness of her sheath. She moved gradually downwards until she held every inch of his hardness inside her, then she sat motionless for a moment, tensing her thigh muscles to grip him even tighter within her body. He stared at the wonderful sight before him. Their pubic hairs were meshed wetly together and the divine image was framed by her stockings and suspender belt. He wasn't to enjoy the vision for long.

Sinitia moved her position and knelt across him to face Demonia, lowering the perfection of her ebony bottom towards his mouth. Soon, he was lapping again at the warm succulence of a soaked pussy as Demonia moved her body up and down, fucking herself on his engorged cock. Sarah resumed her place between his legs and licked his balls and the occasionally exposed stem of his cock voraciously, the combination of sensations driving him to distraction.

He allowed his hands to wander over the smooth flesh of the two women who sat astride him, their movements indicating that they were caressing each other, and the sounds that filled his ears clearly indicating that they were kissing each other passionately. He felt Sarah's tongue flutter over his anus and he thrust upwards involuntarily, the ache within his loins developing rapidly into an uncontrollable surge as once again he came, his seed jetting into Demonia's pulsating sheath. A muffled groan from above his head suggested that Sinitia had joined him in his pleasure as his cock throbbed heavily within the tight grip of sex-flesh. A second, loud cry from Demonia compounded his delight.

They fell apart, their bodies soaked with sweat. They had been making love for less than twenty minutes and already Alex was exhausted. He began to feel uncomfortable in the heat of the sun as it burned through the plate glass of the windows, his cock now lying flaccid against his stomach. The three women looked at him expectantly, but he couldn't do anything more. Not yet anyway.

They seemed to sense his fatigue, and decided to take solace in each other's arms. Alex moved to the side of the beds and watched as they curled themselves around each other and formed a circle on the two mattresses, licking delicately between each other's legs. Hands strayed, fingers probed and the girls moaned softly as they pleasured one another. The sight of the writhing, sumptuous bodies rapidly brought Alex back to a state of extreme arousal.

Sinitia moved herself so that she knelt with her bottom presented to his lustful gaze. Demonia lapped at her lovely pussy and Sinitia's head was buried between Sarah's legs. Alex knelt behind her, his cock jutting massively once more and gripping it by the root aimed the head at the pouted lips of her cunt. He sank into her easily, his long shaft disappearing within the black folds of sex-flesh like a hot knife into warm butter. Demonia delicately ran her tongue over his balls. He moved slowly in and out of her delightful grip, drawing the full length of his thick stalk from her until just the tip remained held inside her then plunging forward to delve deep within her suckling wetness, forcing her body forward so that her face pressed hard against Sarah's pussy, to the young blonde's apparent delight.

Demonia untangled herself from the exotic circle and moved behind Alex, pressing her hand against his bottom, forcing him to plunge harder into Sinitia's warmth and stimulating his desire by tickling the puckered orifice of his anus with her fingertip. His movements became more rapid and he drove his cock deep within her dark pulchritude, the flesh of her pert buttocks rippling in time with each heavy thrust.

Sarah wriggled her body around so that she lay underneath Sinitia, her tongue quickly finding her pussy and licking greedily over the stretched lips and Alex's incessantly plunging thickness. He slipped his arm around Demonia and his hand cupped her huge breast, the nipple pinched between his fingers. She reached down and gripped his stalk by the root, easing it from the sweet honey-pot before him and guiding the thick, bulbous end to Sinitia's other, tiny hole. 'This is where she desires it most,' she breathed.

Alex was not about to object. He moved his hips forward, watching in delight as his huge cock entered the tightness of the young, black girl's perfect bottom. Sarah was now clamping her mouth over the pouted lips of Sinitia's pussy, suckling her flesh ravenously.

He began to pump in and out rapidly, his need for yet

another release tearing at his very soul. Harder and harder he fucked the beautiful bottom before him. Demonia was now kneeling behind him, drawing her tongue wetly up and down the cleft between his buttocks. No man could have held back under such circumstances.

With a groan he came, the seed once more surging along the long stem of his thick cock to fill the succulent confines of Sinitia's magnificent bottom. His orgasm seemed unending, the power of the sensations causing him to collapse heavily on to her body, crushing her against Sarah. Demonia fell with him, still licking between his buttocks until finally he could take no more.

The morning found them asleep; four naked, exhausted bodies entwined on the two beds. Their hair was matted and their skin scratched and bruised from the excesses of the previous night.

Alex was the first to wake, struggling to free himself from the chaos of arms and legs. He staggered to the bathroom. As he stared at his tired, wrecked image in the mirror he couldn't resist a wry smile to himself.

This was only the beginning.

THE 1996 NEXUS CALENDAR

The 1996 Nexus calendar contains photographs of thirteen of the most delectable models who have graced the covers of Nexus books. And we've been able to select pictures that are just a bit more exciting than those we're allowed to use on book covers.

With its restrained design and beautifully reproduced duo-tone photographs, the Nexus calendar will appeal to lovers of sophisticated erotica.

And the Nexus calendar costs only £5.50 including postage and packing (in the traditional plain brown envelope!). Stocks are limited, so be sure of your copy by ordering today. The order form is overleaf.

Send your order to: Cash Sales Department
Nexus Books
332 Ladbroke Grove
London
W10 5AH

Please allow 28 days for delivery.

Please send me _____ copies of the 1996 Nexus calendar @ £5.50 (US$9.00) each including postage and packing.

Name: _____

Address: _____

_____

_____

_____

☐ I enclose a cheque or postal order made out to Nexus Books

☐ Please debit my Visa/Access/Mastercard account (delete as applicable)

My credit card number is:

_ _ _ _   _ _ _ _   _ _ _ _   _ _ _ _

Expiry date: _____

FILL OUT YOUR ORDER AND SEND IT TODAY!

NEW BOOKS

Coming up from Nexus and Black Lace

Demonia by Kendal Grahame

November 1995   Price: £4.99   ISBN: 0 352 33038 4

Hundreds of years ago, Demonia and her vampiric acolyte Sinitia struck terror into the hearts of young men and women all over the country, stalking the beautiful in order to drain them of their sexual energies. Now they have woken in the heart of modern London.

Melinda and Sophia by Susanna Hughes

November 1995   Price: £4.99   ISBN: 0 352 33045 7

In this, the fifth and final volume dedicated to the beautiful blonde submissive, Melinda enters a new domain where she is subjected to the whims of the Master's cruel, wife Sophia. Even more merciless is the courtesan Bianca, who takes an instant fancy to Melinda's youthful charms.

Serving Time by Sarah Veitch

December 1995   Price: £4.99   ISBN: 0 352 33046 5

Trapped in the House of Compulsion, Fern Terris discovers the depths and delights of discipline. The young temptress finds the touch of canes, belts and tawses opens up new realms of pleasure and the arrival of the mysterious Sonia brings her face to face with a whole new sexuality.

Lydia in the Harem by Philippa Masters

December 1995   Price: £4.99   ISBN: 0 352 33051 1

Bound for England with a complement of lusty mariners, Lydia finds herself and her all-female entourage stranded in Arabia. A charismatic local prince swiftly offers temporary shelter – in his harem – and Lydia, Tiliu, Felicity and Alice are determined to reward him for his generosity.

Rude Awakening by Pamela Kyle
November 1995   Price: £4.99   ISBN: 0 352 33036 8
When you are used to getting everything you want handed to you on a plate, abduction must come as something of a blow. So Alison and Belinda discover as they are stripped, bound, and forced to comply with the wishes of their cruel but intriguing captors.

Jewel of Xanadu by Roxanne Carr
November 1995   Price: £4.99 ISBN: 0 352 33037 6
Raised as a nomad in the Gobi desert, Cirina is used to meeting strangers. Antonio, on a quest for a Byzantine jewel, is special – but their blossoming relationship is cut short when Tartar warriors remove Cirina to the pleasure palace of the Kublai Khan.

Gold Fever by Louisa Francis
December 1995   Price: £4.99   ISBN: 0 352 33043 0
Trapped in a dull marriage in 1860s Australia, Ginny is determined nothing will stop her salacious fun. Enter her perfect match: Dan Berrigan, gold miner turned renegade. Together they strike gold – in more ways than one – but a scandal from her lewd past threatens everything.

Eye of the Storm by Georgina Brown
December 1995   Price: £4.99   ISBN 0 352 33044 9
Hired by handsome eccentric Philippe Salvatore to help aboard his private yacht, Antonia expects an easy life at sea. But it's far from smooth sailing – she must contend with a jealous wife, a dominant mother and bizarre sexual encounters, with the beautifully beguiling transsexual, Emira.

NEXUS BACKLIST

All books are priced £4.99 unless another price is given. If a date is supplied, the book in question will not be available until that month in 1995.

CONTEMPORARY EROTICA

THE ACADEMY	Arabella Knight	
CONDUCT UNBECOMING	Arabella Knight	Jul
CONTOURS OF DARKNESS	Marco Vassi	
THE DEVIL'S ADVOCATE	Anonymous	
DIFFERENT STROKES	Sarah Veitch	Aug
THE DOMINO TATTOO	Cyrian Amberlake	
THE DOMINO ENIGMA	Cyrian Amberlake	
THE DOMINO QUEEN	Cyrian Amberlake	
ELAINE	Stephen Ferris	
EMMA'S SECRET WORLD	Hilary James	
EMMA ENSLAVED	Hilary James	
EMMA'S SECRET DIARIES	Hilary James	
FALLEN ANGELS	Kendal Grahame	
THE FANTASIES OF JOSEPHINE SCOTT	Josephine Scott	
THE GENTLE DEGENERATES	Marco Vassi	
HEART OF DESIRE	Maria del Rey	
HELEN – A MODERN ODALISQUE	Larry Stern	
HIS MISTRESS'S VOICE	G. C. Scott	
HOUSE OF ANGELS	Yvonne Strickland	May
THE HOUSE OF MALDONA	Yolanda Celbridge	
THE IMAGE	Jean de Berg	Jul
THE INSTITUTE	Maria del Rey	
SISTERHOOD OF THE INSTITUTE	Maria del Rey	

EROTIC SCIENCE FICTION

BLUE ANGEL SECRETS	Margarete von Falkensee	☐
CONFESSIONS OF AN ENGLISH MAID	Anonymous	☐
PLAISIR D'AMOUR	Anne-Marie Villefranche	☐
FOLIES D'AMOUR	Anne-Marie Villefranche	☐
JOIE D'AMOUR	Anne-Marie Villefranche	☐
MYSTERE D'AMOUR	Anne-Marie Villefranche	☐
SECRETS D'AMOUR	Anne-Marie Villefranche	☐
SOUVENIR D'AMOUR	Anne-Marie Villefranche	☐

SAMPLERS & COLLECTIONS

EROTICON 1	ed. J-P Spencer		☐
EROTICON 2	ed. J-P Spencer		☐
EROTICON 3	ed. J-P Spencer		☐
EROTICON 4	ed. J-P Spencer		☐
NEW EROTICA 1	ed. Esme Ombreux		☐
NEW EROTICA 2	ed. Esme Ombreux		☐
THE FIESTA LETTERS	ed. Chris Lloyd	£4.50	☐

NON-FICTION

HOW TO DRIVE YOUR MAN WILD IN BED	Graham Masterton	☐
HOW TO DRIVE YOUR WOMAN WILD IN BED	Graham Masterton	☐
LETTERS TO LINZI	Linzi Drew	☐
LINZI DREW'S PLEASURE GUIDE	Linzi Drew	☐

- -

Please send me the books I have ticked above.

Name . . . .

Address . . . .

. . . .

. . . .

. . . . Post code . . . .

Send to: **Cash Sales, Nexus Books, 332 Ladbroke Grove, London W10 5AH.**

Please enclose a cheque or postal order, made payable to **Nexus Books,** to the value of the books you have ordered plus postage and packing costs as follows:
   UK and BFPO – £1.00 for the first book, 50p for each subsequent book.
   Overseas (including Republic of Ireland) – £2.00 for the first book, £1.00 for the second book, and 50p for each subsequent book.

If you would prefer to pay by VISA or ACCESS/MASTER-CARD, please write your card number and expiry date here:

. . . .

Please allow up to 28 days for delivery.

Signature . . . .

- -